PENGUIN BOOKS

A PATCHWORK PLANET

Anne Tyler was born in Minneapolis in 1941 but
grew up in Raleigh, North Carolina. She graduated
at nineteen from Duke University, and went on to do
graduate work in Russian studies at Columbia
University. Her eleventh novel, *Breathing Lessons*,
was awarded the Pulitzer Prize in 1988. Tyler is a
member of the American Academy of Arts and
Letters. She lives in Baltimore.

A Patchwork Planet

ANNE TYLER

A Patchwork Planet

Penguin Books

PENGUIN BOOKS
Published by the Penguin Group
Penguin Books Canada Ltd, 10 Alcorn Avenue, Toronto,
Ontario, Canada M4V 3B2
Penguin Books Ltd, 27 Wrights Lane, London W8 5TZ, England
Penguin Putnam Inc., 375 Hudson Street, New York,
New York 10014, U.S.A.
Penguin Books Australia Ltd, Ringwood, Victoria, Australia
Penguin Books (NZ) Ltd, cnr Rosedale and Airborne Roads, Albany,
Auckland 1310, New Zealand

Penguin Books Ltd, Registered Offices: Harmondsworth, Middlesex,
England

First published in Viking by Penguin Books Canada Limited, 1998
Published in Penguin Books, 1999
1 3 5 7 9 10 8 6 4 2

*Publisher's note: This book is a work of fiction. Names, characters, places
and incidents either are the product of the author's imagination or are used
fictitiously, and any resemblance to actual persons living or dead, events, or
locales is entirely coincidental.*

Manufactured in Canada.

Canadian Cataloguing in Publication Data
Tyler, Anne
A patchwork planet

ISBN 10-14-027552-5

I. Title.

PS3570.Y45P37 1999   813'.54   C98-932920-8

American Library of Congress Cataloguing in Publication Data Available

Visit Penguin Canada's web site at **www.penguin.ca**

A Patchwork Planet

I AM A MAN you can trust, is how my customers view me. Or at least, I'm guessing it is. Why else would they hand me their house keys before they leave for vacation? Why else would they depend on me to clear their attics for them, heave their air conditioners into their windows every spring, lug their excess furniture to their basements? "Mind your step, young fellow; that's Hepplewhite," Mrs. Rodney says, and then she goes into her kitchen to brew a pot of tea. I could get up to anything in that basement. I could unlock the outside door so as to slip back in overnight and rummage through all she owns—her Hepplewhite desk and her Japanese lacquer jewelry box and the six potbellied drawers of her dining-room buffet. Not that I would. But she doesn't know that. She just assumes it. She takes it for granted that I'm a good person.

Come to think of it, I am the one who doesn't take it for granted.

. . .

On the very last day of a bad old year, I was leaning against a pillar in the Baltimore railroad station, waiting to catch the 10:10 a.m. to Philadelphia. Philadelphia's where my little girl lives. Her mother married a lawyer there after we split up.

Ordinarily I'd have driven, but my car was in the shop and so I'd had to fork over the money for a train ticket. *Scads* of money. Not to mention being some appointed place at some appointed time, which I hate. Plus, there were a lot more people waiting than I had expected. That airy, light, clean, varnished feeling I generally got in Penn Station had been crowded out. Elderly couples with matching luggage stuffed the benches, and swarms of college kids littered the floor with their duffel bags. This gray-haired guy was walking around speaking to different strangers one by one. Well-off guy, you could tell: tan skin, nice turtleneck, soft beige car coat. He went up to a woman sitting alone and asked her a question. Then he came over to a girl in a miniskirt standing near me. I had been thinking I wouldn't mind talking to her myself. She had long blond hair, longer than her skirt, which made it seem she'd neglected to put on the bottom half of her outfit. The man said, "Would you by any chance be traveling to Philadelphia?"

"Well, northbound, yes," she said, in this shallow, breathless voice that came as a disappointment.

"But to Philadelphia?"

"No, New York, but I'll be—"

"Thanks anyway," he said, and he moved toward the next bench.

Now he had my full attention. "Ma'am," I heard him ask an old lady, "are you traveling to Philadelphia?" The old lady answered something too mumbly for me to catch, and instantly he turned to the woman beside her. "Philadelphia?" Notice how he was getting more and more sparing of words. When the woman told him, "Wilmington," he didn't say a thing; just plunged on down the row to one of the matched-luggage couples. I straightened up from my pillar and drifted closer, looking toward Gate E as if I had my mind on my train. The wife was telling the man about their New Year's plans. They were baby-sitting their grandchildren who lived in New York City, she said, and the husband said, "Well, not New York City proper, dear; White Plains," and the gray-haired man, almost shouting, said, "But my daughter's counting on me!" And off he raced.

Well, *I* was going to Philadelphia. He could have asked me. I understood why he didn't, of course. No doubt I struck him as iffy, with my three-day growth of black stubble and my ripped black leather jacket and my jeans all dust and cobwebs from Mrs. Morey's garage. But still he could have given me a chance. Instead he just flicked his eyes at me and then swerved off toward the bench at the end of the room. By now he was looking seriously undermedicated. "Please!" he said to a woman reading a book. "Tell me you're going to Philadelphia!"

She lowered her book. She was thirtyish, maybe thirty-five—older than I was, anyhow. A schoolmarm sort, in a wide brown coat with a pattern like feathers all over it. "Philadelphia?" she said. "Why, yes, I am."

"Then could I ask you a favor?"

I stopped several feet away and frowned down at my left wrist. (Never mind that I don't own a watch.) Even without looking, I could sense how she went on guard. The man must have sensed it too, because he said, "Nothing too difficult, I promise!"

They were announcing my train now. ("The delayed

10:10," the loudspeaker called it. It's always "the delayed" this or that.) People started moving toward Gate E, the older couples hauling their wheeled bags behind them like big, meek pets on leashes. If the woman in the feather coat said anything, I missed it. Next I heard, the man was talking. "My daughter's flying out this afternoon for a junior semester abroad," he was saying. "Leaving from Philadelphia; the airline offers a bargain rate if you leave from Philadelphia. So I put her on a train this morning, stopped for groceries afterward, and came home to find my wife in a state. It seems our daughter'd forgotten her passport. She'd telephoned from the station in Philly; didn't know what to do next."

The woman clucked sympathetically. I'd have kept quiet myself. Waited to find out where the guy was heading with this.

"So I told her she should stay put. Stay right there in the station, I said, and I would get somebody here to carry up her passport."

A likely story! Why didn't he go himself, if this was such an emergency?

"Why don't you go yourself?" the woman asked him.

"I can't leave my wife alone that long. She's in a wheelchair: Parkinson's."

This seemed like a pretty flimsy excuse, if you want my honest opinion. Also, it exceeded what I would consider the normal quota for misfortunes. Not only a lamebrain daughter, but a wife with a major disease! I let my eyes wander toward the two of them. The woman was gazing up into the man's face, pooching her mouth out thoughtfully. The man was holding a packet. He must have pulled it from his car coat: not a manila envelope, which would have been the logical choice, but one of those padded mailers the size of a paperback book. Aha! Padded! So you couldn't feel the contents! And from where I stood, it looked to be stapled shut besides. *Watch yourself, lady,* I said silently.

As if she'd heard me, she told the man, "I hope this isn't some kind of contraband." Except she pronounced it "counterband," which made me think she must not be a schoolmarm, after all.

"No, no!" the man told her. He gave a huff of a laugh. "No, I can assure you it's not counterband."

Was he repeating her mistake on purpose? I couldn't tell. (Or maybe the word really *was* "counterband.") Meanwhile, the loudspeaker came to life again. The delayed 10:10 was now boarding. Train wheels squealed below me. "I'll do it," the woman decided.

"Oh, wonderful! That's wonderful! Thanks!" the man told her, and he handed her the packet. She was already rising. Instead of a suitcase, she had one of those tote things that could have been just a large purse, and she fitted the strap over her shoulder and lined up the packet with the book she'd been reading. "So let's see," the man was saying. "You've got light-colored hair, you're wearing a brown print coat. . . . I'll call the pay phone where my daughter's waiting and let her know who to watch for. She'll be standing at Information when you get there. Esther Brimm, her name is—a redhead. You can't miss that hair of hers. Wearing jeans and a blue-jean jacket. Ask if she's Esther Brimm."

He followed the woman through the double doors and down the stairs, although he wasn't supposed to. I was close behind. The cold felt good after the packed waiting room. "And you are?" the man was asking.

Affected way of putting it. They arrived on the platform and stopped short, so that I just about ran over them. The woman said, "I'm Sophia—" and then something like "Maiden" that I couldn't exactly hear. (The train was in place but rumbling, and passengers were clip-clopping by.) "In case we miss connections, though . . . ," she said, raising her voice.

In case they missed connections, he should put his name and phone number on the mailer. Any fool would know that much. But he seemed to have his mind elsewhere. He said, "Um . . . now, do you live in Baltimore? I mean, are you coming *back* to Baltimore, or is Philly your end destination?"

I almost laughed aloud at that. So! Already he'd forgotten he was grateful; begun to question his angel of mercy's reliability. But she didn't take offense. She said, "Oh, I'm a *long*-time Baltimorean. This is just an overnight visit to my mother. I do it every weekend: take the ten-ten Patriot Saturday morning and come back sometime Sunday."

"Well, then!" he said. "Well. I certainly do appreciate this."

"It's no trouble at all," she said, and she smiled and turned to board.

I had been hoping to sit next to her. I was planning to start a conversation—mention I'd overheard what the man had asked of her and then suggest the two of us check the contents of his packet. But the car was nearly full, and she settled down beside a lady in a fur hat. The closest I could manage was across the aisle to her left and one row back, next to a black kid wearing earphones. Only view I had was a schoolmarm's netted yellow bun and a curve of cheek.

Well, anyhow, why was I making this out to be such a big deal? Just bored, I guess. I shucked my jacket off and sat forward to peer in my seat-back pocket. A wrinkly McDonald's bag, a napkin stained with ketchup, a newspaper section folded to the crossword puzzle. The puzzle was only half done, but I didn't have a pen on me. I looked over at the black kid. He probably didn't have a pen, either, and anyhow he was deep in his music—long brown fingers tapping time on his knees.

Then just beyond him, out the window, I chanced to notice the passport man talking on the phone. Talking on the phone? Down here beside the tracks? Sure enough: one of those little cell phones you all the time see obnoxious businessmen showing off in public. I leaned closer to the window. Something here was weird, I thought. Maybe he smuggled drugs, or worked for the CIA. Maybe he was a terrorist. I wished I knew how to read lips. But already he was closing his phone, slipping it into his pocket, turning to go back upstairs. And our train was sliding out of the station.

I looked again at the woman. At the packet, to be specific.

It was resting on top of her book, which sat in her feather-print lap. (She would be the type who stayed properly buttoned into her coat, however long the trip.) Where the mailer was folded over, staples ran straight across in a nearly unbroken line. But staples were no problem. She could pry them up with, say, a nail file or a dime, and slip them out undetectably, and replace them when she was finished. *Do it*, I told her in my head. She was gazing past her seatmate, out the right-hand window. I couldn't even see her cheek now; just her bun.

Back in the days when I was a juvenile delinquent, I used to break into houses and read people's private mail. Also photo albums. I had a real thing about photo albums. The other kids who broke in along with me, they'd be hunting car keys and cigarettes and booze. They'd be tearing through closets and cabinets all around me, while I sat on the sofa poring over somebody's wedding pictures. And even when I took stuff, it was always personal stuff. This little snow globe once from a nightstand in a girl's bedroom. Another time, a brass egg that stood on scaly claw feet and opened to show a snapshot of an old-fashioned baby inside. I'm not proud of this. I'd sooner confess to jewel theft than to pocketing six letters tied up with satin ribbon, which is what I did when we jimmied the lock at the Empreys' place one night. But there you are. What can I say.

So when this Sophia woman let the packet stay untouched—didn't prod it, didn't shake it, didn't tease apart the merest corner of the flap—I felt something like, oh, almost envy. A huge wave of envy. I started wishing *I* could be like that. Man, I'd have been tearing into that packet with my bare teeth, if I'd had the chance.

The conductor came and went, and the row houses slipping by turned into factory buildings and then to matted woods and a sheet of gray water, but I was barely conscious of anything beyond Sophia's packet. I saw how quietly her hands rested on the brown paper; she was not a fidgeter. Smooth, oval nails, pale pink, and plump white fingers like a woman's in a religious painting. Her book was turned the wrong way for me to read the title, but I knew it was something worthwhile and educational. Oh, these people who prepare ahead! Who think to bring actual books, instead of dashing into a newsstand at the last minute for a *Sports Illustrated* or—worse yet—making do with a crossword puzzle that someone else has started!

It bothered me more than I liked to admit that the passport man had avoided me.

We were getting close to Wilmington, and the lady in the fur hat started collecting her things. After she left, I planned to change seats. I would wait for Sophia to shift over to the window, and then I'd sit down next to her. "Morning," I would say. "Interesting packet you've got there."

"I see you're carrying some kind of packet."

"Mind if I inquire what's in that packet?"

Or whatever. Something would come to me. But when the train stopped and the lady stood up, Sophia just turned her knees to one side to let her out. She stayed seated where she was, on the aisle, so I didn't see any natural-seeming way to make my move.

We left Wilmington behind. We traveled past miles of pipeline and smokestacks, some of them belching flames. I could tell now that it was rap music the kid beside me was listening to. He had the volume raised so high that I could hear it winding out of his earphones—that chanting and insisting sound like the voices you hear in your dreams.

"Philll-adelphia!" the conductor called.

Of course Sophia got ready too soon. We were barely in sight of the skyline—bluish buildings shining in the pale winter sunlight, Liberty Towers scalloping their way up and up and up—but she was already rising to wait in the aisle. The exit lay to the rear, and so she had to face me. I could see the pad of flesh that was developing under her chin. She leaned against her seat and teetered gently with the swaying of the car. *Critics are unanimous!* the back of her book said. The mailer was almost hidden between the book and her cushiony bosom.

I put on my jacket, but I didn't stand up yet. I waited till the train had come to a stop and she had passed me. Then I swung out into the aisle lickety-split, cutting in front of a fat guy with a briefcase. I followed Sophia so closely, I could smell the dusty smell of her coat. It was velvet, or something like velvet. Velvet always smells dusty, even when it's fresh from the cleaners.

There was the usual scuffle with that automatic door that likes to squash the passengers—Press the button, dummies!— and the usual milling and nudging in the vestibule, and then we stepped out into a rush of other people. It was obvious that Sophia knew where she was going. She didn't so much as glance around her but walked fast, coming down hard on her heels. Her heels were the short, chunky kind, but they made her as tall as I was. I had noticed that while we were standing on the train. Now she was slightly taller, because we'd started up the stairs and she was a step above me.

Even once we'd reached the waiting room, she didn't look around. Thirtieth Street Station is so enormous and echoing and high-ceilinged—a jolt after cozy Baltimore—that most people pause to take stock a moment, but not Sophia. She just went clicking along, with me a few yards to the rear.

At the Information island, only one person stood waiting. I spotted her from far across those acres of marble flooring: a girl in a denim jacket and jeans, with a billow of crinkly, electric red hair. It fanned straight out and stopped just above her shoulders. It was *amazing* hair. I was awestruck. Sophia, though, didn't let on she had noticed her. She was walking more slowly now, downright sedately, placing her toes at a slight angle outward, the way women often do when they want to look composed and genteel. Actually, she was starting to get on my nerves. Didn't that bun of hers just sum her up, I thought—the net that bound it in and the perfect, doughnut shape and the way it sat so low on her head, so matronly and drab! And Esther Brimm, meanwhile, stood burning like a candle on her stick-thin, blue-denim legs.

When we reached the island I veered right, toward a display of schedules on the counter. I heard Sophia's heels stop in front of Esther. "Esther Brimm?" she asked.

"Ms. Maynard?"

Husky, throaty voice, the kind I like.

"Your father asked me to bring you something. . . ."

I took a schedule from the rack and turned my face casually in their direction. Not till Esther said, "Right; my passport," did Sophia slip the mailer from behind her book and hold it out.

"Thanks a million," Esther said, accepting it, and Sophia

said, "My pleasure. Have a good trip." Then she turned away and clicked toward the Twenty-ninth Street exit.

Just like that, I forgot her. Now I was focused on Esther. *Open it!* I told her. Instead she picked up the army duffel lying at her feet and moved off toward the phones. I meandered after her, studying my schedule. I pretended I was hunting a train to Princeton.

The phones were the unprivate kind just out in the middle of everything, standing cheek to jowl. When Esther lifted a receiver off its hook, I was right there beside her, lifting a receiver of my own. I was so near I could have touched her duffel bag with the toe of my sneaker. I heard every word she said. "Dad?" she said.

I clamped my phone to my ear and held the schedule up between us so I could watch her. This close, she was less attractive. She had that fragile, sore-looking skin you often find on redheads. "Yes," she was saying, "it's here." And then, "Sure! I guess so. I mean, it's still stapled shut and all. Huh? Well, hang on."

She put her receiver down and started yanking at the mailer's top flap. When the staples tore loose, rat-a-tat, she pulled the edges apart and peered inside—practically stuck her little freckled nose inside. Then she picked up the phone again. "Yup," she said. "Good as new."

So I never got a chance to see for myself. It could have been anything: loose diamonds, crack cocaine . . . But somehow I didn't think so. The phone call was what convinced me. She'd have had to be a criminal genius to fake that careless tone of voice, the easy offhandedness of a person who knows for a fact that she's her parents' pride and joy. "Well, listen," she was saying. "Tell Mom I'll call again from the airport, okay?" And she made a kissing sound and hung up. When she slung her duffel over her shoulder and started toward one of the gates, I didn't even watch her go.

The drill for visiting my daughter was, I'd arrive about ten a.m. and take her on an outing. Nothing fancy. Maybe a trip to the drug store, or walking her little dog in the park. Then we'd grab a bite someplace, and I'd return her and leave. This happened exactly once a month—the last Saturday of the month. Her mother's idea. To hear her mother tell it, Husband No. 2 was Superdad; but I had to stay in the picture to give Opal a sense of whatchamacallit. Connection.

But due to one thing and another—my car acting up, my alarm not going off—I was late as hell that day. It was close to noon, I figure, before I even left the station, and I didn't want to spring for a cab after paying for a train ticket. Instead I more or less ran all the way to the apartment (they lived in one of those posh old buildings just off Rittenhouse Square), and by the time I pressed the buzzer, I was looking even scruffier than my usual self. I could tell as much from Natalie's expression, the minute she opened the door. She let her eyes sort of drift up and down me, and, "Barnaby," she said flatly. Opal's little dog was dancing around my ankles—a dachshund, very quivery and high-strung.

"Yo. Natalie," I said. I started swatting at my clothes to settle them a bit. Natalie, of course, was Miss Good Grooming. She wore a slim gray skirt-and-sweater set, and her hair was all of a piece—smooth, shiny brown—dipping in and then out again before it touched her shoulders. Oh, she had been a beauty for as long as I had known her; except now that I recalled, there'd always been something too placid about her. I should have picked it up from her dimples, which made a little dent in each cheek whether or not she was smiling. They gave her a look of self-satisfaction. What I'd thought when we first met was, how could she *not* be self-satisfied? And her vague, dreamy slowness used to seem sexy. Now it just made me impatient. I said, "Is Opal ready to go?" and Natalie took a full minute, I swear, to consider every aspect of the question. Then: "Opal is in her room," she said finally. "Crying her eyes out."

"Crying!"

"She thought you'd stood her up."

"Well, I know I'm a little bit late—" I said.

She lifted an arm and contemplated the tiny watch face on the inner surface of her wrist.

"Things just seemed to conspire against me," I said. "Can I see her?"

After she'd thought that over awhile, she turned and floated off, which I took to mean yes.

I made my own way to Opal's bedroom, down a long hall lined with Oriental rugs. I waded through the dachshund and knocked on her door. "Opal?" I called. "You in there?"

No answer. I turned the knob and poked my head in.

You'd never guess this room belonged to a nine-year-old. The bedspread was appliquéd with ducklings, and the only posters were nursery-rhyme posters. By rights it should have been a baby's room, or a toddler's.

The bed was where I looked first, because that's where I figured she would be if she was crying. But she was in the white rocker by the window. And she wasn't crying, either. She was glaring at me reproachfully from underneath her eyebrows.

"Ope!" I said, all hearty.

Opal's chin stayed buried inside her collar.

I knew I shouldn't think this, but my daughter had never struck me as very appealing. She had all her life been a few pounds overweight, with a dish-shaped face and colorless hair and a soft, pink, half-open mouth, the upper lip short enough to expose her top front teeth. (I used to call her "Bunnikins" till Natalie asked me not to—and why would she have asked, if she herself hadn't noticed Opal's close resemblance to a rabbit?) It didn't help that Natalie dressed her in the kind of clothes you see in Dick and Jane books—fussy and pastel, the smocked bodices bunching up on her chest and the puffed sleeves cutting into her arms. Me, I would have chosen something less constricting. But who was I to say? I hadn't been much of a father.

I did want the best for her, though. I would never intentionally hurt her. I walked over to where she was sitting and squatted down in front of her. "Opal-dopal," I said. "Sweetheart."

"What."

"Call off your dog. He's eating my wallet."

She started to smile but held it back. Her mother's two dimples deepened in her cheeks. The dog really was nibbling at my wallet. George Farnsworth, his name was; heaven knows why. "George Farnsworth," I said sternly, "if you're short of cash, just ask straight out for a loan, okay?"

Now I heard a definite chuckle. I took heart. "Hey, Ope, I'm sorry I'm late," I said. "First I had car trouble, see—"

"You *always* have car trouble."

"Then my alarm clock didn't go off—"

"It *always* doesn't go off."

"Well. Not always," I told her. "Then once I got to Penn Station, you'll never guess what happened. It was like a secret-agent movie. Guy is walking up to people, pulling something out of his coat. 'Ma'am,' "—I made my voice sound menacing and mysterious—" 'would you please take this package to Philadelphia for me?' "

Opal didn't speak, but I could tell she was listening. She

watched me with her pinkish-gray eyes, the lashes slightly damp.

" 'Take it to my daughter in Philly; all it is is her passport,' he said, and I thought to myself, *Ha! I just bet it's her passport!* So when this one woman said she would do it, I followed her at the other end of the trip."

"You followed her?"

"I wanted to see what would happen. So I followed her to her rendezvous with the quote-unquote daughter, and then I hung around the phones while the daughter placed a call to—"

"You hung around the phones?"

I was beginning to flounder. (This story didn't have what you'd call a snappy ending.) I said, "Yes, and then—um—"

"You were only dawdling in the station all this time! It's not enough you don't look after your car right and you forget to set your alarm; then you dawdle in the station like you don't care *when* you see me!"

It was uncanny, how much she sounded like her mother. Her mother in the old days, that is—the miserable last days of our marriage. I said, "Now, hon. Now wait a sec, hon."

Which was also from those days, word for word. Some kind of reflex, I guess.

"You promised you'd come at ten," she said, "and instead you were just . . . goofing around with a bunch of secret agents! You totally lost track of where you were supposed to be!"

"In the first place," I said, "I take excellent care of my car, Opal. I treat it like a blood relative. It's not my fault if my car is older than I am. And I did not forget to set my alarm. I don't know why it didn't go off; sometimes it just doesn't, okay? I don't know why. And I honestly thought you'd like hearing about those people I was so-called goofing around with. I thought, *Man, I wish Opal could see this*, and I followed them expressly so I could tell you about it later over a burger and french fries. Wouldn't that be great? A burger and fries at Little Pete's, Ope, while I tell you my big story."

It wasn't working, though. Opal's eyes only got pinker, and for once she had her mouth tightly shut.

"Look at George Farnsworth! *He* wants to go," I said.

In fact, George Farnsworth had lost interest and was lying beside the rocker with his nose on his paws. But I said, "First we'll take George for a walk in the Square, and then we'll head over to—"

"It sounds to me," Natalie said, "as if Opal prefers to stay in."

She was standing in the doorway. Damn Oriental rugs had muffled her steps.

"Am I right, Opal?" she asked. "Would you rather tell him goodbye?"

"Goodbye?" I said. "I just got here! I just came all this way!"

"It's your decision, Opal."

Opal looked down at her lap. After a long pause, she murmured something.

"We couldn't hear you," Natalie said.

"Goodbye," Opal told her lap.

But I knew she didn't mean it. All she wanted was a little coaxing. I said, "Hey now, Ope . . ."

"Could I speak with you a minute?" Natalie asked me.

I sighed and got to my feet. Opal stayed where she was, but I caught her hidden glimmer of a glance as I turned to follow Natalie down the hall. I knew I could have persuaded her if I'd been given more time.

We didn't stop in the living room. We went on through to the kitchen, at the other end of the apartment. I guess Natalie figured my jeans might soil her precious upholstery. I had never seen the kitchen before, and I spent a moment looking around (old-fashioned tilework, towering cabinets) before it sank in on me what Natalie was saying.

"I've been thinking," she was saying. "Maybe it would be better if you didn't come anymore."

This should have been okay with me. It's not as if I enjoyed these visits. But you know how it is when somebody all at once announces you can't do something. I said, "What! Just because one Saturday I happen to run a little behind?"

Her eyes seemed to be resting slightly to the left of my left shoulder. Her face was as untroubled as a statue's.

"I'm traveling from a whole other city, for God's sake!" I told her. "A whole entirely other state! No way can you expect me to arrive here on the dot!"

"It's funny," she said reflectively. "I used to believe it was very important for Opal to keep in touch with you. But now I wonder if it might be doing her more harm than good. All those Saturdays you've come late, or left early, or canceled altogether—"

"It was only the once or twice or three times or so that I canceled," I said.

"And even when you do show up, I imagine it's started to dawn on her how you live."

"How I live! I live just fine!"

"A rented room," she mused, "an unskilled job, a bunch of shiftless friends. No goals and no ambitions; still not finished college at the age of thirty."

"Twenty-nine," I corrected her. (The one charge I could argue with.)

"Thirty in three weeks," she said.

"Oh."

There was a sudden silence, like when the Muzak stops in a shopping mall and you haven't even been hearing it but all at once you're aware of its absence. And just then I noticed, on the windowsill behind her, our old china cookie jar. I hadn't thought of that cookie jar in years! It was domed on top and painted with bars like a birdcage, and it looked so dowdy and homely, against the diamond-shaped panes. It made me lose my train of thought. The next thing I knew, Natalie was gliding out of the kitchen, and I had no choice but to follow her.

Though, in the foyer, I did say, "Well." And then, in the hall outside, I turned and said, "Well, we'll see about this!"

The door made almost no sound when she closed it.

My train home was completely filled, and stone cold to boot. Some problem with the heating system. I sat next to a Spanish-type guy who must have started his New Year's partying a tad bit early. His head kept nodding forward, and he was breathing fumes that were practically flammable. Across the aisle, this very young couple was trying to soothe a baby. The husband said, "Maybe he's hungry," and the wife said, "I just fed him." The husband said, "Maybe he's wet." I don't know why they made me so sad.

After that, it seemed all around me I saw families. A toddler peeked over his seat back, and his mother gave him a hug and pulled him down again. A father and a little girl walked toward me from the club car, the little girl holding a paper cup extremely carefully in both hands. The foreigner and I were the only ones on our own, it seemed.

The father glanced at us as he came close (at the foreigner's head bobbing and reeling, and me with my jacket collar flipped up and a wad of cottony white stuff poking out of a tear in one sleeve), and then he glanced away. It made me think of the passport man, refusing to meet my eyes. And that made me think of the woman in the feather coat. Sophia. So honorable,

Sophia had been; so principled. So well behaved even when she thought nobody was looking.

Oh, what makes some people more virtuous than others? Is it something they know from birth? Don't they ever feel that zingy, thrilling urge to smash the world to bits?

Isn't it possible, maybe, that good people are just *luckier* people? Couldn't that be the explanation?

2

THE COMPANY I work for is called Rent-a-Back, Inc. How I got into it is a whole other story, but basically we provide a service for people who are old or disabled. Any load you can't lift, any chore you don't feel up to, why, just call on us. Say you want your lawn chairs piled in your garage in the fall. Or your rugs rolled up and stored away in the spring. We can do that. A lot of our customers have a standing order—like, an hour a week. Others just telephone as circumstances arise. Whatever.

On the Saturday of my dud trip to Philadelphia, I came home to find a message from my boss on my answering machine. "Barnaby, it's Virginia Dibble. Could you get back to me as soon as possible? We have an urgent request for this evening."

I really liked Mrs. Dibble. She was this dainty, fluttery lady a whole lot older than my mother, but I'd seen her tote a portable toilet down two flights of stairs when we were short-handed. So even though I wasn't in such a great mood, I dialed her number. "What's up?" I asked her.

"Oh, poor, poor Mrs. Alford," she started right in. "She needs a Christmas tree put together."

"A what?"

"An eight-foot artificial Christmas tree. It's in her attic, she says, and she needs it brought down and assembled."

"Mrs. Dibble," I said. "It's New Year's Eve."

"Oh, you have plans?"

"I mean, it's a week after Christmas. What does she want with a tree?"

"She says her seven grandchildren are stopping by for a visit. They're spending the night on their way home from skiing, and she wants the house to look cheery, she says, and not old-ladyish and glum."

"Ah."

Grandchildren ruled the world, if you judged by most of our clients.

"She needs it decorated too," Mrs. Dibble was saying. "She says she can't manage the upper branches, and if she climbed onto a step stool, she's scared she might break a hip."

Breaking a hip was what else ruled the world—the fear of it, I mean. Big bugaboo, in the circles I traveled in.

I said, "Couldn't she tell her grandchildren she did have a tree but took it down? Plenty of folks get rid of their trees on December twenty-sixth, tell her!"

But I knew what Mrs. Dibble's answer would be ("We're the muscles, not the brains," she always said); so I didn't wait to hear it. "Besides," I said, "my car is in the shop and I won't have it back until Monday."

"Oh, Martine can drive," Mrs. Dibble told me. "I thought I'd send the two of you, so as to finish that much faster. Can you do it if Martine picks you up?"

"Well," I said. "I guess."

"All the others have New Year's plans. I'll call Martine back again and tell her to come fetch you."

There were eleven full-time employees at Rent-a-Back. That meant nine people that I knew of had New Year's plans. And these were not particularly successful people. Several might even be looked upon as losers. But still, they'd found something to do with themselves on New Year's Eve.

I lived in the eastern part of the city, in the basement of a duplex out Northern Parkway. Martine lived down on St. Paul. It would take her twenty-some minutes to reach me; so I had time to fix myself a peanut butter sandwich. (My only meal all day had been a bag of chips in Penn Station.) Then I grabbed a Coke and went to eat on the patio, where I could see a sliver of the driveway. I never hung around my apartment if I could help it. It was nothing but a rec room, really, which the family above me rented out because they needed the income.

By now the sky had clouded over and darkened. When the patio lamps switched on, they made a noticeable difference, even though it couldn't have been much later than four o'clock. The patio had these tall pole lamps that were activated by motion. If anybody came near, they would all at once light up. Then after thirty seconds they shut off again. Usually, I enjoyed teasing them. I would take a step, freeze, take another step. . . . Once, when the Hardestys were gone and I was grilling steaks with this girl I'd met, I told her there was no way to make the lamps stay lit nonstop (which was a flat-out lie) and we would have to keep moving if we wanted to see what we were eating. So there we were, shifting hugely in our chairs, lifting our forks with these exaggerated gestures that the lamps would be sure to notice. Then after supper we got to making out and the lamps, of course, went dark, and we forgot about them till she stood up to pull her T-shirt off, and *whang!* they all flared on again. I laughed until my stomach hurt.

That afternoon, though, I wasn't feeling so playful. I just sat hunched over my sandwich in a shreddy mesh lawn chair, and pretty soon the lamps clicked off.

I'd finished eating by the time Martine pulled in. She was driving her boyfriend's battered red pickup, high off the ground and narrow through the eyes. I set my Coke can in a planter and came around to climb in on the passenger side. "Hey, Martine," I said. "No date for New Year's Eve?"

"He's in bed with the throwing-up flu," she said, backing into the street. "What's *your* excuse, Mr. Peanut Butter Breath?"

"I've turned against women," I told her.

"Ha!"

She shifted gears and took off.

Martine drove sitting on a cushion; that's how small she was. Heaven knows what had possessed her to sign on at Rent-a-Back. She must have weighed ninety pounds at the most—tiny little cat-faced girl with sallow skin and boxy black hair squared off above her earlobes. But tough, I have to admit. A Sparrows Point kid, from steelworking stock. Scraped sharp knuckles on the steering wheel; gigantic black nylon jacket that smelled of motor oil. "How was your trip to Philly?" she asked, and her voice had a raspy scratch to it that made me want to clear my throat.

I said, "It stunk."

"Stunk!"

"First thing wrong," I said, "was I had to take the train. Car is acting up again."

"What is it this time?"

"Steering."

"Well, it serves you right for owning an endangered species," she said.

"Tell that to my grandpa," I said. "He's the one who owned it in the first place. You think I'd go out on purpose and buy a Corvette Sting Ray? So I had to plunk down money for a train ticket. Then when I get to Philly, what does Natalie do? Sends me straight back home again. Says she's decided to stop my visits altogether."

"Why, she can't decide that!" Martine said.

"She claims I do Opal more harm than good."

"You just get ahold of your lawyer!"

"Right."

I actually didn't have a lawyer, but it seemed like too much work to explain that. Instead I slouched in my seat and watched the scenery slog by: bald brick houses, pale squares of grass, bushes strung with Christmas lights that were just now winking on.

"Anyway," I said, "her husband is a lawyer. No doubt they have some kind of fraternity or something, some secret circle she can mobilize against me. Oh, Lord. I don't know why I ever hooked up with such a woman."

"Well? Why did you?" Martine asked.

"I believe it was her hairline," I said.

Martine laughed.

"Seriously," I said. "She had this sterling-silver barrette pulling her hair straight back on top so you could see her forehead. Her clean, shiny forehead. It kind of hypnotized me, you might say."

Martine swerved around a liquor truck that was parking at someone's curb.

"I've got to start viewing the whole picture more," I said. "I can't go on falling for people's foreheads."

"With me, it's mouths," Martine said.

"Really."

I began chewing on a thumbnail, incidentally covering my own mouth with my fist.

"First time I met Everett, all I saw was his mouth. That curvy upper lip of his. Did I ask if he had a steady job, or whether he was the type who'd want to get married?"

I said, "Married?" and tucked both fists between my knees.

"Did I ask why he was still living with his mom, who dotes on him and serves him breakfast in bed and makes his truck payments for him when he can't come up with the money?"

"Geez, Pasko," I said. "I never figured on you getting married, exactly."

"Why not?" she asked.

"Well, I don't know. . . ."

"You think I'm not old enough? I'm twenty-six and a half!"

"Well, sure, you're *old* enough, I guess."

"Or you think I'm not frilly and girly enough? Not pretty enough? What?"

"Huh? No! Honest! I think you're very, um . . . " It didn't help that just then she sent me this crosspatch, unalluring scowl, but I said, "Very . . . attractive! Honest!"

"Everett says I remind him of a ten-year-old boy."

Everett had a point—one of the few times I'd agreed with him. I said, "Hogwash."

"When I told him I wanted lingerie for Christmas, he asked if they made black lace training bras."

I started to grin but stopped myself.

"Maybe we should both come up with some New Year's resolutions," Martine said. "Promise ourselves we won't go on acting like such saps."

"Well, maybe so," I said.

But I guess she could tell from my voice that I didn't have the heart for it. You get close to being thirty, and these resolutions start to seem kind of hopeless.

I wished Natalie hadn't felt called upon to remind me of my birthday.

Mrs. Alford lived in Mount Washington, in a white clapboard Colonial that was fairly good-sized but shabby, like most of our clients' houses. (Anybody rich would have hired full-time help, not just Rent-a-Back. And anybody poverty-stricken couldn't afford even us.) She was watching from behind her storm door, with a cardigan clutched around her shoulders. A woman shaped like a pigeon: tidy little head and a deep, low-set pouch of a bosom. When we started up the steps she opened the door and called, "Good evening, Barnaby! Evening, Martine! Isn't it nice you could come on such short notice!"

"Oh, for you, anytime, Mrs. A.," I told her. I walked past her into the foyer and stood waiting for instructions. Her house smelled of steam heat and brothy foods and just, well, oldness. A Christmas tree wouldn't fool her grandchildren for an instant. But she was so cheerful and determined, peering up at us half blind and smiling brightly, her hair smoothly combed, her lipstick neatly applied. "The tree is in the attic, in a white box with a red lid," she said, "and the ornaments should be nearby, but I'm not sure exactly where. I haven't used them lately, because last year I went to my daughter's for Christmas, and the year before . . . Now, what did I do the year before?"

"Never fear, Mrs. A. We'll track those suckers down no matter where they are," I told her.

"Mind you don't step through the ceiling, though."

"Would we do a thing like that?"

The way Rent-a-Back operated was, we tried to send each

client the same two or three workers again and again. So Martine and I already knew our way around Mrs. Alford's house. We knew how to get upstairs, and we knew more or less where the pull-down ladder was, above the second-floor hall. But I don't think either of us had ever been in her attic before. We clambered up—Martine on my heels, nimble as a monkey—into a hollow of cold air and darkness. I groped overhead till I connected with the lightbulb cord, and then all this junk sprang into view: trunks and suitcases and lamps, andirons, kitchen chairs with no seats, electric fans so outdated you could have fit a whole hand inside their metal grilles. None of it any surprise, believe me. I had toured a lot of attics in my time. I said, "Well, there's flooring in the middle, at least," and Martine said, "White box, red lid. White box, red lid," meanwhile maneuvering past a console radio, a standing ashtray, an open carton full of doorknobs. "Here it is," she said.

But I had caught sight of something else: a dress form, over by the chimney. It wasn't an ordinary dress form; not a canvas torso plumped with padding. This was a life-size wooden cutout, head and all, flat as a paper doll. The face was oval and astonished—round blue eyes, two dots for nostrils, and a pink O of a mouth—with brown corkscrew curls painted in at the edges. The arms stuck out at a slant and ended above the elbows; the legs stood in a brace arrangement that kept the figure upright. "Why! It's a Twinform," I told Martine.

"Hmm?"

"It's a Gaitlin Faithful Feminine Twinform! Invented by my great-grandfather."

Martine glanced over. She said, "Well, how would that be useful, though?"

"Listen to this," I told her. I read from the little brass plaque on the base. " 'Gaitlin Woodenworks, Baltimore, Maryland. Patent Applied For.' "

"How would you know how big around to sew your dresses?"

"It's not for sewing dresses. It's for putting together your outfit before you wear it. Like, if you're planning to go to a party or something . . . Well, it does sound kind of dumb. But once upon a time, you could find a Twinform in every bedroom. Now they've disappeared. I've never seen one in person before."

"Those old-time inventions slay me," Martine said. "People used to try so hard, seems like. Used to aim for the most roundabout method of doing things. Could you come give me a hand here, Barn?"

I turned away from the Twinform, finally, and went to help her.

The Christmas tree carton was a manageable size, with holes at each end to hang on by, but it turned out to be fairly heavy. I said, "Oof!" Martine, though, didn't make a sound. (Both our girl employees behaved that way, I'd noticed—kept their breaths very even and quiet where a guy would have openly grunted.) "Better let me go first," I said when we reached the ladder, but Martine said, "What: you think I can't handle it?"

"Fine," I told her. "After you." And then had the satisfaction of watching her pretend it was no big deal when sixty pounds of Christmas tree hit her in the chest as she got halfway down.

Mrs. Alford was waiting for us in the living room—her cardigan thrown aside, her speckled hands twisting and pulling and itching to get started. "Oh, good," she said. "But what about the ornaments, I wonder?"

I said, "Half a minute, Mrs. A.," and we lowered the carton to the rug.

"You did see where they were, though," she said. "You found the boxes."

"We will; don't worry," Martine told her.

"I hope they're not in the basement, instead."

Martine and I looked at each other.

But no, they were in the attic. When we went back up, we spotted them on top of a disconnected radiator—two cardboard boxes marked *Xmas* in shaky crayon script. They weighed a lot less than the tree had. We could carry one apiece with no trouble.

As I was heading toward the ladder, I threw another glance at the Twinform. "Of course, it didn't allow for Fat Days," I told Martine, "or Short Days, or any of those other days when women take forever deciding what to wear."

Martine said, "What?" Then she said, "*I* take about two minutes deciding."

Which was abundantly obvious, I could have told her.

By the time we got back to the living room, Mrs. Alford had emptied the tree carton and heaped all the branches in a tangle on the rug. She said, "Over in that corner is where we always put it. We mustn't let it block the window, though. My husband hates for the tree to block the window."

I'd heard so much of that—the deceased coming back in present tense—I hardly noticed anymore.

Martine set up the stand, while I fanned out the branches to get them looking more lifelike. It wasn't the first time I'd put one of these together (a lot of our clients had switched to artificial), but I'd never quite adjusted to how soft the needles were. Each time I plunged my hand in among them, I felt disappointed, almost—expecting to be prickled and then failing to have it happen.

Mrs. Alford was telling us about her grandchildren. "The

oldest is sixteen," she said, "and I'm sure she couldn't care less whether I have a tree or not, but the little ones are at that dinky, darling, enthusiastic stage. And they'll only be here for one night. I have to make my impression in a limited space of time, don't you see."

Then she laughed merrily so we wouldn't think she was serious, but of course she didn't fool either of us for a second. She was dead serious.

This one worker we had, Gene Rankin: he walked off the job after only three weeks. He said he couldn't stand to get so tangled up in people's lives. "Seems every time I turn around, I find myself munching cookies in some old lady's parlor," he said, "and from there it's only a step or two to the ungrateful-daughter stories and the crying jags and the offers of a grown son's empty bedroom." Mrs. Dibble told him he would get used to it, but she just said that because she didn't want to train another employee. You never get used to it.

The tree turned out to be so big that we had to pull it farther from the wall once we started hooking the lower branches on. Martine wriggled in behind it and called for what she needed. "Okay, now the red-tabbed branches. Now the yellow," and I would hand them over. Mrs. Alford went on talking. She was seated on a footstool, hugging her knees. "When the sixteen-year-old was that age," she said, "—that dinky, darling age, I mean—why, I set a sleigh and a whole team of reindeer up on top of our roof. I climbed out the attic window and strung them along the ridgepole. But I was quite a bit younger then."

"Sheesh. I've never been *that* young," I said.

I must have sounded gruffer than I'd meant to, because Martine told Mrs. Alford, "Pay no mind to Barnaby. He had a bad trip to Philly."

"Oh, was this a Philadelphia week?" Mrs. Alford asked.

"Natalie says he can't come visit anymore," Martine told her.

"Well, I'm sorry to hear that, Barnaby."

Martine crawled out from behind the tree and shucked her jacket off. Beneath it she wore overalls and a long-sleeved thermal undershirt that looked orphanish and skimpy, with the cuffs all stretched and showing her little wrists, as thin as pencils. "See if you can find some lights in one of those boxes," she told me.

But Mrs. Alford had beaten me to it. She was hauling them forth hand over hand—the old-fashioned kind of lights, with the big, dull bulbs. "It's a terrible thing, divorce," she said. "Especially when the child is caught in the middle."

I said, "I don't know that she's in the *middle*, exactly."

"He ought to talk to his lawyer," Martine said.

"Of course he ought!" Mrs. Alford said. "When my nephew and his wife split up—"

"Or go to Legal Aid."

"Oh, Legal Aid is a lovely organization!"

"Hmm," I said, making no promises.

"Or another possibility: my brother is a lawyer," Mrs. Alford told me. She hooked a scratched blue bulb onto the lowest branch. "Retired, needless to say, but still . . ."

I changed the subject. I said, "Mrs. Alford, you know that Twinform you have in your attic."

"Twinform?" she asked. She moved to the branch on her right.

"I was wondering. Did you buy it yourself? Or was it handed down through your family?"

"I'm not entirely certain what you're talking about," she said.

"That wooden person standing near your chimney. Kind of like a dress form."

"Oh, that. It was my mother's."

"Well, guess where it was manufactured," I told her. "My great-grandfather's woodenworks."

"His woodenworks, dear?"

"His shop that made wooden shoe trees and artificial limbs."

"Mercy," Mrs. Alford said.

I could see she was only being polite. She moved away from the tree and started unpacking ornaments, most of them homemade: construction-paper chains gone faded and brittle with age, pine cones glopped with red poster paint. "Someday I should get that attic cleared out," she said. "When would I use a dress form? I've never sewn a dress in my life. The most I've done is quilt a bit, and now that my eyes are going, I can barely manage that much. I've been working on a quilt of our planet for the past three years; isn't that ridiculous?"

"Oh, well, what's the hurry?" I asked. (No point explaining all over again that the Twinform wasn't meant for sewing.)

"One little measly blue planet, and it's taking me forever!"

"But here's the weird part," I said, reaching for one of the chains. It made a dry, chirpy sound, like crickets. "How the Twinform came into being was, an angel showed up and suggested it."

"An angel!" Mrs. Alford said.

"Or so my family likes to claim. They say she walked into the shop one day: big, tall woman with golden hair coiled in a braid on top of her head. Said she wanted shoe trees, but when Great-Granddad showed her a pair, she barely glanced at them. 'What women really need,' she said—these are her very words; Great-Granddad left a written account—'What women really need is a *dress* tree. A replica of their entire persons. How often have I put on a frock for some special occasion,' she said—'frock,' you notice—'only to find that it doesn't suit and must be exchanged for another at the very last moment, with another hat to match, other jewelry, other gloves and footwear?' And then she walked out."

Martine was staring at me, with her mouth a little open. Mrs. Alford said, "Really!" and hooked a modeling-clay cow onto a lower branch.

"It was the walking out that convinced them she was an angel, I believe," I said. "If she'd stayed awhile—if she'd haggled over prices, say, or bought a little something—she'd have been just another customer making chitchat. But delivering her pronouncement and then leaving, she came across as this kind of, like, oracle. She stayed in Great-Granddad's mind. Before the week was over, he'd built himself a prototype Twinform and paid a neighbor's artistic daughter to paint the face and hair on. See, you got your very own features custom painted, was the clincher."

Mrs. Alford handed me a bent cardboard star covered with aluminum foil, not one point matching any of the others. I stepped onto the footstool and propped the star against the top of the tree.

"That's the reason," I said, "after the Twinform made him rich, Great-Granddad started his Foundation for the Indigent. And that's why the Foundation has an angel on its letterhead."

Martine said, "Oh, I always thought that angel was just a *general* angel!"

"Nope, it's a very specific angel, I'll have you know," I said.

"I don't understand," Mrs. Alford said. "Are you talking about the Gaitlin Foundation?"

"Right," I said.

"Do you mean to say you're one of *those* Gaitlins?"

"Well, when they claim me, I am."

"I had no idea!"

"I'm the black sheep," I told her.

"Oh, now," Mrs. Alford said, "you could never be a black sheep."

"Just try telling my family that," I said. "My family would take it kindly if I changed my name to Smith."

"They wouldn't!"

The tree was finished, by now—all the ornaments in place, not counting a paper snowflake that Mrs. Alford was hanging on to in an absentminded way. She looked distressed but also pleased, and alert for further tidbits. (People always imagine that our family must be loaded, although if they put two and two together, they would realize the Foundation had siphoned off most of the loot.)

"He's exaggerating," Martine said. Probably she was afraid I'd bring up my criminal past, which our clients, of course, had no notion of. "Barnaby's very close to his family! Seems every time I talk to him, he's just back from seeing his grandparents."

"Those are my Kazmerow grandparents," I said. "Not Gaitlins."

"Plug in the lights, Barnaby."

"The Gaitlins I see only on major holidays," I told Mrs. Alford. "Thanksgiving. Christmas. Ever notice how closely Christmas follows Thanksgiving? Seems I've barely digested my turkey when I'm back for the Christmas goose, sitting in the same eternal chair, telling the same eternal relatives that yes, I'm still a manual laborer; still haven't found my true calling; still haven't heard from my angel yet; maybe next year."

"You have an angel too?" Mrs. Alford asked.

"All the Gaitlins have angels," I said. "They're required. My brother Jeff saw his when he was younger than I am now."

"What'd she tell him?" Martine wanted to know.

"She told him to get out of the stock market, just before Black Monday."

"Isn't that kind of . . . money-minded for an angel?"

"Yes," I said. "I've always had my doubts about her. Besides which, she was a brunette. I maintain angels are blond."

Mrs. Alford was giving me this dazed look. I said, "Don't worry, Mrs. A.; I'm not serious," and I took the snowflake from her and hung it. (It was pancake-sized, slightly crumpled, snipped from gift wrap so old that the Santas were smoking cigarettes.) "I don't think my family's serious, either, when you get right down to it," I said. "Shoot, they don't even go to church! My dad's an outright atheist! The angels are just one of those, like, insider things that help them imagine they're special. You know? I bet your family has some of those."

"Well . . . ," she said dubiously.

I bent to plug in the lights, and when I straightened up, the tree was sending out this dusty, faded glow and Mrs. Alford had her hands clasped under her chin. "Oh! How pretty!" she said.

Some of the branches were drooping—the ones where the modeling-clay animals hung. Some of the paper chains' links had sprung open. The pine cones had lost quite a few of their scales, so that they had a snaggle-toothed look. But Mrs. Alford said, "Isn't it perfect?"

I said, "It certainly is."

By the time we got back to the truck it was dark, and a chilly drizzle was falling. Martine had to switch her windshield wipers on. While she drove, I filled in the time sheets, one for her and one for me, and I tore the carbon copy off hers and stuck it in her overhead visor. Then I sat back and said, "Ah, me."

The lights from the oncoming traffic kept swinging across Martine's face, turning her skin even yellower than usual.

We passed a city bus, empty except for the driver, its windows glowing foggily like the bulbs on Mrs. Alford's tree. We passed a little strip mall, all closed for the night and eerily fluorescent, with swags of frowsy tinsel swinging in the wind.

I said, "This weather will mess up a lot of New Year's plans."

"It won't mess up mine," Martine said.

"I thought you didn't have any."

"Who told you that?"

"Didn't you say Everett was sick?"

"Yes, but I'm going to this party at my brother's. Him and his wife are throwing a party, and I said I'd help with the kids."

Martine had a whole slew of nephews that she was forever amusing—taking them to the zoo or the circus or letting them spend the night in her apartment. I don't know where she got the energy. I could never be like that. I could barely recall what my own one nephew's name was.

I said, "Ah, me," again, and this time Martine glanced over.

I said, "In Penn Station today, this guy was going around asking people to carry something to Philadelphia for him."

"Whoa! A mad bomber."

"He claimed it was a passport for his daughter," I said.

"Yeah, right."

And then . . . I don't know why I said this next thing. I'd been planning to tell the story just the way it happened, I swear. But what I said was, "So when he asked *me*, I told him yes."

"You didn't."

"I did too!" I said. (For a second, I thought she was doubting my word.) "He said I had an honest face," I said. "How could I resist?"

"For all you knew, he was planning to blow up your train."

"Well, obviously he didn't succeed," I said, "since I'm here to tell the tale. No, I'm pretty sure it was a genuine passport.

Of course, I didn't actually check it out. This lady next to me, blond lady, she kept saying, 'Oh, just take a peek, why don't you? Just take a little peek!' But I wouldn't do it."

We slowed and turned into my driveway. Our headlamps lit the patio with two long spindles of mist.

"So anyway," I said.

I felt this inward kind of slumping, all at once, like, *What's the point? What's the* point? "I carried his package to Philly and gave it to his daughter," I said, "and that was that."

Martine had put the truck in neutral now, and she was facing me. For someone so small, she had an awfully large nose—an imposing nose, casting a shadow—and her eyebrows were large, too, and fiercely black, above her sharp black eyes. She said, "Hey. Barn. You want to come to my brother's?"

"Who, me?"

"You know they'd love to have you. You could help me with the treasure hunt."

"Oh," I said. "Nah. Thanks anyway."

Then I clapped her on the shoulder (little blade of bone under yards of slippery black nylon) and hopped out of the truck.

This time when the patio lamps lit up, they just annoyed me. I crossed the flagstones and went down the basement steps without stopping; unlocked my door and walked in, peeling off my jacket and dropping it to the floor, flipping on the wall switch as I headed toward the kitchen. Actually, it was more of a wet bar than a kitchen. But it did have a little under-counter fridge, and I reached inside for a beer and popped the lid. Then I turned on the TV that was sitting on top of the bar. Perky guy in a bow tie was wondering what this rain would do to the New Year's Eve fireworks. I settled on the couch to watch.

The couch was a sleeper couch, still folded out from last night, the blankets all twisted and strangled. The only other furniture was a platform rocker upholstered in slick red vinyl that stuck to me in the summer and turned clammy in the winter. I didn't even have a bureau—just stored my clothes on the shelves beneath the bar. My stove was a two-burner hot plate, and my bathroom was a rust-stained sink and toilet partitioned off in one corner; shower privileges upstairs. Every Saturday morning, Mimi Hardesty came tiptoeing down to do the family's laundry in the washing machine to the right of the furnace. Every evening, the Hardesty children roughhoused overhead, thumping and bumping around till the light fixture on my ceiling gave off little tingly whispers like a seashell.

Well, I make it sound worse than it was. It wasn't so bad. I think I was just at a low point that night. *Here I am*, I thought, *close to thirty years old and all but homeless, doing my own daughter more harm than good. Living in a world where everybody's old or sick or handicapped. Where my only friend, just about, is a girl—and even her I lie to.*

Not a useful lie, either. Just a boastful, geeky, unnecessary lie.

I think it was Mrs. Alford's fault. Or not her fault, exactly, but this job could get me down sometimes. People's pathetic fake trees and fake cheer; their muffled-sounding, overheated-smelling houses; their grandchildren whizzing through on their way to someplace better.

That employee who quit on us: Gene Rankin. He had a smart idea. He carried a kitchen timer dangling from his belt. He would set it to beeping at burdensome moments and, "Oops!" he would say to the client. "Emergency. Gotta go."

That was the way to do it.

. . .

How I started working for Mrs. Dibble: I was nineteen years old, fresh out of high school, looking for a summer job before I entered college. Only nobody wanted to hire me because, let's be honest, the high school I had attended was sort of more of a reform school. Not to mention that a lot of folks in the immediate area were mad at me for breaking into their houses and reading their mail. So my father asked around among his Planning Council members. (By then my father was head of the Foundation.) Eventually he persuaded this one guy, Brandon Pearson, to put me to work in his hardware chain. But I could tell Mr. Pearson had warned his staff about my evil nature. They watched my every move and they wouldn't let me near any money, even though money had never been my weakness. They gave me the most noncrucial assignments, and the manager nearly had a stroke once when he found me duplicating a house key for a customer. I guess he thought I might cut an extra copy for myself.

My second week on the job, a lady in a flowered dress came in to buy a board. Mrs. Dibble, she was, although of course I didn't know it at the time. She said she wanted this board to be two feet, two and a half inches long. So I told her I would cut it for her. I wasn't aware that a customer had to buy the whole plank. (Besides, she had these nice smile wrinkles at the corners of her eyes.) I grabbed a saw from a wall display and set to work. Made kind of a racket. Manager came running. "What's this? What's going on here?"

"Oh, he's just cutting me a teeny piece of shelving!" Mrs. Dibble sang out.

"What on earth! You weren't hired to do that," Mr. Vickers told me. "What do you think you're up to?"

That's when I should have stopped, I know. But I didn't like the tone he was using. I pretended not to hear him. Kept on sawing. When I'd finished, there was this enormous, ringing silence, and then Mr. Vickers said, clearly, "You are fired, boy."

"Oh!" Mrs. Dibble said. "Oh, no, don't fire him! It was all because I asked him to! I begged him and implored him; I pleaded on bended knee!"

But Mr. Vickers had his mind made up, I could tell. No doubt he was glad of the excuse.

I wasn't too devastated. I couldn't have stood the place much longer, anyhow. So I told Mrs. Dibble, "It's all right."

But Mrs. Dibble started burrowing in her purse. She came up with a cream-colored business card, and, "Here," she said, and she handed it to me.

RENT-A-BACK, INC., the card read. "WHEN YOUR OWN MUSCLES AREN'T QUITE ENOUGH." VIRGINIA DIBBLE, PRES.

"Your new place of employment," she told me.

"Aw," I said. "Mrs.—um—"

"All our clients are aged, or infirm, or just somehow or other in need, and what they're in need of is precisely your kind of good-heartedness."

"Ma'am—" Mr. Vickers said.

And I said, "Mrs. Dibble—"

I guess Mr. Vickers was going to say, "Ma'am, I think you should know that this boy is a convicted felon, or would have been convicted if his folks hadn't bought his way out of it."

And I was going to say, "Mrs. Dibble, I don't have a muscle to my name, if you're talking about heavy lifting."

But she didn't give either one of us the chance. "Nine a.m. tomorrow," she said, tapping the card with her index finger. "Come to this address."

Later, when she got to know me better, she told me it was my philosophical attitude that had won her. "It was the way you didn't protest at what happened," she told me. "You didn't put up any fuss. You seemed to be saying, 'Oh, all right, if that's how life works out.' I admired that. I thought it was very Zen of you." And she patted me on the arm and sent me one of her warm, wrinkly smiles.

She had no idea how she had just disappointed me. Till then, I had been telling everybody I saw—I'd told practically total strangers—that I'd been given my new job on account of my good-heartedness.

On TV, they were asking pedestrians for their New Year's resolutions. People said they had resolved to lose ten pounds, or stop smoking, or stop drinking. They'd resolved to join a gym or take up jogging. Seemed it was always something body-related. Except for this one guy—slouchy black guy in a hooded parka. He said, "Well, I just can't decide. Could be I'll start going to church again. Could be I'll apply to truckdriving school. I just can't make up my mind."

As if he were allowed no more than one resolution within a given year.

I finished my beer and set the can on the floor beside the phone. My answering machine was blinking, but I didn't expect any great messages at this hour. Unless some acquaintance was throwing a party and suddenly recollected my name. I leaned over and pressed the button.

"Barnaby," my mother said, "this is your mom and dad."

What a thrill.

"We just wanted to say Happy New Year, sweetie. Hope it's the start of good things for you—good news, good plans, a whole new beginning! Call us sometime, why don't you? Bye."

Click.

I flopped back on my bed and looked up at the ceiling. *Hope it's the end of all the trouble you've caused us*, was what she was really saying. *Hope at long, long last you're planning to mend your ways; hope you'll meet a decent girl this year and find a job we're not embarrassed to tell the neighbors about. Hope you get your instructions from your angel, finally.*

Now, why did this next thought occur to me?

I don't know, but it did.

Sophia Whatsit. Maynard. The woman on the train. Suppose Sophia Maynard was my angel.

Silly, of course. I'd been snickering at that angel stuff since I was old enough to think straight. If that was not the Gaitlins in a nutshell, I always told them: imagining they had connections even in heaven!

But still.

I saw her gold hair, her feather coat, her bun that was not so unlike (it occurred to me now) a coiled braid.

The trouble was, I seemed to be the first Gaitlin in history who didn't have a clue what my angel had wanted to tell me.

SHE WAS WEARING the feather coat again, and boots this time instead of last week's pumps. (Overnight a light snow had fallen—that considerate kind of snow that sticks to lawns but melts on streets and sidewalks.) Would an angel wear quilted black nylon boots with white fluff around the tops? Well, sure; no reason she couldn't. And she could sit on a bench in Penn Station reading a *Baltimore Sun* too, while she was at it.

I drifted closer, pretending I wanted to look through the window behind her. The 10:10 was on time for once, according to the notice board. All I could see was a segment of bare track, but I rested one knee on the bench and set my forehead to the glass and peered down. I think she felt crowded. She gathered herself together somehow; hid behind her paper. I backed off and turned away to show I posed no threat.

Of course, if she really was my angel, she would know that on her own.

Check out what *I* was wearing: a white oxford shirt and brown corduroys. No tie (there were limits, after all), but I had exchanged my leather jacket for my one tweed sports coat and trimmed my own hair as best I could and shaved that very morning. I was so clean-shaven, my face seemed to belong to someone else. Kind of plastic-feeling. A whole new surface to it. My skin felt stretched across my bones.

When the loudspeaker called out my train, I started down to the platform ahead of all the others so she wouldn't think I was following her. And I kept my back to the stairs after I arrived. I could feel her approaching, though, like a current of air, a change of temperature in a room. Her presence, descending the steps. I fixed my eyes on a point far up the tracks.

Two young women stood nearby. Sisters, from the look of them, both dark and pretty and dressed in layers of black. The taller one was trying to convince the little one to come all the way to New York with her. The little one insisted she was getting off in Philly. I tallied up the other passengers: twenty or so, at the most. With luck, it wouldn't be hard for Sophia to find a seat all her own. Then I would come along, nonchalant, couldn't care less. "Is this seat taken?" Or maybe not ask. Just sit, kerplunk, looking elsewhere, before she could claim she was saving a place for a friend.

Not that she would tell an actual lie, you wouldn't think.

But just to be on the safe side.

At the end of the track our train appeared, only a dot yet but growing. I stepped closer to the edge of the platform. The man next to me wore earphones looped beneath his jaw instead of over his head, which made him look like the bearded version of Abraham Lincoln. Just past him, Sophia rummaged through her bag for her ticket. Never mind that it was nowhere near time to have it ready.

The train drew up beside us, ding-dinging. Abe Lincoln

and the two sisters entered through the door nearest me, but I walked over to where Sophia stood. Several people got off, and then a woman with a baby got on. Sophia followed her. I came next. I was too close behind and hung back, biding my time.

It was unfortunate that the car was almost empty. This way, she would wonder why I didn't sit by myself. Well, too bad. She chose a seat at her right and for one awful moment seemed about to stay on the aisle but then, with a kind of flounce, she moved over. A good thing, too, because I was holding up a whole line of people behind me. Quick as a wink, I settled beside her. She kept her face turned toward the window. Her newspaper was nowhere in sight. She must have stowed it in her bag.

Passengers came shuffling down the aisle, and I watched the backs of their heads once they'd passed. A kid with a Mohawk, all prickly white scalp and pierced ears. Two nuns in short navy headdresses and square coats and thick-soled shoes. An old, bent man, creeping. I was trying so hard to sit still, to keep my elbow from touching Sophia's, that I was almost rigid. (As a rule, I twitched and jittered, jiggled a foot, drummed my fingers.) Face it: I felt kind of shy. Kind of unconfident.

Scared to death, to be honest.

The train lurched and started moving. Sophia delved into the bag at her feet and came up with a section of newspaper. It was folded open to the business page. Business! Lord above. I wondered why I was kidding myself. Did I just not have enough to occupy my mind? Or what?

We were passing people's wintry backyards, filled with scrap lumber and rusty shovels and plastic wading pools propped on their sides, everything skimmed with snow. The conductor came through saying, "Tickets, please." When Sophia handed him hers, I saw that she wore a Timex watch with a wide black leather wristband.

She wouldn't have any message for me. She was merely annoyed that I'd sat down beside her; and here I was, like a fool, waiting for her to inform me how to begin my life.

Wouldn't she laugh at me if she knew!

When Great-Granddad saw *his* angel, she lit the air of the woodenworks. *A golden dust, she dispersed, floating in the gloom,* he reported. *Lingering for an hour, at least, after she left the room.* The rhyme was intentional. He wrote up his encounter in the form of an epic poem whose scheme was A, A, A . . . till he ran out of words to rhyme with A, evidently, and then B, B, B . . . , and so forth. Not what you would call a literary masterpiece. Even so, my family treasured it. They kept it in a glass-doored bookcase in my father's study. A gray cloth ledger with maroon leather corners, containing three pages of penciled business accounts followed by seventeen pages of "A Providential Visitation, April 1898." Since then, the tradition was for *all* the Gaitlins to file reports on their angels—though Great-Granddad's was the only poem. Myself, I planned to stick to prose, when the time came. And right from paragraph one, I would stress my reliability, my solid and trustworthy nature. It's a mistake to go all misty and poetic when you're trying to convince your readers you've seen an angel.

Sophia said, "Excuse me, please."

She had her bag in both hands now, and she was perched on the edge of her seat, knees angled toward me, getting ready to rise. I said, "Oh!" and stood up and stepped into the aisle. She sidled out, bulky and wide-hipped, and started toward the front of the car. Was she leaving me? What was she doing? I sat back down and watched her bypass first one empty seat and then another; so I was partly reassured. She didn't stop at the rest room, either, but vanished through the end door. Maybe she was buying a snack. And her ticket stub was still in its overhead slot, her newspaper still in her seat. I was pretty sure she'd be returning.

I checked to see what news items she'd been reading. Plans for a merger between two banks. A growing concern over Maryland's bond rating.

She was probably some kind of financial wheeler-dealer. And I was out of my mind; and this train trip had cost me a whole lot of money for nothing, not to mention the goodwill of my best-paying customer. Mrs. Morey had wanted me to take down all her curtains for laundering today. I'd told her at the very last minute that I would be out of town. "Out of town!" she said. "You can't be out of town! This isn't a Philadelphia week; it's the first Saturday of the month!"

Oh, my life was a wide-open book to half the old ladies in Baltimore.

There was a sudden rise in the noise level, and I looked toward the front of the car and saw Sophia stepping through the door, gliding back in my direction at a stately, level pace. She hadn't left me, after all. I felt so grateful that when I noticed something in her hands, I thought for a second she was bringing me a gift. But it was only a Styrofoam cup of coffee. She paused next to me, and I jumped up, and—oh, God.

Jostled against her coffee. Spilled it all down her front.

"Geez!" I said. "I'm so—geez! I'm such an oaf!"

"That's all right," she murmured, but in a faint and reluctant tone that made it clear it was not all right. And who could blame her? Dark splotches stained the feather coat. Even her hands were wet. She shook one hand in the air, meanwhile hanging on to the cup with the other. "Allow me," I said, and I took the cup away from her—both of us still standing, braced against the swaying of the train—so that she could get a tissue out of her bag. She wiped her hands and then ducked into her seat and started dabbing at the splotches on her coat. I slid in after her. "I could kick myself," I said. Even through the Styrofoam I could tell that the coffee was hot, which made things all the worse. "I hope you didn't get burned," I told her.

She said, "No . . . ," and stopped scrubbing her coat and looked over at me. In a friendlier tone, she said, "Really. I'm fine. I should have let the counterman put a lid on, the way he wanted."

"Well, how could you have foreseen you'd be sitting next to a klutz?" I said. I passed her the cup. Then I removed the screw of soaked tissue from her hand and stuffed it into my seat pocket. "It was nerves, I guess," I told her. "I think I'm a little nervous."

"Nervous! About a train trip?"

I looked into her eyes. *Don't you know?* was the thought I sent her, but she gazed pleasantly, blankly back at me. Her eyes were blue. Her mouth was large and well shaped, lipsticked in too bright a shade of red, and the light from the window behind her gilded the powdery down along her jawline.

I said, "I'm, ah, heading up to Philly to see my little girl on not my normal visitation day."

"Oh," she said. "Well, I'm sure it will all work out."

Was this an official prophecy? No, of course not. Get a grip, Gaitlin. She took a sip of her coffee and shifted in her seat so she could pull her newspaper from beneath her. I said, "And besides!" (I was desperate. I didn't want to let the conversation die.) "Not only is it not my normal day; I'm not supposed to see her *any* day, ever again."

Her eyes came back to me. "Why is that?" she asked, finally.

"Last time I had car trouble, and I got there late, and her mother claimed it broke her heart," I said.

Then I said, "My little girl's heart, I mean. Not her mother's. Lord knows, not her mother's."

Sophia laughed. I caught the faint scent of flowers mingled with the coffee, as if she'd been chewing roses.

"So today I'm going up blind," I said. "I don't even know if Opal's going to be there."

Which was true enough, certainly. I hadn't given Opal a thought. I'd assumed that once I reached Philadelphia, I would turn around and catch the next train home. But I said, "Kids need their fathers. You can't just break off ties like that."

"You can't, indeed," she told me. "How old is she?"

"She's—um—nine? Yes, nine."

"Oh, at nine they definitely need their fathers."

"The trouble is," I said (for lack of any other subject), "I doubt my visits are anything she looks forward to. I've been seeing her once a month, is all. Last Saturday of every month. When they're that young, they can change completely in a month! Not to mention she's a girl. What do I know about girls? Do you have any daughters yourself?"

"Oh, no," Sophia said. She hesitated. Then she said, "I'm not married, actually."

I'd have been flabbergasted to hear she was, but I just said, "At least you've *been* a little girl." (Though in fact I wasn't so sure.) "You remember how it feels."

"Well, but I suspect I wasn't typical," she told me. "I was an only child. I think that tends to keep children childlike longer, don't you?"

"Opal's an only child too," I said. "Oh—sorry. My name's Barnaby Gaitlin."

"Sophia Maynard," she told me.

"Sophia, if you had your say," I said, "what would you advise a guy in my general position to do about his life?"

"I'd advise you to persevere, of course," she said.

"Persevere?"

"Why, certainly! I can guarantee that no matter what, Opal wants to keep seeing her daddy."

"Oh. Opal," I said.

Actually, Opal had never called me "daddy." "Daddy" sounded like someone else—someone who'd treat her to Shirley Temples in stodgy, flocked-wallpaper restaurants. I was starting to feel like some kind of impostor.

"But I don't have to tell you that," Sophia was saying, "because look at you!"

"Pardon?"

"You're already on your way to visit her!"

"Ah. Except that, well, this visit was really just a . . . random activity, so to speak."

"I know just what you mean," Sophia said.

"You do?"

"Sometimes intuition is our truest guiding force, don't you agree?"

"Intuition? Hmm," I said, paying close attention now.

"You can be *led* to get on a train, not even knowing why," she said.

"Is that a fact."

"And once you arrive at your ex-wife's, you're going to be led to say exactly the words that will change her mind."

"But see," I said, "I'm not sure that . . . at this point, I don't believe my family situation is the central issue anymore."

"I'm going to tell you a story," Sophia said.

I grew very still. I said, "Okay."

"Two weeks ago, I went to visit my mother. Well, I do that every week; she's elderly and she lives alone. But this time she was in such a fretful mood; so fractious. I made her some tea, and she said, 'This tea tastes moldy.' 'Moldy?' I said. 'It's a new box! How could it taste moldy?' She said, 'I don't know, but it does.' I said, 'Very well, Mother.' This was not fifteen minutes after I had got there, mind. I was still exhausted from my trip. But I said, 'Very well, Mother,' and I picked up my purse and went out to buy more tea bags. I was walking toward this little store nearby, but once I reached it, do you know what I did? I walked right past. I kept walking till I came to Thirtieth Street Station, and I hopped on a train and rode home. And all the way, I was thinking, *Heavens, what have I done?* Then something told me, *This is what you were led to do; so it must be right.* Well, my point is, that evening Mother telephoned, which she almost never does—she has that old-time attitude toward long distance—and she said, 'Sophia, I apologize. I don't know what got into me. All day I've been regretting my behavior, and I promise that when you come next week I will watch my p's and q's.' And true to her word, when I went back up last Saturday she was an entirely different person."

I couldn't figure out how this related to *me*. I said, "Well. That's very interesting."

She must have sensed my disappointment, because she said, "You think I acted terrible, don't you?"

"No, no. Not at all."

"You're shocked I would walk out on her like that."

"I'm not a bit shocked," I told her. "I know all about these aged parents. The kind that want everything done for them, and the kind you can't do a thing for, and the humble, self-denying kind, and the cranky, picky, dissatisfied kind . . . I must have seen every existing model. They're who my company deals with, mostly."

"What company is that?" Sophia asked.

"Rent-a-Back, it's called. We go around to people's houses, perform whatever chores they aren't quite up to."

"Oh! What a valuable service!"

"Well, we try," I said. (I wanted to look as good as possible.) "How about you?"

"I work in a bank. Equity loan department," she said. And while I was adjusting to this, she gave a little laugh and said, "Nothing like as helpful as what your company does!"

"Oh, I don't know," I said. "A loan can be extremely helpful."

She made a face, turning her mouth down. (She had no idea.) "And can people just telephone and you send somebody over?" she asked. "Or do they have to be on a schedule of some kind?"

"Either way. We offer both arrangements," I told her.

"Would a client be able to get her groceries carried in? Her garbage taken out to the alley? Little humdrum things like that?"

"Oh, the humdrum is our specialty," I told her. Then it dawned on me that she might have her mother in mind; so I added, "We operate just in Baltimore, though."

"I was thinking about my Aunt Grace. She's in Baltimore; and independent? You wouldn't believe how independent. But she's getting hard of hearing, and she's frail as a stick, besides; has trouble with her bones. She can break a bone in midair, if she's not careful."

"Osteoporosis," I said knowledgeably.

" 'Aunt Grace,' I tell her, 'you need a companion! Someone live-in, to fetch and haul!' But *oh*, no, no. Not Aunt Grace. 'I prefer to have my house to myself,' she says, and of course you can't really blame her."

"Yes, we see that every day," I said. Then, trying to get back to the subject, I said, "But anyhow. You believe in intuition."

"I most assuredly do." She nodded several times, cradling her coffee cup in both hands.

"You believe a person will just be led to the proper action."

"Absolutely," she told me.

I made myself keep quiet a moment. I allowed her a block of silence to fill; I put on an expression that I hoped would seem receptive. She didn't seize her chance, though. She just took a sip of her coffee. Beyond her head, bare trees skimmed past.

"So," she said, finally.

I sat up so straight, you'd think I'd been electrocuted.

But all she said was, "Tell me more about your company."

"My company," I repeated.

"How many workers does it employ? Would you call it a success?"

"Oh, yes, it's done very well," I said.

And then I gave up and just went with the flow—told her about our two newspaper write-ups and our letters from grateful clients and their relatives, their sons and daughters living elsewhere who could finally sleep at night, they said, now that we had taken over their parents' heavy lifting. Sophia kept her eyes on my face, tilting her head to one side. I could see how she would make an excellent loan officer. She had this way of appearing willing to listen all day.

I described my favorite customers—the unstoppable little black grandma whose children phoned us on an emergency basis whenever she threatened to overdo ("Come quick! Mama swears she's going to wash her upstairs windows today!"); and our "Tallulah" client, Maud May, who smoked cigarettes in a long ivory holder and drank martinis by the quart and called me "dahling." Then the weird ones. Ditty Nolan, who was only thirty-four and able-bodied as I was but couldn't face the outside world; so everything had to be brought to her. Or Mr. Shank, a lonesome and pathetic type, who took advantage of our no-task-too-small, no-hour-too-late policy to phone us in the middle of the night and ask for someone to come right away for some trifling, trumped-up job like securing a bedroom shutter that was flapping in the wind.

By the time we reached Wilmington, I'd progressed to Mrs. Gordoni, who couldn't afford our fees but needed us so badly (rheumatoid arthritis) that we would doctor her time sheet—write down a mere half hour when we'd been at her house a whole morning. "For a while, none of us knew the others were doing it," I said. "Then it all came out. Our two girl employees, Martine and Celeste: they weren't filing any hours at all for her, which is a whole lot easier to catch than just underreporting."

"Isn't that nice," Sophia said. "You don't often see that kind of heart in the business world."

"Well, I wasn't trying to brag," I said. "I mean, we generally do charge money for our labors."

"Even so," she said, and she gave me a long, serious stare and then nodded, as if we had shared a secret. But I didn't know *what* secret. And before I could say any more, the conductor walked through, announcing Philadelphia.

Still, even then, I hadn't quite lost hope for some kind of revelation. I went on weighing and considering her most casual remark, giving her every chance to redirect my course. As we stepped off the train, for instance, she said, "Notice how much faster people move, here," and I blinked and looked around me. Faster? People? Move? What was the deeper significance of that? But all I saw was the usual crowd, churning toward the stairs in the usual bobbling manner. "It always takes me by surprise, what a different atmosphere Philadelphia has from Baltimore," she said, and I said, "Atmosphere. Ah," and stumbled as I started up the steps, I was so intent on analyzing the atmosphere.

In the terminal, I stopped and faced her, wondering if her goodbye, at least, might be instructive. "Well," I said, "I enjoyed our conversation."

"Yes! Me too!" she told me. But she continued walking, and so I was forced to follow. She said, "I thought that was so fascinating about your company. Where are you headed?"

"Where am I headed," I repeated, sounding like a moron.

"Does your daughter live nearby?"

"Oh. Yes, she's off Rittenhouse Square."

"So's my mother. Shall we share a cab?"

"Well . . ."

It hadn't occurred to me that my actions would be observed at the other end of my trip. I said, "No, thanks; I—"

"Though it *is* a nice day to walk," she said.

A nice day?

We followed a group of teenagers through the Twenty-ninth Street exit, but I was dragging my heels, pondering how to get out of this. Suppose, by some horrible coincidence, Sophia's mother lived in Natalie's building! What then?

The weather did seem to have improved, I found when we reached the sidewalk. The temperature had risen some, and the sun was trying to shine. I said, "It's still kind of damp underfoot, though." I was looking toward the line of taxicabs, hoping she would change her mind and take one. But she walked right past them, and it was true she had those boots on.

On Market Street, she asked, "Are you bringing your daughter a present?"

"No," I said. I flipped my jacket collar up. (Tweed was not half as warm as leather.) "This was such a sudden decision," I said. "She's probably not even home! I should just cut my losses and grab the next train back."

"Darn," Sophia said, not appearing to hear me. "If I'd thought, we could have picked up something in the station. They have all those boutiques there."

"Well, no great loss," I told her. "I wouldn't have had the slightest idea what to get her, anyhow."

"You could have bought a stuffed animal. Something of that sort. All little girls like stuffed animals."

We veered around a man pushing a grocery cart full of rags. Sophia's pace had grown leisurely and wafting. I had a sense of being dragged backward. "When *I* was nine," she said, "my favorite toy was a stuffed raccoon named Ariadne."

"Ariadne!"

"Well, I was extremely fanciful. I liked the Greek myths and all that. It's because I was an only child. I was quite the little reader, as you might imagine."

She had the only child's elderly way of speaking too, I noticed. But I didn't point that out to her.

"My father kept forgetting Ariadne's name," she was saying. "Most often he called her Rodney. 'Sophia! Come and get Rodney! She's out here on the porch, and there's supposed to be a storm!' "

She laughed.

I looked at her then and knew, for a fact, that she was not my angel. She was an ordinary, middle-class, middle-aged bank employee with no particular life of her own, and it showed what a sorry state *my* life had come to that I could have imagined otherwise even for an instant.

If I'd had the nerve, I would have turned around then and there. Already half my Saturday had gone to waste. But it would have seemed peculiar, just wheeling and racing off with no good reason. So I dug my hands in my pockets and kept going.

I really hated this city, come to think of it—these wide,

pale, bleak sidewalks littered with blowing rubbish, and the bombed-out-looking buildings.

I said, "Where does your mother live, exactly?"

"On Walnut Street," Sophia said. "How about your daughter?"

"Locust," I said.

Thank goodness.

A truck roared past, and we walked awhile without speaking before Sophia asked, "Is your ex-wife a Philadelphian?"

"No," I said, "but her husband is."

"Oh, so she's remarried."

"Right."

"That must be difficult for you."

"Difficult? Why would you say that?" I asked.

"Seeing her with someone else, I mean. I suppose inevitably there's a bit of—"

"I never give it a moment's thought," I said, and then I stopped short, at the corner of Twenty-second Street, and said, "Well, here's where I'll be—"

But Sophia turned down Twenty-second and kept walking. I had hoped she would continue east. "It must have been an amicable divorce, then," she called over her shoulder.

I said, "Oh . . . ," and took a few extra steps to catch up. "It was *sort* of amicable," I said. (No sense going into the gory details.)

"Were you very young when you married?"

"Lord, yes. I was way too young. And she was even younger. We got married on her twentieth birthday."

Then I happened to glance down the street, and who was walking toward us? Natalie. She was wearing a red coat and holding Opal's hand. It was unsettling, because I'd just had a flash of how she had looked on our wedding day: all dressed up for the registry office, so pale and prim and solemn in a red coat that was not this same one, I guess, but close enough; close enough.

She hadn't seen me yet. She was speaking to Opal, turning to look down at her, and it was Opal (gazing straight ahead) who spotted me first. Opal wrenched her hand free and cried, "Barnaby!" and ran to meet me. There was enough of a breeze so she had lost that careful, prissy look. Her hair was tumbled, her cheeks were pink, and her jacket was flying behind her. She barreled into me and threw her arms around my waist, which she wouldn't ordinarily have done. She wasn't a very *warm* child, in my limited experience. But she said, "It's not true you're stopping your visits, is it?"

"Who, me?" I asked, and I looked past her to Natalie. She approached more slowly, with a hair-thin line of puzzlement running across her forehead as she noticed Sophia. (Maybe she imagined we were together.) I said, "Hey there, Nat."

"Mom said you weren't going to come anymore," Opal told me. She grabbed hold of one of my thumbs and started tugging on it, bouncing slightly on the balls of her feet in an edgy, agitated manner I'd never noticed in her till now. "She said you'd talked it over and you'd be stopping your visits. But I knew you wouldn't do that. Would you? You'd want to keep on seeing me! Wouldn't you?"

"Well, sure I would," I said. It hadn't occurred to me that she would take this so personally. I felt kind of touched. In a funny way, I felt almost hurt. My throat got a hurtful, heavy feeling halfway down to my chest.

And Natalie must have felt the same, because she said, "Oh, honey. Of course he would! I didn't realize you would mind so much."

Then a hand arrived on my arm, so light it took a moment to register, and I turned and found Sophia smiling into my eyes. It was the most serene and radiant smile; the most *seraphic* smile. "Goodbye, Barnaby," she said, and she dropped her hand and walked away.

I never did explain her presence to Natalie. I honestly don't know what I would have said.

4

MY FAVORITE MOMENT of the day comes before the sun is up, but conditions have to be right for it. I have to be awake then, for one thing. And the weather has to be clear, and the lights lit in my room, and the sky outside still dark. Then I switch the lights off. If I'm lucky, the sky will suddenly change to something else—a deep, transparent blue. There's almost a sound to it, a quiet sound like *loom!* as the blue swings into focus. But it lasts for only a second. And it doesn't happen that often.

It happened on my thirtieth birthday, though. I took that for a good omen. My thirtieth birthday fell on a Monday, which was garbage day for more than half our clients. I hadn't gotten around to setting out their trash cans the night before, because I'd indulged in this private little one-man birthday bash, instead. So there I was, up before dawn in spite of myself, just opening my door, which is the only place in my apartment

I can even see the sky from; and I switched my lights off, and *loom!*

I decided turning thirty might not be so bad, after all. I thought maybe I could handle it. I went off to work whistling, even though I had that balsa-mouth feeling that comes from too many beers.

It was a bitter-cold day, the kind that turns your feet to stone, and after I'd dealt with the trash cans I went home and wrapped myself in a blanket and tried to get back to sleep. Only trouble was, the telephone kept ringing. I let the machine answer for me. First call, Mrs. Dibble wanted me to take the Cartwrights grocery shopping. Second call, she needed a sack of sidewalk salt run over to Ditty Nolan. Third call was my grandparents. "Barnaby, hon," my grandma said, "it's me and Pop-Pop, just wanting to wish you a—"

I leaned over the edge of the bed and picked up the phone. "Gram?" I said.

"Well, hey there! Happy birthday!"

"Thanks. Is Pop-Pop on too?"

"I'm here," he said. "Hope you got plans to celebrate."

"Oh, yeah; well, yeah," I said in this vague sort of way, because I couldn't tell if they knew about the dinner Mom was fixing. I never could be certain. Some years she invited them, but other years she thought up reasons not to. (My grandpa had driven a laundry truck till poor vision forced his retirement, and Gram still clerked in a liquor store. "God gave" them—their wording—only one child, my mother, and they were very proud of her, but the feeling didn't seem to be mutual.) I said, "Probably I'll just, you know, drop by home for dinner or something."

"That's my boy!" Gram said. "That's what I like to hear! A visit'll mean the world to them, hon."

"Yes, Gram," I said.

Then Pop-Pop asked, "How's the car doing?"

"Oh, chugging along just fine," I said. "Had to take it in and get the steering linkage tightened, but no big deal."

"Why, you could have done that yourself!" he said. "That's what *I* always did, when she was mine!"

"Maybe next time," I told him.

I'd given up trying to convince him I wasn't a born mechanic.

The way the conversation ended was, I would stop by and see them later in the week. They had a little something for me. (A book of coupons good for six take-out pizzas, I already knew. It was their standard birthday gift, and one I counted on.) Then after I hung up I called Mrs. Dibble, because my conscience had started to bother me over the Cartwrights. They tended to feel rushed when somebody else took them shopping. "So," I said. "Cartwrights' groceries, Ditty Nolan's salt. What: she's expecting snow?"

"I have no idea," Mrs. Dibble told me. "We're just the . . ."

We're just the muscles, not the brains. I said goodbye and stood up to unwind myself from my blanket.

The Cartwrights were a good example of why Rent-a-Back was so sought after. They weren't all that old—early sixties, which in this business was nothing—but Mr. Cartwright had permanently ruined his right ankle several years before while stepping off a curb in Towson. So he couldn't drive anymore, and Mrs. Cartwright had never known how and did not intend to learn, she said, at this late date. Nor could they afford a chauffeur. Rent-a-Back offered just what they needed: somebody (usually me) to drive their big old Impala to the grocery store, and unfold Mr. Cartwright's walker from the trunk when we got there, and follow behind as the two of them inched down the aisles debating each and every purchase. I could have just waited at the front of the store, but I got a kick out of listening to their discussions. Today, for instance, Mr. Cartwright expressed a desire for sauerkraut, but Mrs. Cartwright didn't feel he should have it. "You *always* think you want sauerkraut," she told him, "and then you're up half the night with indigestion and it's me who has to bring you the Tums. You know how cabbage in any form gives you indigestion."

Mr. Cartwright said he knew no such thing, but I knew it. And I knew green peppers repeated on him too, and I knew what their shoe sizes were and their grandchildren's video game preferences, and I had advised on the very coat that Mrs. Cartwright was wearing today. (It was this navy one or a gray, almost white, which I had pointed out would show the dirt.)

In the window bays near the registers I noticed big sacks of sidewalk salt, and I thought of picking one up for Ditty Nolan. But the Cartwrights might feel slighted, seeing me attend to another customer on their time. So what I did was drive them home (Mr. Cartwright next to me, Mrs. Cartwright perched in the rear but leaning forward between us to advise on traffic conditions) and carry in their groceries, and then I got in my own car and drove back to the store for salt. Then I went to Ditty Nolan's.

I don't know why Ditty Nolan was scared to go out. She hadn't always been that way, if you could believe Ray Oakley. Ray Oakley said Ditty's mother had fallen ill with some steadily downhill disease while Ditty was off in college, and Ditty came home to nurse her and never left. Even after the mother died, Ditty stayed on in the Roland Park house where she had grown up—must have had a little inheritance, or how else would she have managed? For sure, she didn't go out to work. And when I rang her doorbell, she had to check through the front window first and then undo a whole fortress of locks and sliding bolts and chains before she could let me in. "Barnaby!" she said.

She was thin and pretty and unnaturally pale, with wispy tow hair that hung to her shoulders. Her dress was more a spring type of dress—flower-sprinkled and floaty—which wasn't so unreasonable for someone who avoided all weather.

"I brought your salt," I told her.

"Oh, good," she said, stepping back. "Come on inside."

I followed her in and dropped the sack to the floor. I said, "Has there been some kind of forecast I haven't heard about?"

"Forecast?" she asked. She was wandering away to some other part of the house. Her voice came threading back to me.

"Is it supposed to snow or something?"

"Not that I know of," she said.

She returned, holding an envelope. My name was on the front. "Happy birthday," she said.

"Oh! Well, thanks."

I should have guessed: the salt was just an excuse. She knew every birthday at Rent-a-Back and never let one pass without notice. I opened the envelope and looked at the card inside. "This was really nice of you," I told her.

She waved my words away. Long, fragile hands, untouched by the sun. "What a pity you have to work today," she said. "I hope you're having a party later on."

"Just supper at my folks' house."

"Is your little girl going to join you?"

"Well, no," I said. "But look at what she sent."

From my rear jeans pocket I pulled out Opal's gift—a leather money clip, the kind you make from a kit. I hadn't put any money in (if you thought about it, it was kind of an *ironic* gift), but I liked carrying it around. "The mailman brought this Saturday," I said, "along with a handmade card with a drawing of me on the front that really did resemble me. You could even see the stitches on my blue jeans."

"Oh, isn't that sweet!" Ditty said.

"I was so tickled that I called her up long distance," I said. "Knocked her mother for a loop, as you might imagine. But I think Opal liked it that I bothered."

"I'm sure she loved it," Ditty said.

I put the money clip back in my pocket. "You want me to add the salt to your account?" I asked.

"Yes, please," she said. "And then maybe when the weather gets bad, you could come sprinkle my walks. I can't have the UPS man falling down and suing me."

Ray Oakley always claimed, every year when she gave him *his* birthday card, that she had a little crush on him. But I knew better than that. She didn't have a crush on any of us. It's just that service people were the only human beings she saw anymore.

My parents lived in Guilford, in a half-timbered, Tudor-style house with leaded-glass windows. Out front beside the gas lantern was this really jarring piece of modern sculpture: a giant Lucite triangle balanced upside down on a pole. My mother went after Culture with a vengeance.

I showed up for dinner late, hoping my brother had gotten there first; but no such luck. Mine was the only car in the driveway. So I spent some time locking my doors and double-checking the locks, studying my keys to see which pocket they should go in. Eventually I was detected, though. My father called, "Barnaby?" and I turned to find him standing on the front steps. Against the light from the hall chandelier he looked like a stretched-out question mark, with his stooped, hunched, narrow shoulders. "What's keeping you?" he asked.

"Oh, I'm just . . ."

"Come on in!"

I climbed the steps, and he stood back to let me by. He was taller than me and more graceful by far—had a Fred Astaire kind of elegance that my brother and I had totally missed out on. Nor did we get his soft fair hair or his long-chinned parchment face. My mother's genes had won every round.

"Happy birthday, son," he told me, giving my arm a squeeze just above the elbow.

"Well, thanks."

That about wrapped it up. We had nothing further to talk about. As we crossed the hall, Dad sent a desperate glance toward the second-floor landing. "Margot?" he called. "Barnaby's here! Aren't you coming down?"

"In a minute."

The living room had an expectant look, like a stage. A fire crackled in the fireplace, and somebody's symphony poured from the armoire where the stereo was hidden. Over the mantel hung more of my mother's Culture: a barn door, it could have been, taken off its hinges and framed in aluminum strips.

"Well, now," my father said.

He seized the poker and started rearranging embers.

"Which birthday is this, anyway?" he asked, finally.

"Thirtieth," I told him.

"Good grief."

"Right."

Then we heard my mother's footsteps on the stairs. "Happy birthday!" she cried, hurrying in with her arms outstretched.

"Thanks," I said, and I gave her a peck on the cheek.

She had dressed up, but in that offhand way that Guilford women do it—A-line skirt, tailored silk shirt, navy leather flats with acorns tied to the toes. Her one mistake was her hair. She dyed her hair dead black and wore it sleeked into a tight French roll. It made her look white-faced and witchy, but would I be the one to tell her? I enjoyed it. You see a woman who's reinvented herself, who's shown a kind of genius at picking up the social clues, it's a real pleasure to catch her in a blunder. I watched as she bustled about—snatching my jacket, darting off to the closet, rushing back to settle me on the couch. "We haven't seen you in ages," she said when she'd sat down next to me. Then she jumped up: cushion tilted off-center in the armchair opposite. "You're skin and bones!" she said over her shoulder. "Have you lost weight?"

"No, Mom."

"I'll bet anything you're not eating right."

"I'm eating fine," I said.

If I'd lost weight every time Mom claimed, I'd have been registering in the negative on the bathroom scale.

Now she was off to pull open a desk drawer. The woman could not sit still. Always something discontented about her, something glittery and overwrought that set my teeth on edge. "Where *is* it?" she asked, rummaging about. She came up with an envelope. "Here," she said, and she sat back down and laid it in my hand. "Your birthday present," she said.

"Well, thanks."

"Maybe you can find yourself some decent clothes."

"Maybe so," I said, not troubling to argue. I folded the envelope in two and slid it into my jeans pocket. (I didn't need to look to know it was a gift certificate from some menswear store or other, someplace Ivy League and expensive.) "Thanks to you too, Dad," I said.

"You're very welcome."

He was propping the poker against the bricks, and the sight of his thin, sensitive fingers also set my nerves on edge, and so did the music diddling about as if it couldn't decide where to go. I turned to my mother and said, "So. Are Gram and Pop-Pop coming?" Which was purely to annoy her, because I already knew the answer.

"No, they're not," she told me, brazening it out. "But your brother is, of course. And I invited Len Parrish too. He's stopping by for birthday cake after; he couldn't make it for dinner."

No surprise to me. Len was one of those boyhood friends mothers always love, but he had gone on to big doings and left me far behind. I said, "Well, I wouldn't hold my breath, if I were you."

"He told me he'd come, Barnaby. I'm sure he'll keep his word."

The doorbell rang. "Oh! Jeff!" my mother said, and she jumped up and rushed to the hall, while Dad and I exchanged relieved grins. Things would proceed more smoothly now. Not only was my brother a better conversationalist, but he had a wife and baby who would help to dilute the atmosphere. Especially the baby.

Or actually, he wasn't a baby. It shows how out of touch I was. When Jeff and Wicky entered the room, this little kid was toddling between them—a pudgy tyke in a suit like his dad's and a polka-dot bow tie. "Look at that!" I said, getting to my feet. "Walking! At his age!"

"He's *been* walking for months," Mom said. "He's nearly two, for heaven's sake."

"Happy birthday," Wicky told me, kissing the air beside my left cheek. She smelled of toothpaste. She and Jeff made a model couple—Wicky an attractive blonde in clothes that were twins to my mother's, Jeff dark and square-set and handsome in a stockbroker sort of way. He wasn't really a stockbroker; he worked at the Foundation with Dad. But he had on one of those stockbroker shirts with the pinstripes and plain white collar.

"Where'd you park?" I asked him. "You didn't park behind me, did you?"

"The birthday boy!" Jeff said, clapping me on the shoulder.

"Is your car blocking my car in?"

"Relax," he told me. "I can move it at a moment's notice."

"Damn! You *are* blocking me in!"

But he was already heading toward the cocktail cart, where Dad had started rattling ice cubes. Wicky, meanwhile, bent to scoop up my nephew. "Give your Uncle Barnaby a birthday kiss, Jape," she said, holding him out in my direction.

Jape? Oh, right: they called him J.P. Jeffrey Paul the Third. J.P. stole a peek at me and then buried his face in Wicky's shirt-front. "Silly," she said. "It's your uncle! Uncle Barnaby! How does it feel to be thirty?" she asked me.

"Feels like hell," I told her.

"Oh, it does not! Look at me: I'm thirty-three. I feel better than I did at twenty."

"Well, you probably didn't drink a case of beer last night," I told her.

"True enough," Wicky said.

"Oh, Barnaby!" Mom cried. "A whole case? You didn't!"

These little rituals were so reassuring. I could always get a rise out of Mom.

Dad was taking drink orders. Jeff wanted Scotch, and the women wanted white wine. I said, "I'll have whatever J.P. is having," because I'd been only half kidding about last night. Then I was struck by the horrible thought that J.P. might still be breast-feeding. But no, he was having ginger ale, in a plastic cup with a bunny decal. Mine came in a glass, though. Dad handed it to me with a flourish.

"So! Barnaby! How's it feel to turn thirty?" Jeff asked.

"What an original question," I said. "Did you think it up all by yourself?"

"Oh, touchy, touchy," he told me. "Don't worry, it's not a bad age. Twenty-seven was worse, as I recall."

"Twenty-seven?"

"That's when it first hit me that thirty was on the way. By the time it actually came, I'd adjusted."

Count on Jeff: he plans ahead.

The whole bunch of us were standing, like people at a cocktail party. J.P. began spitting experimentally into his bunny cup. Wicky brought forth a sheaf of Christmas photos to show Mom. (She and Jeff and J.P. had spent Christmas in South Carolina with her folks, pretty much breaking Mom's heart.) Dad and Jeff talked about, I don't know, the Deserving Poor, I guess. "Exactly," Jeff said heavily, rocking from heel to toe. "I couldn't agree with you more. Exactly."

I went over to the fireplace and considered the barn door awhile. Then I drifted into my father's study. I stood sipping my drink in front of his bookcase, pretending to be absorbed by the titles. *The Gaitlin Foundation's First Quarter-Century, 1911–1936. The Gaitlin Foundation: Fifty Years of Compassion, 1911–1961.* Dry as dust, I already knew, and dotted with black-and-white photos of Planning Council members in stiff dark suits.

On the shelf below was the ledger containing Great-Granddad's epic poem and, next to that, his son's contribution, done up by some obliging printer to look like a ledger too. Same gray cloth, same maroon leather corners, the title trimmed with spires and dangles of lace. *Light of Heaven* was the title. Grandfather must have fantasized that someone besides Gaitlins would read what he had to say, because he explained things the family already knew. *My wife, Abigail McKane Gaitlin, was exceedingly devout,* he wrote. From the sound of it, he had been visited by one of Creation's dullest angels—a sweet-faced young secretary who arrived for a job interview at a "perilous moment" in his personal life and instructed him to appreciate his wife and children, after which she vanished. Reading between the lines, I always assumed that what we had here was an instance of attempted sexual harassment in the workplace, but that could have been wishful thinking; I was so eager for some sign of colorfulness in my family. The nearest thing to a renegade that we could claim was my great-aunt Eunice, who left her husband for a stage magician fifteen years her junior. But she came home within a month, because she'd had no idea, she said, what to cook for the magician's dinners. And anyhow, Great-Aunt Eunice was a Gaitlin only by marriage.

Just look at Dad's ledger; look at Jeff's. *A Possible Paranormal Experience*, my father's contribution, described the woman who stopped him on Howard Street and asked him for a match. While he was explaining that he didn't smoke, the police arrested the gunman who'd been lurking around the next corner. (But the gunman was only Charles Murfree, the unbalanced grandson of those selfsame Murfrees who'd gone bankrupt after purchasing our Twinform patent, and he'd been stalking my family for decades, off and on. Wouldn't you say, therefore, that if not for Angel Number One, Dad never would have been endangered in the first place?) My brother called *his* report *A Tradition Repeated*, which was appropriate in view of its many redundancies. I guess he was just doing his utmost to stretch a one-sentence encounter into a respectable length. (And a fragmentary sentence, at that. "Looking mighty spooky," his angel had announced, briskly refolding the stock market page before she stepped off the elevator.)

Close behind me, Wicky said, "Stop right where you are!" I practically jumped out of my skin, till I realized she was talking to J.P. He had padded in without my noticing; he was reaching for the crystal paperweight on the desk. "Don't touch, Jape," Wicky said. "What are you up to?" she asked me.

"Oh, just browsing," I said.

She came over to stand next to me, carrying J.P. in her arms. "*A Tradition Repeated*," I told her, gesturing toward Jeff's ledger.

I was hoping to get her reaction—her private, unvarnished views on Our Lady of the Stock Market—but she must have thought I was commenting on the whole shelf-load, because she said, "Yes, they're very inspirational, aren't they?"

Diplomatically, I took a sip of my drink. Except that the glass was empty and the ice cubes crashed into my nose.

"I feel so bad for your mom," Wicky said. "Now that angels are the latest thing, she worries you-all's will look faddish."

"You feel bad for my *mom?*" I asked. I was trying to find the connection.

"She was telling me, just the other day: 'It used to be that angels were unusual, but now they're in every bookstore; they're on every calendar and wall motto and needlepointed cushion; they're little gold pins on every lapel. Ours will be lumped right in with all those tacky newcomer angels,' she told me."

"They aren't *hers*," I said. "Mom is not even a Gaitlin! What's she all het up about?"

"Well, you know how she is."

I certainly did. If Mom had had her way, she wouldn't have merely married a Gaitlin; she'd have arranged to have a Gaitlin blood transfusion.

We went back out to the living room, where Dad and Jeff were discussing the new software they'd bought for the office. Mom headed off to the kitchen to see about dinner. J.P. wanted more ginger ale, but Wicky told him no. "It's the learning curve that worries me," Dad said, and Jeff said, "Yes, I'm very concerned about the learning curve."

The symphony on the stereo was building louder and louder, ending and ending forever. It reminded me of some huge, frantic animal crashing around the bars of its cage.

How come I always got the feeling that somebody was missing from our family table? I had thought so from the time I was little, toting up the faces at dinner every night: Mom, Dad, Jeff, me . . . It was such a pitiful showing. We didn't make enough noise; we didn't seem busy enough, embroiled enough. In the old days, I had thought we needed more kids. Two was a pretty lame amount, it seemed to me. Maybe we should have had a girl besides. I'd have liked that. It might have helped me understand women a little better. But my parents never obliged me.

Then later, when I got married, I figured Natalie would liven things up—I mean, at holiday meals and such. She didn't, though. For one thing, she was too quiet. Too demure, too well mannered; spine never touched the back of her chair. Also, she didn't last all that long. Eighteen months from wedding to bust-up. Opal was out of the picture before she got her own place setting, even. As for my sister-in-law, by the time she appeared I'd quit hoping. It's not that I had anything against her, but I had come to realize we would never be the kind of family I'd envisioned.

So there I sat at my birthday dinner, just going through the motions. "Great, you made the potato dish." That sort of thing. "Please pass the rolls." Mom had to tell her story about the New Year's Baby That Wasn't: how I had all but promised to be the very first birth of the year (name in the papers, free diaper service, six-month supply of strained spinach), but then, of course—of course!—had loafed about and procrastinated and shown up three weeks late. And that got Wicky started on Punctual-to-the-Minute J.P. We all turned, synchronized, to beam at J.P. in his high chair. "Not to imply that he was a *speedy* birth," she said. Wonderful: the Difficult Delivery Story. The rest of us were excused from inventing another topic for a good quarter hour. We fixed our eyes on her gratefully and nodded and tut-tutted.

Then I started having this problem that afflicts me every so often. I'm listening to someone talk, I'm the picture of attentiveness, and all at once I just know I'm about to burst out with something rude or disgustingly self-centered. I might say, for instance, "You think your labor pains are so interesting? Let me describe this tight feeling that's seizing up my temples." Because I did have a tight feeling. I felt overly aware of the art piece above the sideboard—actual knives and forks and spoons, bent into angular shapes and leaning out from the canvas in a threatening manner. "You wouldn't believe how my nerves are just . . . jangling!" I might have said. But apparently I didn't say it, because everyone was still nodding at Wicky.

At the end of the meal, Mom rose to clear the table, shooing away all offers of help. "I won't serve the cake just yet," she said as she set out the cream and sugar. "We'll wait for Len."

"Or go ahead without him, why don't we," I suggested.

"Oh, he'll be here by the time I get the coffee poured."

Dreamer.

While Mom was matching cups to saucers, Wicky remembered my birthday present and took it from her purse: a red silk paisley tie wrapped in red tissue. I hadn't worn a tie since Grandmother Gaitlin's funeral, but I put it on right away—knotting it around my bare neck, since my shirt didn't have a collar. "Thanks, Wicky. Thanks, Jeff," I said. "Thank you very much, J.P." Then I said, "Want to see what Opal gave me?" I dug the money clip from my pocket and passed it around. Everyone admired it. I said, "You should have seen the card that came with it. There was a really good drawing of me on the front."

"Oh," my mother said, "that child is just growing up without us! It's not fair."

"I was thinking she might come stay with me for a week or two this summer," I said. "She's getting old enough, I figure. I ought to be taking part in her life a little more."

"Stay in that basement room of yours?" Mom asked.

"Well, yes."

"I hardly think so, Barnaby. Maybe here, instead."

"There's nothing wrong with my place!"

Mom just pursed her lips and poured me a cup of coffee.

I'd been planning to mention my angel next. I mean, just jokingly. Tell how I'd half imagined she had instructed me to be more of a father. But somehow the moment had passed. A silence fell. The only sound was the clinking of spoons against cups. Finally Wicky started a story about one of her famous cooking disasters, but she interrupted herself to mop up J.P.'s spilled milk; or maybe she just lost heart. I said, "Mom? Do I get cake, or don't I?"

"Well, but what about Len?"

"Whose birthday is this, anyhow?" I asked.

"I hate to just go ahead," she said, but she stood up and went out to the kitchen. She came back with the cake held high in front of her: chocolate icing and a blaze of candles. We're not much for singing in my family, but Wicky started "Happy Birthday," and so the others raggedly joined in. "Make a wish! Make a wish!" Wicky chanted at the end. Poor Wicky; she was carrying more than her share of the burden here. Although J.P., banging his spoon on his tray, might be willing to help in a couple more years.

I blew out all the candles in one breath. (I said I'd made a wish, but I hadn't.) Then I grabbed the knife. "There's an extra plate for Len," Mom told me. "Just set a piece aside, and he can eat it when he gets here."

She was watching the path of my knife, sitting on the front two inches of her chair and coiled to spring the instant I flubbed up; but I disappointed her and cut the first slice perfectly. I sent it across to Wicky and said, "Haven't we been through this before?"

"Through what before?" Mom asked.

"Waiting for Wonder Boy and he never showed up? I seem to remember we did the same thing last year."

"I don't know why you always take that tone about him," Mom said. She waved a slice of cake on to Jeff. "You used to be inseparable, once upon a time."

"Once upon a time," I agreed.

"I believe you're jealous of his success."

"Success?" I asked. I stopped slicing the cake and looked over at her. "You call it a success, selling off fake plantation houses on streets called Foxhound Footway and Stirrup Cup Circle?"

"At least he wears a suit to work. At least he makes a decent living. At least he has a college degree."

"Well, if that's what turns you on," I told her.

She said, "Did you sign up for that course?"

"What course?"

"That night course at the college, remember? I suggested you might sign up for it and earn a few more credits."

"Oh, that," I said.

"Well, did you?"

"No."

"Why not?"

"Just never got around to it, I guess."

I handed a piece of cake to Dad. He accepted it with a pinched and disapproving expression, his gray eyes pronounced in their sockets; but it would be Mom he disapproved of, not me. He couldn't abide for people to act upset. And Mom was obviously upset. She was stripping all her rings off, a very bad sign. Setting them at the head of her place in little jingling stacks with trembling fingers: her wedding and engagement rings, Grandmother Gaitlin's dinner ring, her Mother's Day ring with its two winking red and blue birthstones. She said, "But the semester must have started already!"

I gave her a plate and said, "Probably has."

She pushed the plate away.

"Cakies, Jape-Jape!" Wicky caroled, aiming a forkful of crumbs at J.P. But J.P. was staring openmouthed at Mom, a thread of dribble spinning from his gleaming lower lip.

I cut the last slice, my own. A big one. I told my brother, "Not to be piggish or anything . . . ," and my brother rolled his eyes.

"Twelve, credits," my mother said, too distinctly. "Twelve, little, college, credits, and you could kiss Roll-a-Bat goodbye."

"Rent-a-Back," I said. I licked the frosting off a candle.

"You could buy yourself a decent suit and go to work for your father."

"Now, Margot," my father said. "If college were all that stood in his way, I'd dream up something for him to do tomorrow. Maybe he'd rather work elsewhere; have you considered that?"

"Of course he'd rather work elsewhere!" my mother cried. "Are you blind? He's spitting in your face! He's spitting in the *Foundation's* face! He has deliberately chosen employment that has no lasting point to it, no reputation, no future, in preference to work that's of permanent significance. And he's doing it purely for spite."

I had been steadily chewing, but I couldn't let that pass. I swallowed twice (the cake might as well have been sand) and turned to my father. "It isn't spite," I told him. "It's only that I feel uneasy around do-gooders. You know? When somebody tells me he, oh, say, spent his Christmas Day volunteering in a soup kitchen, I feel this kind of inner shriveling away from him. You know what I mean?"

"Barnaby!" my mother cried. "Your own father's a do-gooder! Think what you've just said to him!"

"And who cares if my job has no future?" I asked him. He was at one end of the table and she was at the other. I could speak to him directly and shut Mom out. "I need to pay my rent and grocery bill, is all. I'm not looking to get rich."

He seemed to find this idea startling; or at any rate, he blinked. But before he could comment, I said, "Besides. I wouldn't call Rent-a-Back pointless. It serves a very useful purpose."

"Well, certainly, for a fee!" my mother said triumphantly. "For people who can pay you a fee and then die, and that's the end of it!"

J.P. was starting to make cranky, whimpering noises. Wicky rose and tried to lift him from his high chair, but he was fussing and squirming. She said, "Jeff, could you give me a hand here?"

"What am I supposed to do?"

"Can't you get his legs out from under? I shouldn't have to manage all on my own."

"You need to slide the tray off first, for God's sake," Jeff told her.

"Well, you could slide it off yourself instead of just sitting there, dammit!"

I set down my fork and turned to my mother. "I'll tell you what's really bothering you," I said. (Oh, I always did get sucked in sooner or later.) "You think a thing is worthwhile only if it makes the headlines. *Prominent Philanthropist Donates Five Hundred Thousand.* You think it's a waste of time just to carry some lady's trash out for her."

"Yes, I do," Mom said. "And it's a waste of money too. *Our* money."

"Well, I knew we'd get around to that sooner or later."

"Our eighty-seven hundred dollars," she said, "that you have never paid us back a cent of because you earn barely a subsistence wage at that so-called job of yours."

"Margot," my father said. "He doesn't have to pay us back."

"Of course he has to pay us back! It isn't your average household expense: buying off your son's burglary victims!"

"*He is not required to pay us back, and you are behaving abominably!*" my father said.

The silence was that sharp-edged kind that follows gunshots or shattering claps of thunder. J.P. stopped whimpering. Jeff and Wicky froze on either side of him. My mother sat very straight-backed in her seat. It was a lot more obvious now that she was just a Polish girl from Canton, scared to death Jeffrey Gaitlin might find her common.

Strange how always, at moments like these, the table finally felt full enough.

I had my brother come out with me and move his car so I could make my getaway. At first he tried to stall, saying they were about to leave themselves if I would just hold my horses. But I said, "I need to go *now*," and so he came, muttering and complaining.

"Geez, Barn," he said as he trailed me down the steps. "You take everything so personally. Mom was just being Mom; it's no big deal."

"I knew she'd bring up that money," I told him.

"If you knew, why let it bother you?"

We stopped beside my car, and I zipped my jacket. "What's our next occasion? Easter?" I asked. "Remind me to be out of town."

"You should lighten up," Jeff said. "They don't ask all that much of you."

"Only that I change into some totally other person," I told him.

"That's not true. If you made the least bit of effort; showed you cared. If you dressed a little better when you came to see them, for instance—"

"I'm dressed fine!" I glanced down at myself. "Well, so maybe the tie doesn't go. But the tie wasn't my idea, was it."

"Barnaby. You're wearing a pajama top."

"Oh," I said. "You noticed?"

I had thought it didn't look much different from a regular plaid flannel shirt.

"And both knees are poking through your jeans, and you haven't shaved in a week, I bet—"

"I did have a haircut, though," I said, hoping he would assume that meant a barber had done it.

He squinted at me and said, "When?"

"Look, pal," I said. "Could we just get a move on here? I'm freezing!"

And I strode off toward my car, which forced him to go to *his* car, sighing a big cloud of fog to show how I tried his patience. His car was one of those macho four-by-fours. You'd think he rode the range all day, herding cattle or something.

A four-by-four, and a Princeton degree, and a desk half the size of a tennis court on the top floor of the Gaitlin Foundation. None of which I wanted for myself, Lord knows. Still, I couldn't help thinking, as I unlocked my car door, how comfortable it must be to be Jeff. Things just seemed to come easier for him. Me, I'd been in trouble from adolescence on. I'd been messing up and breaking things and disappointing everyone around me, while Jeff just coolly went about his business. It's as if he were an entirely different race, a different species, more at home in the world. More blessed.

What I sometimes told myself: *I'll be that way too, as soon as my real life begins.*

But I can't explain exactly what I meant by "real life."

I slid behind the wheel, slammed my door shut, watched in my rearview mirror as Jeff backed toward the street. When I moved to start my engine, though, I heard a honk behind me. I checked in the mirror and found a sleek black Lexus just turning into the driveway and blocking Jeff's exit.

Len Parrish, after all.

I opened my door and climbed out. Jeff was rolling forward again with the Lexus following, barely tucking its tail in off the street before it had to stop short behind our two cars. "Hold it!" I called, waving both arms, but Len went ahead and doused his lights. I walked over to the Lexus. "Don't park! I have to leave!"

He lowered his window. "Nice to see you too, Gaitlin."

"You're blocking me in! I'm going. You'll have to let me by."

Instead he got out of his car. A good-looking guy, wide-shouldered and athletic, in a fitted black overcoat. He wore a broad, lazy grin, and he asked me, "How's the birthday boy?"

"Fine, but—"

"Jeff!" he said, because my brother had come to join us.

"Hello, Len," Jeff said. The two of them shook hands. (I just stood there.)

"Guess I'm a little late," Len said.

"Well, Mom's saved a piece of cake for you," Jeff told him.

"Come back inside and help me eat it, Barnaby," Len said.

"I can't," I said. "I have to be going."

"Aw, now. What's the rush?"

Here's what's funny: Len Parrish went along with me on every teenage stunt I ever pulled. He was with me the night I got caught, in fact, but he wasn't caught himself, and I never breathed a word to the police. After the helicopter buzzed us, I tried to jump from the Amberlys' sunporch roof to the limb of a maple tree. Made a little error in judgment; I'd had a puff or two of pot. Landed in the pyracantha bush below. No injuries but a few scratches, thanks again to the pot, which kept me loose-limbed as a trained paratrooper all the way down. The police got so diverted, they failed to notice Len and the Muller boys slipping out the Amberlys' back door.

I didn't blame Len in the least. I'd have done the same, in his place. But it irked me that my mother thought he was such a winner. Him in his expensive coat and velvety suede gloves. He pulled off one of the gloves now to stroke the hood of my car. In the dark, my car looked black, although it was a shade called Riverside Red. "Grit," he said. He withdrew his hand and rubbed his fingers together.

"You want to move your vehicle, Len?"

"What you need is a garage," he said. "Rent one or something. Take better care of this baby."

"I'll go see to it this instant," I told him. "Just let me out of the driveway."

"At least you ought to wash her every now and then."

I slid in behind the wheel and shut the door. Jeff returned to his car, and Len at last ambled toward the Lexus, while I watched in my mirror. The minute the driveway was clear, I shifted into reverse and backed out.

Len should try this himself, if he thought Corvettes were that great. It just so happened mine was made in 1963, the year they had a split rear window. Stupidest idea in automotive history.

I was happy enough to be leaving that I returned Len's wave very cheerfully, before I took off toward home. Now he and Mom could have their little love feast together. Shake their heads about I-don't-know-what-Barnaby-will-come-to. Cut themselves another slice of cake.

I thought of my rooftop fall again. It was possible I could have escaped, if the tippy toe of my sneaker hadn't caught on some kind of metal bracket that was sticking up from the gutter. I remembered exactly how it felt—the barely perceptible hitch as my toe and the bracket connected. I recalled the physical sensation of something happening that couldn't be reversed: that feeling, all the way down, of longing to take back my one single, simple misstep. But it was already too late, and I knew that, absolutely, even before I hit the pyracantha bush.

Eighty-seven hundred dollars. It never failed to come up at some point. Mom might say, for instance, that they planned to remodel the kitchen as soon as they could afford it; and while a stranger would find that an innocent remark, I knew better. Of course they could afford it—if they couldn't, who could?—but she wanted to make it plain that they still felt the effects of that unforeseen drain on their finances. The waste of it, the fruitlessness. The niggling dribs and drabs handed out to neighbors. Sixty dollars for a ballerina music box, which I'd thrown down a storm drain in a moment of panic. Ninety-four fifty to mend the lock on a cabinet door. The most expensive item was an ivory carving of a tiny, naked Chinese man and woman getting extremely familiar with each other. I broke it when I stuffed it between my mattress and box spring. Mr. McLeod said it was priceless but settled for six hundred, grumbling. You'd have thought he'd be embarrassed to claim ownership.

I was heading up Charles Street now, slightly above the speed limit. Racing a traffic light that turned red before I reached it, but I hooked a right onto Northern Parkway without touching the brakes.

And it wasn't only the reparation money. Get Mom wound up and she would toss in the tuition at Renascence, besides. A little harder to figure the precise amount, there. As Dad pointed out, they'd have paid for my schooling in any case. But Mom said, "Not a school like Renascence, though, with its four-to-one student-teacher ratio and its trained psychologists."

I didn't count the tuition myself; I reasoned that Renascence was their idea, not mine. First inkling I had of it was, Mom said to pack my clothes because the next day I was leaving for a special school that was perfect for me: roomy accommodations out in the country and a supervised environment. Except I heard "roomy" as "loony." ("It's perfect for you: loony accommodations.") I flipped and said I wouldn't go. Never did want to go, even after they cleared up the misunderstanding. So I couldn't be held responsible for the Renascence bill, right?

Unfortunate name, Renascence. People were always correcting my pronunciation. "Uh, don't you mean *Ren*aissance?" And nobody got reborn there, believe me—nobody I ever heard of. The aim stated on the school's letterhead was "Guiding the Gifted Young Tester of Limits," but what they should have said was "Stashing Away Your Rich Juvenile Delinquent." The only thing "special" about the place was, they kept us twelve months a year. No awkward summer vacations to inconvenience our families. Also, we had to wear suits to class. (Which explains why I favor pajama tops now.) And every time we cursed, we had to memorize a Shakespeare sonnet. Boy, that'll clean up your language in a hurry! Not to mention instilling a permanent dislike of Shakespeare.

I remember this one sonnet I learned, the first week I was at Renascence. It started out, *When, in disgrace with fortune and men's eyes* . . . I thought it was me he was talking about. I swear it just about tore me apart the moment I saw those words on the page.

Well. As I said, it was my first week. And anyhow, the guy went on to say, *Haply I think on thee*, which was certainly *not* about me. I didn't have any "thee" in my life; no way. The girls I hung out with in those days were more body mates than soul mates, and you couldn't claim that anyone in my family was my "thee."

I wondered how my family would react if I ever paid that eighty-seven hundred back. How my mother would react, to be specific. She'd probably fall over in a faint.

Sometimes I thought if I could just show her, just once and for all *show* her, I would be free of her.

I reached my apartment, finally. Switched on the lights, unzipped my jacket, punched the button on my answering machine. Mrs. Dibble needed an errand run for Miss Simmons, provided I got home before six. Too late now; so I took off my jacket and started emptying my jeans pockets. Mimi Hardesty, upstairs, left a message about an eentsy bit of laundry she wanted to do in the morning even though it wasn't a Saturday. Then Mrs. Dibble again. Never mind about Miss Simmons—she'd sent Celeste, instead—but tomorrow I should meet with a brand-new client. A Mrs. Glynn. "It was her niece who made the request," she said. "She told me you two had talked on the train. Good work, Barnaby! You must be quite a salesman. The niece says her aunt will need hours and hours; that was her exact phrase. She inquired about our weekly rates. She wants you to come to her aunt's house tomorrow evening."

Mom's envelope was made of paper so thick that it unfolded by itself as I set it on the counter. I lifted the flap and peered inside. Whoa! Not a gift certificate, but cash—a hundred dollars. Five twenties new enough to stick together slightly when I fanned them out. Well, good; I didn't need clothes, anyhow. I hadn't yet redeemed my certificate from Christmas.

I restacked the bills and fitted them into Opal's money clip. Then I stood weighing the clip in my hand, looking down at it and thinking.

Let's say I made a hundred dollars extra every week. Say I lined up this aunt of Sophia's with her hours and hours of chores; say I stopped dodging the clients I didn't care for, the assignments I didn't find convenient, and added a clear hundred dollars to my weekly income. Eighty-seven weeks, that meant. Eighty-six with the birthday money; eighty-five and eighty-four if we could count next birthday and next Christmas too.

I would hand it to Mom in cold cash: eighty-seven crisp new hundred-dollar bills. I'd slide them out of the money clip and slap them smartly on her palm.

Everybody else's angel had delivered a single message and let it go at that. Wouldn't you know, though, *my* angel seemed to be more of the nagging kind.

5

MRS. GLYNN lived on a shady street just south of Cold Spring Lane, in a brown shingle-board house with peeling green shutters. I was supposed to meet Sophia there at five-thirty, which would give her time to drive over after work; but when I pulled up early, about a quarter past, she was already waiting out front. She was leaning against the hood of her car—a silver-gray Saab. I had always thought Saab owners were shallow, but now I saw I might have been mistaken.

I parked behind her and stepped out. "Yo! Sophia," I said, and then I wondered if I should have called her Miss Maynard. Mrs. Dibble had her rules about how we addressed our clients. Except that Sophia wasn't a client, strictly speaking. And she didn't appear to mind; she just smiled and said, "Thanks for coming, Barnaby."

Today she was wearing a different coat, black wool with a Chinese type of collar. It made her hair look blonder. Also, it seemed to me she had more makeup on. This must be her loan officer outfit. I said, "I thought bankers' hours were shorter. You mean you have to work till five like everybody else?"

"Yes, alas," she told me. We started up the front steps. "It was nice of you to agree to meeting my aunt first," she said. "I need to sort of talk her into this, as I explained to your employer."

"Oh, no problem," I told her.

"Is that who she is?" Sophia asked.

"Who who is?"

"Mrs. Dibble," Sophia said. She pressed the doorbell, and a dog started yapping somewhere inside. "Is Mrs. Dibble your employer?" she asked me.

"Yes, she owns the whole company. Started it from scratch and owns it lock, stock, and barrel."

"Because I had somehow understood that the company was yours," she said.

"Mine? No way." I had to raise my voice, since the yapping was coming closer. "I'm just a peon, is all."

"Well, surely more than a peon," she said. "It must take quite a bit of skill, dealing with your older clients."

"Oh, a fair amount. Shoot, some of us have Ph.D.s, times being what they are," I said. "Not me, though, I don't mean." I was consciously trying to be truthful, so she wouldn't get any more wrong ideas. But before I could explain that I didn't even have my B.A., the front door swung open and Sophia's aunt said, "There you are!"

She was no bigger than a minute—a tiny, cute gnat of a woman with a wizened face and eyes so pouchy they seemed goggled. She wore a navy polka-dot dress that hung nearly to her ankles, although on someone else it would have been normal length, and loose, thick beige stockings and enormous Nikes. Over her forearm she carried a Yorkshire terrier, neatly folded like a waiter's napkin. "This is my doorbell," she said, thrusting him toward me. "I'd never have known you were out here if not for Tatters."

"Aunt Grace," Sophia said, "I'd like you to meet Barnaby."

"Bartleby?" her aunt said sharply.

"*Barnaby*."

"Well, that sounds more promising. Won't you come in?"

"My aunt, Mrs. Glynn," Sophia told me, but Mrs. Glynn had already turned to lead us into her parlor. There was something about her back that let you know she was hard of hearing. And clearly the place was getting to be too much for her. The lace curtains were stiff with dust, and the walls were darker in the corners, and the air had the brownish, sweet, woolen smell that comes from a person sleeping extra-long hours in a tightly closed space.

"Sophia thinks I'm too doddery to do for myself anymore," Mrs. Glynn said. She waved us toward the couch. When she perched in a wing chair opposite, her Nikes didn't quite touch the floor. She set the dog down next to her, tidily arranging his paws. "Lately she's been after me to hire a companion. I say, 'What do I want with a companion? I'd just end up waiting on *her*, like as not, and we'd bicker and snipe at each other all day and I wouldn't know how to get rid of her.' "

"Well, there you see the value of Rent-a-Back," I told her. I was speaking in that narrower range of tone that carries well. (I had it down to a science.) "We can go about our business without a word, if you want. You can leave a key at the office, and we'll let ourselves in while you're out; be gone before you get home again."

"It's not that I'm antisocial," Mrs. Glynn said. "Am I, Sophia."

"Goodness, no, Aunt Grace. Just independent."

"Pensive? Well, I do like to have my thinking time, but—"

"*Independent*, is what I said."

"Oh. Independent. Yes."

She faced me squarely, raising her chin. "But we're not here to talk about me. We're here to talk about you. Are you a Baltimore boy, by any chance?"

"Yes, ma'am. Born and bred," I said.

"Is that right. Would I know your parents? What's your last name, anyhow?"

"Gaitlin," I told her.

"Gaitlin." She thought it over. "As in the Foundation?" she asked.

"Yes, ma'am."

"Really."

There was a pause. Sophia smoothed her skirt across her lap. Mrs. Glynn said, "Why don't you work for them, then?"

"It's a long story," I said.

"Lost art? Why is that?"

"A *long story*. Complicated."

"Aha," she said. "So you, too, are independent. Refuse to take any handouts from rich relations. Well, I don't blame you a bit, young man. Good for you!"

"Thanks," I said.

"Stand on your own two feet. Right? Now you see why I don't want a live-in companion."

"Oh, yes."

"Sophia's even offered to come stay with me herself, bless her heart," Mrs. Glynn said. She reached over to ruffle the Yorkie's bangs. He smiled, showing his tongue—a little pink dollop of a tongue like on a child's teddy bear. "I told her, 'What, and spoil a perfectly good relationship?' Sophia is my one and only niece. It's not as if I had relatives to squander."

"I thought I could live in her guest room," Sophia told me, "but Aunt Grace wouldn't hear of it."

"She'd be watching me every minute," Mrs. Glynn said. "Oh, I know: meaning the best! But trying to change what I ate or when I went to bed. Wouldn't you?" she asked Sophia fondly. "As it is, you're worse than a mother."

"It's true," Sophia said. "I'm a worrywart."

"She's a worrywart!" Mrs. Glynn announced. She came up with it so triumphantly, I was pretty sure she hadn't heard Sophia. "Pushing the multivitamins. Nagging me to exercise. Trying to make me stash my money in a bank."

"Aunt Grace distrusts banks," Sophia told me.

"Of course I distrust banks!" Mrs. Glynn said. This she seemed to have caught with no trouble, although Sophia had barely murmured it. "I lived through the Great Depression! I'd be out of my mind to trust a bank! I keep my liquid assets in the flour bin."

"There," Sophia said. "See what I mean?" she asked me. "She hasn't known a person five minutes and she tells him where she keeps her cash."

"Not just *a* person. A *nice* person, with kind brown eyes and a mouth that tips up at both ends!"

"But you'd tell anybody you met, I believe," Sophia persisted. "You think we're still in the thirties, when people left their front doors unlocked and their car keys in the ignition."

"Now, don't exaggerate," Mrs. Glynn said. "I'm very careful to lock my front door."

"When you happen to think of it!"

I could see they'd had this conversation any number of times. They were obviously enjoying themselves, each delivering her lines with an eye cocked in my direction. I said, "Well, anyhow. At Rent-a-Back, we're used to dealing with independent people. We adjust to fit our customers' needs: as much butting in as they want, or as little."

"Tell about Mr. Shank," Sophia prodded me.

"Mr. Shank?"

"How he calls in the middle of the night just because he's lonely."

"Oh," I said. I was surprised that she'd remembered. "Well, he's got the opposite problem, really—"

"Tell about Mrs. Gordoni. There's this client named Mrs. Gordoni," Sophia said to her aunt, "who can't afford to pay."

"In pain from what?" Mrs. Glynn asked.

"To pay. To pay the fees," Sophia said. "And Barnaby helps her out even so, and underreports his hours."

"I have no problem whatsoever in paying off my bills," Mrs. Glynn told me firmly.

Sophia said, "No, I didn't mean—"

"Whatever the charge, I can more than pay. And however many hours. I believe I'll start with an hour a day. After that, we'll see."

"An hour a day," I said, hunting through my pockets for my calendar. "And would that be mornings, or afternoons?"

"Afternoons, if you have them."

"Yes, ma'am. Or somebody will. Me or one of the others."

"One of the others? Wait. Wouldn't it be you who came?"

"I'll come if possible," I said.

"I'd prefer it to be you."

"Well, I'll try," I said.

"For one thing, you're left-handed," she told me.

I was, in fact, although I had no idea how she had figured that out. Sophia said, "What does left-handed have to do with it?"

"I just feel left-handers are more reliable, that's all."

Sophia made a sound somewhere between a laugh and a sigh. I said, "Yes, ma'am, I'm very reliable," as I flipped through calendar pages. "How is three o'clock?" I asked. "I have that open every weekday. Or four o'clock except for Fridays, so on Fridays we could—"

"No, I think later," Mrs. Glynn said decisively. "I think five-thirty. Could you do that?"

"Sure thing," I told her, penciling it in. Five-thirty was our slow time—dinner hour for many of the older folks. "Will you be here then? Or you want to give us a key."

"You can take a key for unexpected occurrences," she said, "but generally I'll be here. Why don't you start next Monday? By then I'll have a list written out."

She rose from her chair, and we did too. Her little dog perked up his ears and made a chortling sound. "I knew you were left-handed because you put Sophia on your right when you sat down," Mrs. Glynn told me. "My husband was left-handed. He liked to have me on his right at all times—sitting, walking, even sleeping. He said it freed his sword arm to defend me."

When she smiled up at me, the bags beneath her eyes grew bigger than ever. She had to sort of peek out over them. It made her seem mischievous and gleeful, like an elf.

Mrs. Glynn's five hours would help out quite a bit with the eighty-seven hundred, but they wouldn't be enough on their own, of course. I told Mrs. Dibble I needed more jobs. "You know Mrs. Figg? The Client from Hell? You can send me over there after all; I've changed my mind. And forget what I told you about wanting off Saturday nights."

"Hmm," Mrs. Dibble said. "Someone must be saving up for something."

I just said, "Oh, a few extra dollars would always come in handy."

For the sake of a few extra dollars, I agreed to a double trash-can route when Jay Cohen came down with mono. I spent an entire day shifting furniture for Mrs. Binney, who stood about with one finger set prettily to her chin and said, "On second thought . . ." I loaded the Winstons' station wagon at four o'clock in the morning for their annual drive to Florida. (They wouldn't let me do it the night before—scared of thieves. And of course they were the type who believed in setting off before dawn.)

I even went so far as to telephone Len Parrish, because he had mentioned needing part-time help on his newest housing development. Someone to show off the model home—just a warm body, he'd said. But not *my* warm body, evidently, because first he behaved like Mr. Important ("Barn! You caught me just as I was heading out the door! Sorry I can't chat."), and then he claimed he'd already hired someone. I didn't know whether to believe him or not. "Hey, guy," he said. "How you *doing*? How's the *car*? We should get together for a drink at some point. I'm going to give you a call."

I wondered if he planned to declare the drink on his taxes. (Not that I really expected him to call.) One time, Len had told me that just about anything he did he considered tax deductible. "Taking a trip to the beach, going to the movies . . . ," he said. "Because it gives me more experience, and I'm therefore better equipped to make informed business decisions. Heck, the way I figure it, *life* is tax deductible!"

Probably it was just as well he didn't have any work for me.

On Monday, I went to Mrs. Glynn's, bringing my canvas gloves because I didn't know what chores she had in mind. But as it turned out, her list contained only the most undemanding tasks. *Fetch all tureens and platters from tops of kitchen cabinets, replace on shelves within my reach. Move armchair from sunporch to living room.*

I was tightening the screws on a saucepan rack when Sophia showed up. I heard Tatters yapping at her. She had come straight from work, apparently. Breezed into the kitchen in her dressy black coat and asked me, "How's it going?"

"Going fine," I told her.

"I just thought I'd stop by and make sure the two of you were getting along."

"Well, we haven't had all that much to do with each other," I said. I could speak in a normal tone, because Mrs. Glynn had returned to the parlor after ushering in Sophia. "So far I've just been following what she's got on her list," I said. "But I'm not sure there's enough here to fill the whole hour."

"Oh, this is just the beginning, when she's not used to the luxury of having you around. Believe me: there's a lot to be done! I can name some things if she can't. I've been nagging her for years now to pack up my uncle's lawbooks in the sunporch."

She was watching me replace the saucepans. They were filmed with dust—Mrs. Glynn must not cook much—so I gave each one a rub with my shirtsleeve before I hung it. Then I worried that would strike Sophia as sloppy. I said, "Do you suppose she would want to run these through the dishwasher?"

"Well, maybe," Sophia said. But she didn't go ask. She said, "My ulterior motive here is to get Aunt Grace's belongings organized somewhat and then move her to an apartment. Something nearer to my place, so I could keep an eye on her. She's nearly eighty years old, after all."

I decided to give up on the dishwasher idea. I hung another pan. "Eighty, huh?" I said. "Is she actually your aunt, or is she a great-aunt?"

"No, she's my aunt. My father's sister. I was a late arrival,"

Sophia said. "My mother was in her forties when she had me. By now she's almost eighty herself, and I'm only thirty-six."

I was ready for the next job: fixing a loose knob on a cupboard in the pantry. I headed off to see to it, taking the screwdriver with me.

"I guess *you* think thirty-six is old," Sophia said in the pantry doorway.

"Gosh, no," I told her politely. "Not when I've been hanging out with people in their nineties." I jiggled the knob and then squatted down in front of it.

"How old are you, Barnaby?"

"I turned thirty last week."

"Oh. Well, happy birthday."

"Thanks."

"Did somebody throw you a party?"

"Just my parents had me to dinner," I said. I opened the door slightly to study the inner side of the knob.

"How about your little girl?"

"How about her."

"Did she come down for the dinner?"

"Nah. Well, she'd already given me my present, see. And besides, I knew I'd be going up there Saturday."

"Yes, I looked for you on the train," she said.

"You did?"

"I remembered you always visit her the last Saturday of the month."

"This time I drove," I said. "I generally do, if my car's not on the blink."

"Oh, you drove."

"It's cheaper."

"I should do that too, I suppose. If I weren't so nervous on interstates," she said.

I was trying to tighten a screw now, but it kept slipping away from me. Sophia was making me self-conscious. I'm not a bona fide handyman; I do these little fix-it jobs by trial and error. So I looked at her, and she must have understood, because she said, "Well. I'll let you get on with it."

Then she straightened up from the doorway and left, and a moment later I heard her out front, telling her aunt goodbye.

My second day on the job, Mrs. Glynn had me take her to the grocery store. She was a quicker shopper than the Cartwrights but a much worse back-seat driver. Although we were in my car (she'd given hers up years ago, she said), she slammed a Nike down hard every time we neared a stoplight, and she wouldn't talk at all but concentrated fiercely on the traffic. Even in the store, conversation was tough, because the background noise made her hearing worse. When I asked her, in the canned-fruit aisle, whether she liked mandarins, she said, "I like *any* kind of instrument," and at the register she took offense when the clerk offered plastic or paper. ("*Naturally* I can pay for it, or why else would I be here?" she snapped.) But we did okay. Used up slightly more than an hour—though I didn't note the extra on my time sheet—and at the end, she told me I'd been a help. "I hate to rely on Sophia for every little thing," she said. "Not that she isn't sweet as pie about it, but *you* know."

Wednesday, I bought a new curtain rod and installed it in her dining room where the old one had started to sag. Thursday, she asked me to pack up those lawbooks of her husband's. So I drove off to the liquor store for some boxes, and when I got back, I found Sophia in the sunporch. She had her coat off and her sleeves rolled up, and she'd covered the desk with cleaning supplies—rags and a can of furniture polish. "Hello, Barnaby," she said. "I thought I'd follow along behind you and wipe off the shelves as you clear them."

"Oh, I can do that," I told her.

"I wouldn't dream of it! You're not her housekeeper, after all."

"No, but a lot of our jobs *edge over* into housekeeping," I said. "We're used to handling pretty much anything that's required. I'll be glad to wipe the shelves."

"Well, aren't you nice," she told me.

But when I returned from the car with the second load of boxes, she'd already emptied one bookshelf onto the desk and started dusting. So I gave up. She must have been one of those people who couldn't bear sitting by while other people worked—unlike her aunt, who was off in the parlor happily talking baby talk to Tatters.

"I have no idea what to do with these books once we get them packed," Sophia told me. "I suppose some charity might want them."

"I'll ask Mrs. Dibble. She keeps a Rolodex for things like that."

"Uncle George has been dead for twenty years or more, and every book he ever owned is still sitting here. I think all his clothes are still in the upstairs closet too."

"That's nothing compared to some of our clients," I said. "This one woman, Mrs. Morey: she sleeps with her husband's bathrobe laid across the foot of the bed, and he's been gone as long as I've known her."

"Oh! How sad!"

"Yeah, well."

"You must see so many sad things in this job."

"Well, quite a few," I said. I stopped to consider, bracing a carton of books against my shoulder. "On the other hand," I said, "I see quite a few happy things too. This same Mrs. Morey, for instance: she just loves her garden. Come spring, you'd think she was in heaven. She says, 'As long as I can walk out in my garden first thing every morning—take that gardener's early-morning walk, to check what's sprouted overnight and what's about to bloom,' she says, '—why, I feel I have something worth staying alive for.' "

Sophia lifted her dustcloth and turned to look at me. She said, "You're a very kindhearted person, Barnaby Gaitlin."

I said, "Me? I am?"

Of course, I no longer believed that Sophia was my angel. Not literally, at least. But still, I paid close attention whenever she told me something in that quiet, firm tone of voice.

Martine said Sophia had designs on me—that she was hanging around at her aunt's all the time in the hope I'd ask her out. I said, "She's *what*?" We were loading the books onto Martine's boyfriend's truck when she came up with this. Granted, Sophia had put in several appearances—at the moment, she was in the attic, checking for more lawbooks—but the notion of any romantic interest was absurd. I heaved a box onto the truck bed and said, "Get serious, Pasko. She's thirty-six years old."

"So?" Martine said.

"She's a . . . lady! She works in a bank!"

"We women can sense these things," Martine said knowingly. I had to laugh. (She was wearing Everett's parka today, the hood trimmed with matted fake fur, and her little face poked out of it like some sharp, quick, rodenty animal.) "I saw how she was eyeing you!" she said. "Lolling around the sunporch, getting underfoot. Asking those made-up questions in that . . . lilting way of hers. 'Ooh, Barnaby, do you think they'll all fit in one truckload?' 'Ooh, Barnaby, won't you strain your back lifting that great heavy box?' "

Sophia had asked nothing of the sort; Martine was imagining things. I said, "You're just envious, is all."

"Envious!"

"You wish *you* could act so well bred and refined."

"Like hell I do," Martine said. She started back up the front walk, calling over her shoulder, "So obvious and flirtatious is more like it."

"Sh!" I said, glancing toward the house. I caught up with her and said, "She's being a good niece; what's wrong with that? Watching out for her aunt."

"Committing her aunt to five hours a week just to have you around," Martine said.

"Now wait," I said. "I really need these extra hours, Martine."

"Well, sure, *you* need them."

Martine was the only person I'd told about my plan to pay back the eighty-seven hundred. (She'd made a bet with me that my parents wouldn't accept it—"They're not exactly poverty-stricken," she'd said—but that just showed how little she knew Mommy Dearest.) "The question is," she said now, "does the *aunt* need them?"

But before I could argue my case any further, Sophia stepped out the front door. "Guess what, Barnaby!" she called. "In the attic are boxes and boxes of books! More than there were in the sunporch, even!"

Her voice had a kind of caroling tone—a kind of, yes, lilting tone, I had to admit. And she tipped her head against the doorframe in this picturesque, inviting way and flashed me a white-toothed smile.

I felt my heart sink. I glanced over at Martine. She didn't

meet my eyes; just climbed the porch steps alongside me. But I saw the smug little kink at the corner of her mouth. I heard the humming sound she made beneath her breath. "Hmm-hmm-hmm," she hummed, high-pitched and airy and innocent, clomping up the steps in her motorcycle boots.

6

ON THE LAST Saturday in February, Opal had a ballet recital. This meant I had to share my monthly visit with my mother. Mom phoned and said she'd been sent an invitation. "I'll do the driving," she told me. "I don't trust that car of yours as far as I can throw it."

"Or here's an idea," I said. "Why don't I just meet you there?"

"You mean, not ride up together?"

"Well . . ."

"Barnaby," she said. "I would hardly suppose you're in any position to buy gas when you don't need to."

Which was when I could have told her, "That's *my* business, isn't it?" so she could come back with, "Not as long as you still owe us eighty-seven hundred dollars, it isn't." For once, though, I kept quiet. I thought about Opal's money clip and I held my tongue. This seemed to throw Mom off her stride. She waited just a beat too long, and then she cleared her throat and said, "I'll pick you up at eight a.m. sharp. You be waiting out front."

I said, "Well. Okay."

"Don't make me come into that place of yours and haul you out of bed. Set your alarm clock. Promise."

"Sure thing," I told her.

I tried to look on the bright side after I hung up. At least now I'd have an ally along—or someone people would assume was my ally. Though myself, I had my doubts.

Saturday morning turned out so clear that I checked the sky for the color-change trick after I got up, but the sun had beaten me to it. And then I found I was out of instant coffee; so I had to make do with a Pepsi; and then my mother came early. I swear I would have been ready by eight, but she came five minutes before. Stalked across the patio in her brisk black wool pantsuit, all spiny-backed and indignant. "Where *are* you, Barnaby?" she asked—and this was after I'd opened the door and was standing in plain view.

"Eight o'clock, you said," I told her. "What are you doing here at five of?"

"Well, come along; don't waste more time arguing," she snapped, and she turned on her heel and marched off again. She knew she was in the wrong.

Her car was a Buick, very posh and plushy. Power windows you couldn't roll down unless *she* had turned the ignition on. She drove well, though; I had to hand her that. She slung that thing around like a grocery cart—slithered out of town and started cruising up I-95 in no time flat. "Of course, at this rate we'll hit the recital way too early," I said when we'd been traveling awhile. "We'll have to sit there making small talk with Natalie and Mr. Wonderful."

"If you didn't want her remarrying, you shouldn't have gotten divorced," Mom told me.

"Did I say I didn't want her remarrying? What do I care what she does? I'd just rather not mingle socially with the guy; that's all."

"At least we were invited," Mom said. "Oh, when I read those letters to Ann Landers, I could cry: those poor bewildered souls who lose all touch with their grandchildren after the divorce. Why should *they* have to suffer? It's no fault of theirs if their sons can't manage to sustain a serious relationship!"

"You certainly have a way with words," I told her.

"Hmm?" she asked, and she veered around a tour bus. "What did I say?" she asked me.

I kept quiet and drummed my fingers on my knees.

"I suppose it's merely your generation," Mom said in a placating tone. "Everybody in your generation seems to view marriage so lightly."

"Generation!" I said. "I don't belong to a generation!"

Oops. The trick was to dodge to one side here; resist a head-on argument. I tried for a save. "Anyhow," I said, "generations nowadays seem to change over about every three years or so, have you noticed? Why is that, I wonder."

But Mom refused to get diverted. She said, "Mind you, I don't exempt Natalie's parents. Jim and Doris Bassett were at least as much to blame as you two were, I always felt. They actively encouraged that divorce!"

I just whistled a tune through my teeth and gazed out the side window. We were crossing a body of water. It looked very broad and peaceful.

"Say what you will," Mom told me, "but at least your father and I accepted your marriage graciously. I treated Natalie like my own! That's why she still asks me to Opal's recitals and such. Even if she does send just a standard mimeographed invitation with my name filled in on the blank."

She treated Natalie *better* than her own, I wanted to say. Miss High-Class Good-Girl Natalie, the daughter of Mom's dreams. But I let it rest. I watched a train skim across a railroad bridge in the distance, and I pondered whether it really was possible, these days, to get something mimeographed.

The recital was in the basement of a church on Chestnut Street. We had the devil's own time finding parking—ended up in a space several blocks away. "Now you see why I wanted to start out early," Mom told me. She tossed the words over her shoulder as she strode ahead of me, her purse clamped in a paranoid way between her arm and her rib cage. All the women around us looked just like her, tailored and crisp, with shoes that you just knew, somehow, had cost a whole lot of money. All the men were homeless. They sat huddled under ragged blankets on top of the grates in the sidewalk, and I couldn't help thinking that I had more in common with them than with my mother.

In the church basement the women were younger, and most of them had husbands in tow. I saw no sign of Natalie or *her* husband, though—not that I tried very hard. I settled in a folding chair and made a telescope out of my program. (Which did seem mimeographed.) My mother started chattering in this chirpy, chipmunk tone she puts on when she feels ill at ease, giving me a whole rundown of an avant-garde play she'd recently dragged my father to. Maybe the sight of the stage had brought it to her mind. "First the actors came out all bundled up in down jackets," she told me, "and as the play went on they stripped off a layer of clothes, see, and then another layer, till by the last act they were down to nothing."

"They were naked?"

"It was meant to be symbolic."

"They just walked around the stage with no clothes on?"

"I promise you, it didn't seem the least bit shocking. These were just ordinary, middle-aged men and women. Some were overweight, even. Your father said he wished the move had been in the opposite direction—*adding* clothes, not taking them off."

I laughed. My mother said, "I don't know why you menfolk always have to have culture just forced down your throats."

Then here was Natalie, wearing a dark-brown dress that made you notice her brown eyes—so secretive and distinctly lidded. "Hello, Mother Gaitlin," she said. "And Barnaby," she added. "You've met Howard, I believe."

Howard stood just behind her, a silver-haired, portly man holding an enormous paper cone of sweetheart roses. He gave a deep nod that was almost a bow, and my mother said, "Yes, certainly," although I wasn't all that sure they *had* met. He and I had, of course, when it couldn't be avoided. When we accidentally crossed paths exchanging Opal or whatever. I said, "How you doing?" and then raised my chin and squinted at the stage while Mom and Natalie took care of so-thoughtful-of-you-to-invite-us and so-good-of-you-to-come.

When we were alone again, Mom said, "That went very well, in my considered opinion."

I felt extremely tired, all at once. I saw that nothing could be said on this earth that wasn't predictable. Even the bands of sunlight slanting through the basement windows were predictable, and the milky white swirls on the green linoleum floor, and the clunky-sounding "Teddy Bears' Picnic" coming over the PA system.

And the recital: well, you can't get much more predictable than a children's ballet recital. The youngest ones were dazed and obedient, milling around in tufts of pink gauze with their eyes fixed trustingly on Madame Whosit in the wings. The middle group—Opal's group—was a bristle of gawky arms and legs struggling to form a straight line. I hadn't realized before that Opal was so big for her age. She stood a full head above the others, down at the end, where (I guessed) she was meant to be less conspicuous. When they all set their heels together and pointed their toes sideways, she was the only one with no space showing between her thighs. In each position she teetered a bit after the others had frozen, and I felt certain that the audience noticed.

But my mother said, "Wasn't that precious?" applauding with just the tips of her fingers once the piece was over.

Between acts the curtain came down, but you could see it poking out first one place and then another as children jostled behind it. It made me think of a pregnancy—Natalie's pregnant stomach, the baby's knee or elbow knobbing the plaid material of her smock.

Not so long ago, amazingly enough.

It felt like a lifetime.

The oldest girls came last and showed us how it *should* be done, but I was too tired to watch. I let the dancers in front of me turn into a blur, and when the rest of the audience clapped, I just folded my arms and studied the acoustic tiles in the ceiling.

We met down in front near the stage at the end of the show—Mom and I, Natalie and Howard, Opal still in her tutu. She was hugging the cone of roses. I said, "I didn't bring any flowers myself. I didn't have a chance to buy some. I would have, but I didn't have a chance."

Before Opal could tell me it was all right, though, Mom rushed in with, "You were the best of the bunch, honey pie!" The level stare Opal gave her struck me as disconcertingly cynical, till I remembered she always looked that way. It was a hand-me-down from Natalie—Natalie's calmness, magnified.

"I messed up on the curtsy," she said, turning to me.

"Well, if you did, nobody noticed," I told her.

"Madame Stepp's going to yell at me."

"Your dance teacher's named Madame Stepp?"

Howard gave a dry cough. "Ah . . . we had thought we might take Opal to a congratulatory lunch," he said. "You're welcome to join us, Barnaby, Mrs. Gaitlin . . ."

"Oh, I guess not," I hurried to tell him. "We should be heading back."

No one argued—not even Mom, thank heaven. "Yes," she said. "I've left poor Jeffrey holding down the fort alone!"

We stood around a moment longer, all of us no doubt picturing Dad in the throes of some kitchen emergency. (Although I knew for a fact that he spent Saturdays at the office.) Then I gave Opal's shoulder a squeeze and said, "So long, Ope. You did great. I'm sorry I didn't bring flowers." And the two of us walked out.

In the car, my mother said, "Natalie's gained some weight, don't you think?" It was her way of acting chummy—showing me she was on my side. I didn't bother answering.

"Of course, she always had that wide, smooth face," Mom went on. "Almost a *flat* face, some might say. I like a bit of an edge to a person's face, don't you?"

"He had no business taking over lunch like that," I said, all at once realizing.

"What, dear?"

"Lunch was *my* time. It's part of my Saturday visit. Then he horns in on it and makes it seem like a favor to ask us along."

"Well, I wouldn't let it upset me," Mom said, slowing for a stoplight.

"I should have said, 'Thanks, but we've already made plans to eat with Opal on her own. Reservations,' I should have said. 'Reservations for three,' so they couldn't say they'd join us. Good grief! It's not as if we're all best buddies!"

"He didn't mean any harm," Mom told me. "He seemed like a very nice man. A bit old, though, don't you agree? Is he a lot older than Natalie?"

"I wouldn't have any idea," I said.

"Of course, Natalie always did have something of a father fixation."

The light changed, but Mom didn't notice till someone behind her honked. Then she gave a start and drove on. She said, "Remember how she used to phone her father at work every day? She phoned him every morning the whole time you were married, even though you were living not twenty feet away from him."

We lived above her parents' garage—practically in their laps. Which didn't help the marriage any, believe me. Every little thing I did—take a day off from classes, say, or come home a tad bit late or not at all—they would watch and judge and comment on to Natalie. But hey, it was rent-free; don't knock it. In fact, I stayed on there after we split up, although it got kind of awkward once I started dating again. Finally her father came over and had a little talk with me; said maybe I should consider moving. I didn't make it easy for him. I said, "Your daughter was the one who walked out, Mr. Bassett. I fail to see why *I* should be dislodged from my established residence." But I did find another place, by and by. Just not the very instant he suggested it.

Now Mr. Bassett was dead of a stroke, and his widow lived in Clearwater, Florida. Everything seemed to have changed in a flash, when I got to looking back on it.

"Opal has Jim Bassett's eyes, have you noticed?" Mom was asking. "His eyes were his best feature—that pale shade of gray. I was thinking after the recital; I looked at Opal and I said to myself, 'Isn't that a coincidence! Her eyes are the color of opals.'"

I pictured Mr. Bassett's eyes when I'd reminded him his daughter had walked out. "But, Barnaby," he had said, "what actual choice did she have?" With his upper lids crinkling, honestly perplexed. Then I pictured Opal's eyes, so measuring and veiled.

I have a problem, sometimes, after I come away from a place. I'll start out feeling fine, but just a few minutes later I'll get to reconsidering. I'll regret that I've said something rude, that I've disappointed people or hurt their feelings. I'll see that I have messed up yet again, and I'll call myself all manner of names. Freak of the week! Nerd of the herd! And I'll wish I could rearrange my life so I'd never have to deal anymore with another human being.

It was nearly two p.m. before I got home. Mom offered to stop for lunch somewhere, but I said no, even though I was starving; so first thing after I walked in the door, I made myself a sandwich. Then I checked my answering machine. Four messages.

Mrs. Dibble said, "Barnaby, I know it's a Philadelphia day, but Mrs. Figg has the idea that you'd promised to move her husband's computer down to their den. I told her she must be mistaken, but you know how she is. Anyway, call me if you get back anytime soon."

Then: "Hello, Barnaby. This is Sophia, at eight-fifteen Saturday morning. Just wondered if you'd be taking the train to

Philly today, by any chance! I thought I could give you a ride to Penn Station. Oh, well! I'll try you later, I guess."

After that, a cranky-voiced woman: "Now, how do I . . . oh, I hate these machines!" Mrs. Figg herself, although clients were not supposed to telephone us directly. "Where have you got to, Barnaby? You said you'd come move my husband's computer!"

And finally Sophia again: "Just trying you one more time before I head for the station! I guess you've decided to go by car. Well, maybe next time." Her tone was airy and casual, with a flicker of a laugh behind her goodbye.

I sighed and punched the Delete button.

I used to have friends to hang out with on weekends. Ray Oakley at work, before he got married. Martine before she met Everett. Or some of the guys from my old neighborhood, but they'd mostly moved away now, or turned all important and busy like Len. And I hadn't dated a girl in months. I *wanted* a girlfriend, but lately it seemed girls were getting younger and younger. They'd begun to seem just plain silly, with their giggly enthusiasm and their surfer-type vocabulary and their twitchy little miniskirts.

And I never counted my clients as friends—not even the ones I liked. Clients could up and die on you.

A few years ago, when they were making a public to-do over laying the last stone at the National Cathedral, I read an interview in the paper with a guy who'd seen the *first* stone laid, in nineteen-oh-something-or-other. He said he'd been just a little boy then, and his father took him to the ceremony. That story caught my fancy, for some reason. I pictured a kid in high button shoes and a ribbon-trimmed hat, hanging on to his father's hand in a great cobbled square among crowds of cheering people. Then one by one the people started dimming. They grew pale and then transparent, and finally they disappeared. The father disappeared and the men in bowler hats and the women in long cloaks, until the only one left was that little boy standing all, all alone.

Sunday, I woke up late, because I'd had a bad night. I'd tossed and turned and dreamed sketchy dreams I couldn't quite remember. It was well past noon before I really got going.

The weather was gray and cold, with needles of sleet that pricked my face as soon as I stepped outside. Ice glazed my windshield. I scraped it off and let the engine warm up, and then I drove very slowly, braking as easily as possible at each intersection. Almost no other cars were on the road. The radio announcer said the sleet would continue till evening. A good thing it was a Sunday, he said, when most of us could stay home.

In Penn Station, no more than six or eight people sat far apart on the benches, buried in coats and scarves and looking grumpy.

First I checked the board. Southbound trains were due in at 1:19, 2:35, and 3:11. It was 1:07 by this time, but the 1:19 was fifteen minutes late, wouldn't you know; so I went off to the newsstand and bought myself a paper. Then I settled on a bench and started reading. When the first arrivals filed in, I watched both doors but I didn't stand up, because I doubted this was my train. And I was right. I didn't see anybody familiar. I went back to reading the sports section.

By 2:35 I'd finished every shred of the paper, but I held off on a return trip to the newsstand till I'd checked out the next batch of passengers. They came in at 2:43, although the board didn't warn us about the delay. (These Penn Station folks could be sneaky sometimes.) First an entire family slogged through—parents, grandparents, several kids, dressed to brave a blizzard. I set my paper aside and stood up. Next came a teenage couple in hooded jackets, toting knapsacks. And next came Sophia.

She was bareheaded—the only one who was, so far. Even in this gray light, her hair had a warm yellow glow. She didn't see me yet. She shifted her bag to her other hand, and she fastened the top button of her coat. Then she happened to glance in my direction. She came to a stop. We stood about ten feet apart. She said, "Barnaby?"

"Hi," I told her.

"How come you're traveling *today*?"

"I'm not."

"Well . . . is something wrong? Is it Aunt Grace?"

"Nothing's wrong," I told her. "I just came to drive you home."

Her mouth took on a tentative look, as if she were about to smile, but she stayed serious. She said, "My car, though."

"What about your car?"

"It's parked here in the lot."

"Never mind," I told her. "We'll pick it up tomorrow, when the sleet's stopped."

She let herself smile then. And I was smiling too. I cupped her elbow to guide her through the station. Her coat sleeve was as soft against my palm as a kitten's belly. It made me feel protective, and capable, and determined. It made me feel grown up.

"WHEN I WAS a young slip of a thing," Sophia's aunt said, "I used to have so much trouble adjusting to a new year. We'd change from, oh, 1929 to 1930, but I'd go on writing '1929' at the tops of my letters for months, for literally months. Now, though, it's no problem whatsoever. I suppose that's because time has speeded up so, I've grown accustomed to making the switch: 1980, 1990 . . . You could tell me to date this check '2000' and I wouldn't bat an eye!"

She was sweeping the check through the air to dry it, although she'd filled it out with a ballpoint pen. I stood waiting beside her desk till she felt ready to hand it over. Apparently she was one of those clients who preferred not to pay their monthly bills by mail. (No sense wasting a stamp, they'd say, when a Rent-a-Back employee would be coming by the house.)

"You'll find out for yourself one day," she said. "Personal time works the opposite way from historical time. Historical time starts with a swoop—dinosaurs, cavemen, lickety-split!—and then slows and takes on more detail as it gets more recent: all those niggling little four-year presidential terms. But with personal time, you begin at a crawl—every leaf and bud, every cross-eyed look your mother ever gave you—and you gather speed as you go. To me, it's a blurry streak by now."

"Yes, ma'am," I said. It began to seem I would never get hold of this check. "I thought you mistrusted banks, though," I said. "How come you're not paying in cash?"

Mrs. Glynn lowered the check and peered at me over her eye pouches. All I'd done was delay things even further. "You haven't heard a word I said," she told me.

"Yes, I have! I promise! Change of dates, time speeding up, personal versus historical . . ."

"You're still so young, you can't imagine any of it will ever apply."

"Believe me, I'm not *that* young," I said.

She raised the check again, but only to blow on the signature. Then she said, "I do mistrust banks. I wouldn't dream of using one if it were up to me. However, my monthly allowance comes from my lawyer, and he insists on sending it to an account. Any money left over, it's *my* decision where I keep it."

Now she was holding the check at arm's length and studying her signature. She seemed to be having trouble placing the name. I shifted from my right foot to my left.

"The lawyer and my niece are in collusion, I believe," she told me. "Sophia's always nagging me: 'What if the house should burn down? Or what if you were robbed? Half of Baltimore knows where you stash your money.' 'Fine, then, I'll change the location,' I say, and she says, 'You are living in the past, Aunt Grace.' 'Indeed I am,' I tell her. I tell her, and I tell that lawyer too, who's young enough to be my grandson. '*You*-all don't remember the Great Depression,' I say, 'when banks were falling like building blocks and grown, respectable men were sobbing in the streets.' "

If the lawyer was young enough to be her grandson, he could be Sophia's age. Were they really in collusion? Did they meet to discuss her problem aunt over drinks, over dinner, in some candlelit restaurant where I myself couldn't afford to buy her so much as a salad?

Nowadays it seemed to me that anyone in his right mind would have to want Sophia for his own.

"But here," Mrs. Glynn said, all at once passing me the check. "Tatters, say bye-bye to Barnaby."

I folded the check and slipped it into my rear jeans pocket. "Thanks, Mrs. Glynn. See you Monday," I told her, and I was out the door before she could get started on a new topic.

Down Keswick, down University Parkway, to St. Paul, and then over to Calvert. It was only the middle of March, but there'd been a burst of unseasonably warm weather—highs near eighty, the last few days—and people were jogging or walking their dogs or just standing talking on street corners, looking aimless and carefree. I felt I was back in high school. In high school, when I went out with girls, it always seemed to be spring; the girls were always wearing spring dresses, and I was in short sleeves.

Sophia lived in a solid old brick row house with wide front steps and a porch. It was just a rental, but she had fixed up the little yard as if she owned it; you could tell even now, when things weren't blooming yet. And last weekend she'd bought two window boxes and set them on the concrete railing, ready to be filled with petunias as soon as all danger of frost was past.

It was her roommate who answered the door. Wouldn't you

know Sophia would have a roommate? Roommates are so wholesome. I picture them in quilted white bathrobes, their faces scrubbed and their teeth freshly brushed, although whenever I'd seen Betty she was wearing one of those pink trouser outfits that're trying not to look like a uniform. She worked in a hospital; she was some kind of pediatric health care person. A bony, spectacled woman with painfully short black hair and paper-white skin. "Sophia will be down in a minute," she told me, and then she went off somewhere and left me to my own devices. She disapproved of me, I sensed. Well, never mind.

I liked Sophia's living room—the staidness of it, the good, worn furniture handed down from relatives. When I sat in her grandfather's big recliner, it gave out a weary wheeze. Through the arched doorway I could see the dining room (claw-footed table, antique breakfront), and I knew that the kitchen, too, was comfortably old-fashioned. The upstairs I had to guess at, but I was willing to bet that she slept in a four-poster bed.

Now I heard her footsteps descending the stairs. When she walked in, I jumped up and said, "Oh! Hi!" as if she'd taken me by surprise. I don't know why I behave like such an idiot, sometimes.

"Hi," she said.

We kissed, and she stepped back.

She was wearing a navy skirt and a flowered blouse. She had this way of looking into my eyes and then quickly glancing down at her own bosom and smiling.

"Come into the kitchen," she told me. "Supper's almost ready."

The kitchen table was set for two, and the Crock-Pot on the counter gave off the smell of tomato sauce. In the mornings before she went to work, Sophia would put supper in the Crock-Pot. Then when she got home all she had to do was fix a vegetable. I don't know when the roommate ate. She never joined us, although if she happened to walk through the kitchen Sophia always offered to lay a place for her.

"How was your day?" Sophia asked, emptying a box of frozen peas into a saucepan.

"Oh, pretty good." I sat in a chrome-and-vinyl chair that must have dated from the forties. "Your Aunt Grace had me take down her storm windows," I said. "I told her it was too early, but she insisted. 'Mark my words,' I told her, 'winter will be back before next week is out,' but you know how she is. Monday, I'm putting her screens in."

"I can't imagine why she bothers," Sophia said. "She never opens her windows anyway."

"No; most of that age group doesn't. Scared of burglars."

"With her, it's she's eternally cold. You'll see: she'll be wearing a sweater in July."

I liked the thought that I'd be seeing Mrs. Glynn in July. That meant I'd be seeing Sophia too. I studied the back of her neck as she worked, and her smooth, netted bun. I hadn't seen a hair net on a bun in years, and now I wondered why; this one was so seductive. All I could think of was slipping it off, letting her hair tumble out of it.

She filled our two plates and then sat down across from me, smoothing her skirt beneath her. Her thighs, I thought, would be very pale and soft and fleshy. I stared at her like someone in a trance, till she asked me, "How's the stew?"

"Oh! Delicious," I said, although I hadn't yet tasted it.

She raised her wineglass. "To us," she said.

"To us," I repeated.

The way she served wine tickled me: one glass for each of us with each dinner, already poured beforehand. Me, I was used to drinking either not at all or far too much. This *moderation* business was a whole new approach.

Upstairs, the roommate's shoes were creaking back and forth. I heard a door slam, then a drawer bang shut. "Is she mad about something?" I asked Sophia.

Sophia shrugged, which was answer enough.

"She thinks I'm a loser, doesn't she."

"Heavens, no! Why do you say that?"

I sliced into a chunk of potato and said, "She's pointed out to you that I'm basically no more than a manual laborer. That I have the fashion sense of a Hell's Angel, and my prospects for advancement are flat zero. Right?"

Sophia flushed and looked down at her bosom again.

"Not to mention I hold the title of World's Oldest Living Undergraduate," I said. Then I said, "Hey. You didn't tell her about the Renascence School and all that, did you?"

"Certainly not," Sophia said.

Even Sophia didn't know everything; just the more dashing highlights. We were in that stage where we were formally presenting each other with our pasts: Sophia's prim, Mary-Janed childhood, my nefarious adolescence. I liked the fondly nostalgic way she said, "When I was a little girl . . . ," and she liked the fact that I'd have struck her as slightly scary if she had met me in my teens. "You were one of those boys who hung around the corner in packs," she'd surmised. "Who piled twelve deep in a car and hooted out the windows. Who smelled of cigarettes when they brushed by me on the sidewalk."

"Oh, I never cared much for cigarettes," I'd told her. "I preferred to smoke the harder stuff."

Just to see her expression of thrilled horror.

Now she said, "Betty's merely a roommate. I got her name off a bulletin board. What do I care what she thinks?"

"Actually," I said, "it's not true that I have no prospects—I mean, if I wanted prospects. I could always get a job at Dad's foundation. Does Betty know about the Foundation?"

"I believe I did happen to mention it," Sophia said.

"Also, I've held the same one job for almost eleven years," I said. "That's more than you can say for a lot of other guys."

Sophia reached across the table and laid a hand over mine. "Barnaby," she said. "It's fine. *Whatever* you do. Really."

I squeezed her fingers.

Granted, Sophia wasn't the type I'd fallen for in the past. She was luxuriously padded, and she carried herself from the hips in a settled and matronly manner. She probably weighed more than I did, in fact, but I found this sexy. It made me conscious of my own wiriness, and the springy, electric energy in the muscles of my legs. Sitting on that vinyl chair, I had all I could do not to leap up and fling myself across the table. But I stayed where I was and just smiled at her, and then I speared a cube of beef.

After supper, we moved to the living room. We settled on her sofa, surrounded by dried flower arrangements and frilled glass candy dishes, and started kissing. Once we drew apart when we heard footsteps crossing the upstairs hall, but it was a false alarm and we resumed where we'd left off. I stroked her creamy skin and I cupped her lush, heavy breasts in the circle-stitched cotton bra that I could feel through the silk of her blouse. When Betty's footsteps crossed the hall again, we had to separate in a hurry and straighten our clothes.

I told Sophia she should come to my place. She turned pink; she knew what I was asking. She said, "Well, maybe soon. Give me a little more time." I didn't push it. I almost preferred it this way for now. I left her house whistling. I imagined she'd be slipping into a quilted bathrobe exactly like her roommate's, and scrubbing her face, and brushing her teeth, and settling down for the night in her four-poster bed.

. . .

It always seemed to happen that we lost a lot of our older folks at the tail end of winter. Just when the worst of the weather was behind us, when you'd think a person would be gathering strength and looking forward to spring, why, we'd get a sudden call from a relative, or we'd find a week's worth of newspapers littering a client's lawn. During the first half of March, Mrs. Gordoni went into the hospital and didn't come out again; Mr. Quentin succumbed to whatever illness he'd been battling for the past six years (he'd never named it, and we weren't supposed to ask); and Mr. Cartwright died of a heart attack. Now I took Mrs. Cartwright shopping all on her own, and she was very different—wavery and bewildered. Funny: I had thought *he* was the dependent one in that couple. But you never know. I took her to the grocery store and she walked the aisles with this testing sort of posture, placing the balls of her feet just so, as if she were wading a creek. "Isn't it ridiculous," she told me, "how even in the face of death it still matters that the price of oranges has gone up, and an impolite produce boy can still hurt your feelings." I didn't know what to say to that. I steered her toward the dairy case.

I thought about one time when I'd driven the Cartwrights to a pharmacy and Mr. Cartwright had paused in the doorway to announce, "This used to be a pharmacy!" in his loud, impervious, hard-of-hearing voice, and the other shoppers had all raised their heads and looked around them for a second, plainly wondering what it was *now*, for heaven's sake. I don't know why he said that. Maybe he was objecting to the heaps of extraneous merchandise, the beach chairs and electric blenders pharmacies seemed to stock these days. Maybe he was just confused. At any rate, remembering the slight jolt that had rippled through the store made me smile, and Mrs. Cartwright glanced up at me just then and happened to notice. I worried she'd be offended, but instead she smiled too. "You're a good boy, Barnaby," she said.

None of my customers had the least inkling of my true nature.

Then Mrs. Beeton died—that nice black lady whose children always fussed so. First I knew of it, I telephoned to see if I should pick up any groceries on my way to her house, and her daughter was the one who answered. Said, "Hello, Barnaby!" and chatted awhile, cheery as you please. Not a clue about her mother. Finally I said, "Could I talk to Mrs. Beeton a minute?" A silence. Then she said, "Let me give you to my husband, okay?" And her husband got on the line—a man I'd never met. "My mother-in-law has passed as of yesterday morning," he told me. I guess her daughter just couldn't say the words.

I'd always admired Mrs. Beeton. She had such a sweet, chuckly face, and this attractive darker outline to her upper lip. Dirt was her personal enemy. Let her catch sight of a cobweb and she would not rest until she'd killed it dead.

And then Maud May broke her hip and had to go to a nursing home. Maud May! My Tallulah client, with her movie-star cigarette holder and her pitchers of martinis and her drawling, leathery voice. I visited her to get instructions—which plants needed watering and so forth—because she swore this was not a permanent state of affairs. "No Vegetable Villa for me," she said; that was what she called nursing homes. "I'm getting out of here if I have to crawl on my hands and knees." Then she dropped to a whisper and asked me to bring her a carton of Marlboros. "Sure thing, Ms. May," I told her. (We're the muscles, not the brains.) But I sounded cockier than I felt. She'd given me a start, lying there so helpless. Why, Maud May was my foreign correspondent, you might call it, from the country of old age. She had this way of *reporting* on it in a distant, amused tone. "I used to think old age would make me more patient," she'd told me once, "but instead I find, oh, Gawd, it's turned me into a grouch." And another time: "Everybody claims to venerate older women, but when I ask what for, they all mention things like herbal medicine, and I can't tell an herb from a mule's ass."

Now she said, "Know what this feels like, Barnaby? Feels like I'm living someone else's life. This is not the *real me*, I want to say."

"Well, of course it's not," I told her.

But I must have spoken too quickly, or too easily or something, because she jerked her head on her pillow and said, "Don't be so goddamn patronizing!"

"Ms. May," I said, "I promise you'll be out of here before you know it. What this other client was telling me just a few days ago: the older you get, the faster the time goes. By now it's all a blur, she says."

"Wrong," Maud May said firmly.

"Wrong?"

"Time has stopped dead still," she said.

Then she gave a snort and said, "No pun intended."

I took Sophia down to Canton to visit my grandparents one evening, because they'd been complaining they never saw me anymore. We sat in their tiny living room (twelve feet wide, the width of the house) and watched TV while Gram shot sideways glances at Sophia. I hadn't warned them I'd be bringing her. I didn't want to answer any questions. So Gram was having to work things out for herself, calculating Sophia's age, gauging how close together we sat. Sweetheart? Friend? Mere acquaintance? Sophia faced the TV, pretending not to notice.

We were watching a game show on what had to have been the world's largest residential television set. The only place it could fit was against the long side wall of the living room. This meant we had to line the couch on the other side wall, with our noses practically touching the screen. Pop-Pop sat at one end, so he had someplace to put his beer can. I sat next to him, Sophia next to me, and Gram on the other end. The rest of the room was filled with plaster statues of the Virgin Mary, and ceramic planters shaped like wheelbarrows and donkeys, and praying hands molded from some kind of resin, and dolls dressed like Scarlett O'Hara. Oh, and I should mention that Pop-Pop wore a V-necked undershirt that showed his scrawny white-haired chest; and Gram was in a tight tank top and baggy army-green shorts. (The thermostat was set at about eighty-five degrees, although outdoors it was winter again.) I was interested in Sophia's reaction to all this, but I couldn't tell from her profile, which was edged with blue light from the game show.

Gram said, "Sophia. Would that be an Italian name?"

"It came from a great-aunt," Sophia told her, turning briefly in her direction.

"Was your great-aunt Italian?"

"No, Scottish."

"Oh."

I knew what Gram was aiming at here. She wanted to find out whether Sophia was Catholic. She poked her headful of pink curlers forward for a moment and looked at me.

"Presbyterian," I told her.

"Oh."

She sat back again. She sighed. Oh, well, you could see her thinking, her own daughter had married Episcopal and the sky hadn't fallen in. "It's a pretty name, anyhow," she told Sophia.

"Thank you."

"I like names that end with an *a*, don't you? Or other vowels. Well, what other vowels? Most often it seems to be *a*. But wait: Margo's name ends with an *o*, for mercy's sake! Barnaby's mother. Or it used to be *o*. Then she met Barnaby's father and added a *t*."

Sophia looked at me. I told her, "Mom thought Margot with a *t* was higher-class."

"First time I saw it written that way was on the wedding invitations," Gram said. "She brought them home from the printer's and I said, 'Who's this?' She said, 'That's me.' Well, I did try to accommodate. Her daddy said it was stuff and nonsense, but I told Jeffrey the next time he came to call, 'Mar-gott will be down in a minute.' He laughed because he thought I was joking, but I was serious. I honestly assumed people pronounced the *t*."

"Watch this next contestant," Pop-Pop told me. "She knows every fact there is to know about Elvis."

"She always was a go-getter," Gram said. "Very energetic. Very brainy. She won so many prizes when she was in school! I can't imagine where that came from."

"Margot, we're talking about," I explained to Sophia. She was looking puzzled.

"Folks would ask, 'Is she a changeling?' Because Frank didn't even graduate high school, and the only reason *I* did was to fill in the time till we married. But there must be a smarty gene somewhere in our family. Look at Barnaby! He's practically an Einstein. Learned to read so young, he used to check in the child development books to see how he ought to be acting."

"I had a very promising past," I told Sophia.

She smiled and turned her eyes back to Gram. On the TV, somebody flubbed a question. The audience gave a groan, and Pop-Pop said, "Why, *I* could've answered that one!"

Gram heaved herself from the couch to fetch us a snack,

and Sophia rose and followed, asking, "Can I help?" She was doing everything right. Gram ought to love her.

Now it was just me and Pop-Pop, two skinny, puny males taking up the much smaller half of the sofa. We got started on one of those man-to-man talks that are all numerals—which cable channels he was subscribing to these days, how many quarts of oil my car was burning—while in the kitchen, above the clatter of dishes, I heard Gram doing her best to figure out who Sophia was, exactly. If I cocked an ear in their direction, I could keep tabs on them while listening to Pop-Pop reel off last week's bowling scores. No, she came from Philadelphia. And yes, she had a job; she worked at Chesapeake Bank. And she rented a place on Calvert Street; shared it with a room-mate. (Gram would find the fact of the roommate reassuring—less chance we were living in sin.) And it probably *did* seem odd that a girl like her hadn't been snapped up yet by some man, but she wanted to be sure she didn't make any mistakes, because marriage was for life, she'd always felt; and in fact, she had once been engaged and another time almost engaged, but it hadn't panned out, which now she realized must have been all for the best.

Then she said, "I met Barnaby on the train to Philly a few months back"—volunteering it, without any prodding from Gram. Evidently it told Gram what she wanted to know, because when they emerged with the food, she was treating us like a couple. It was "you two" this and "you two" that, and, "Next time, the two of you will have to come for a meal."

The snack she'd fixed was a recipe she'd read about in a magazine—Bill Clinton's favorite, corn chips with a dip made of bottled salsa and Velveeta cheese melted in the microwave. She served it on a tray that showed a head-and-shoulders por-trait of John F. Kennedy. "I see we're going with a presidential theme tonight," I said, and Gram jabbed an elbow into Sophia's ribs and asked, "Isn't he a cutup?"—rolling her eyes and giggling as if they shared a secret.

In the car as we were driving home, Sophia said she had liked my grandparents very much. "They liked you too," I said. I was partly proud and partly taken aback. I hadn't expected Sophia to get so *into* it, somehow. After a moment, I said, "You never told me you had been engaged."

She shrugged and said, "It didn't last long."

"Who was the guy?" I asked her.

"Oh, someone at the bank."

"And another time *almost* engaged? What happened?"

"It just didn't work out," she told me. "I'm probably too set in my ways. Too, you know. Definite. Too definite for men to feel comfortable with."

She was wearing the dressy black coat that made her hair look blonder, and the carriage of her head struck me as queenly. I said, "Well, I think definite women are great." She looked over at me and smiled. "If there's anything I'm crazy about, it's definiteness," I said.

She laughed. I got a little carried away; I said, "In fact, I've always dreamed of a having a military wife."

"Oh?" she said. "You mean a soldier?"

"No, someone whose husband's a soldier," I said. "I've seen them in the movies. They know how to do everything that needs doing. They could probably build their own houses, if they had to, and deliver their own babies. If that's not definite!"

"So . . . would this mean that you're planning to enlist?" she asked.

"Enlist! God forbid," I told her.

"Then how . . . ?"

"I only meant . . . ," I said. "Shoot, I'm just talking out

loud." Which was an expression Mrs. Beeton used to use: Don't mind me; I'm just talking out loud.

Dummy.

News of all the deaths spread magically among our other clients. I've never figured out how that happens. It's not as if our people know each other, for the most part. But I could sense the agitation in just about every house I went to. Mrs. Rodney got the notion to update her will; so did Miss Simmons. Mr. Shank called on us even more often than he normally did, on even more trumped-up excuses, and one time insisted that I drive him to the emergency room, when as far as I could see there was not one thing the matter with him. I said, "What is it? Are you short of breath? Chest pains? Weak? Dizzy?" All he would say was, he felt "unusual." For the sake of his unusualness I spent three and a half hours in the Sinai Hospital waiting room, watching homemaking shows on TV. "What I like to do," this lady on one program said, "I like to place a lead crystal bowl on the credenza in my entrance hall. I fill it with tinted water and I float scented votive candles on the surface, to lend a sense of graciousness when I'm entertaining." A roomful of sick people—bleak-faced, bleary-eyed, most in threadbare clothes—stared up at her in astonishment. Mr. Shank turned out to be suffering from stress and was sent home with a prescription for some pills.

Then Mrs. Alford started sorting her belongings. That's always a worrisome sign. For a solid week she had three of us come in daily—me, Ray Oakley, and Martine. ("Two men for the real lifting," was how she put it, "and a girl so as to encourage the hiring of women.") She wanted her basement sorted, then her garage, then her attic. This was in mid-April—a busy time for us anyhow, plus it was near Easter and lots of grown children were expected home and our clients were overexcited and crabby and demanding. But Mrs. Alford couldn't wait, couldn't put it off. Each morning she met us on her front porch, or even halfway down the walk. "There you are! What kept you?" Martine didn't have the truck that week; so I had to pick her up, which once or twice made us late, and Ray Oakley was late by nature. But we're only talking minutes here. Still, Mrs. Alford would be fretting and pacing. Half the time she called Martine "Celeste," which was the name of our other female employee, and I was "Terry."

"It's Barnaby, Mrs. Alford," I said as gently as possible.

"Oh! I'm sorry! I thought your name was Terry and you played in that musical group."

Martine snickered—picturing me, I guess, at the harpsichord or something. "No, ma'am," I told Mrs. Alford. "Must be somebody else."

In my early days at Rent-a-Back, I'd have feared she was losing her marbles. But I knew, by now, that it was just anxiety. I've had an anxious client mistake me for her firstborn son; then next day, she'd be bright as a tack. I didn't let it faze me.

Sorting the basement was easy, because that was mostly stuff to be thrown out. Paint tins that no longer sloshed; mildewed rolls of leftover wallpaper; galvanized buckets so old they'd been patched with metal disks by some long-dead tinker. We crammed them all into garbage cans and hoped the city would collect them. It took us less than a day. I had time to drop Martine off and check my messages before I headed to Mrs. Glynn's.

The garage was where it got harder. Mrs. Alford's husband had left a fully stocked workbench there—the lovingly tended kind, with each tool hung on the backboard within its own painted silhouette. Mrs. Alford must have dreaded to face it, because when we showed up the next morning, she managed to get our names one hundred percent wrong. "Hello, Celeste. Hello, Roy. Hello, Terry." None of us corrected her. On her way up the back steps to the garage, she asked me, "How's the music?" and I said, "Oh, fine," because it seemed easier.

But then she wouldn't let go of it. She said, "Now, what is it you play, again?"

"The . . . tuba," I decided.

"Tuba!" She paused at the top of the steps and looked at me. One hand pitty-patting the speckled flesh at the base of her throat. "Funny," she said. "I had thought it was something stringed."

"No, it's the tuba, all right," I said, wishing I'd never begun this.

"Fancy that! A tuba in a chamber group! I hadn't heard of such a thing."

"Oh," I said. "Ah. Chamber. You hadn't?"

"But what do I know?" she asked me. "I'm such a babe in the woods when it comes to music."

"Well, that's all right, Mrs. Alford."

We walked through her backyard, where daffodils were blooming in clumps. "I haven't been to the garage in years," Mrs. Alford said. "I never go! I don't like to go." She stopped at the door, inserted a key in the lock, and turned the knob. Nothing happened. "Oh, well. I guess we can't get in, after all," she said.

"Allow me," Ray Oakley told her. He set his shoulder to the door—he was a big guy, with a giant beer belly—and gave it a shove and fell into the garage.

"Why, thank you, Roy," Mrs. Alford said, sounding not the least bit grateful.

Mr. Alford's workbench was one of those objects that seem to go on living after their owner dies. And clearly he had been a hoarder. The rows of baby-food jars on the shelves were filled with various sizes of screws in generally poor condition—some bent, some dulled, some rusted. You just knew he'd saved them for decades, even though his wife had probably begged him to get rid of them. I said, "Tell you what, Mrs. A. You go on back to the house and we'll see to this without you."

"But how will you know what to do with it all?" Mrs. Alford asked. A reasonable question. She wandered the length of the workbench, reaching up to touch a coping saw here, a claw hammer there. "My nephew, Ernie: he's very good with his hands," she told us. "I should probably give these to him."

"And the screws and things?"

"Well . . . ," she said.

"Chuck them?"

She went over to the baby-food jars. She picked one up and looked at it.

"We'll settle that," I told her. "You go on back to the house."

This time she didn't argue.

So the garage took us slightly longer, what with locating empty cartons and packing them with tools and writing *Ernie* across the top, and stuffing all the discards into trash bags. "How do people end up with so many *things*?" I asked Martine. "Look here: a bamboo rake with three prongs left to it, total."

"A rotary telephone," Martine said, "labeled *Does Not Work*." She held it up.

"I hope she's not fixing to die on us," I said.

"Why would you think that?"

"I've seen it before. It's something like when pregnant cats start hunting drawer space: old people start sorting their possessions."

"Oh, don't say that! Mrs. Alford's one of my favorites."

I had never given Mrs. Alford much thought one way or another. She didn't have the zing that, say, Maud May had. But I wouldn't want to see her die.

"Sounds to me," Ray Oakley said, "like you two are in the wrong business."

"Listen to him: Mr. Tough Guy," I told Martine.

Then on Wednesday, Ray called in sick, and we had to start the attic on our own. What Mrs. Alford wanted was, we would carry everything down to the glassed-in porch off her bedroom, where she sat in a skirted armchair, waiting to tell us what pile to put it in: Ernie's, or her daughter's, or Goodwill. "How about the Twinform?" I asked her right off.

"Pardon?"

"That mannequin-type thing," I said, because I'd already made up my mind to offer money for it if she put it in the Goodwill pile.

But she said, "Oh, I'll keep that. It reminds me of my mother."

She kept a lot. A humidor that used to be her father's, a pipe rack of her husband's, a cradle that dozens of Alfords had slept in when they were small. Each object we hauled down, she'd make us stand there holding while she told us the story that went with it. And it seemed that the more she remembered of the past, the more she forgot of the present. "Should you be lifting that, Celeste?" she asked Martine, and she mentioned twice again that Ernie was good with his hands. But when I wondered aloud how a big rolltop desk had managed to go up the attic steps in one piece, she was able to recall that it hadn't gone up in one piece. Her husband had dismantled it first. "The top half's attached to the bottom half with four brass screws under the corners," she said, and she went on to recollect that her husband and her brother-in-law had carried the two parts up in the summer of '59. "You'll find a screwdriver on my husband's workbench," she said. Then she said, "Oh, no! His tools are gone now!" and her eyes glazed over with tears.

I said, "Never mind, Mrs. A. I can dig that screwdriver out in half a second. I know just which box I put it in."

She rearranged her face into an appreciative, bright expression. "Why, thank you, Terry," she said. "Aren't you clever!" And she kept her eyes very wide so that the tears wouldn't spill over.

When we were back in the attic, Martine said, "Ray had better not be sick tomorrow, I tell you." We were struggling at the time with the top half of the desk—Martine's hair sticking out in spikes around her face—but I knew it wasn't the lifting that concerned her. We needed someone more hardhearted here, was what.

Thursday, Ray returned, greenish under the eyes and still not good for much, and we stationed him downstairs with Mrs. Alford. While he shoved items from pile to pile and listened to her stories, we did the hauling. Even then, we got waylaid a time or two. We brought down a piano bench, and Mrs. Alford wanted it placed in front of her so that she could sort the sheet music stored inside. When she lifted the lid, the smell of mice floated out. " 'I'm Always Chasing Rainbows,' " she said. She spoke so wistfully, so regretfully, that it took me a second to realize she was only quoting a song title. " 'Don't Bring Lulu.' 'You Must Have Been a Beautiful Baby.' " Once, the house key Martine wore around her wrist clinked against a metal foot-locker we were carrying, and the sound must have touched off a memory in Mrs. Alford's head. Out of the blue, she said, "I used to have a wind chime made of copper circles, but then my neighbor came and told me, 'Please take down your wind chime; please. A wind chime was tinkling the whole entire time I tended my daughter's last illness, and now I can't bear to hear it.' "

We set the footlocker on the floor. "Well, of course I took it down," she said.

"Yes, ma'am," Ray said. "Ernie's pile, or your daughter's?"

Martine and I scooted back upstairs.

Friday, we found Mrs. Alford's brother eating breakfast with her—a tufty-haired, plump old man in a business suit. He'd arrived the night before for the Easter weekend. And Mrs. Alford was her merry self again, graciously introducing us all, ticking off our names perfectly. The three of us went up to the attic and finished clearing it out in no time, after which Mrs. Alford came to the glassed-in porch and said, "This goes to Ernie, this to Valerie, this to Goodwill," zip-zip-zip. She didn't even bother sitting in her armchair. We were done by midafternoon.

I gave Martine a lift home, because she still didn't have the truck. Neither one of us talked much. I was calculating the time, wondering if I could fit some other assignment in before I went to Mrs. Glynn's. Martine was hanging her head out the window and humming to herself. Then all at once she pulled in her head and said, "Know what happened the other day? I was playing catch with my nephews in their backyard. And they were having this discussion—about my brother, I thought it was. 'He says this, he says that.' So I ask, 'What time's he due home tonight?' and they get quiet and sort of embarrassed and they look at each other and I'm thinking, *What? What'd I say?* And one of them tells me, 'Uh . . .' And the other says, 'Uh, actually, we were talking about our baseball coach.' I said, 'Oh. Sorry. I thought you meant your dad.' But it gave me this sudden picture of what it must feel like to be old. I mean, so old that people imagine you've gone dotty. I wanted to say, 'Wait! I just heard you wrong, is all. It was a natural, normal mistake to make, okay?' "

Then she hung her head out the window again, and we went back to our separate lines of thought.

Sophia and I drove up to Philadelphia on the last Saturday in April. This was my second trip to Philly since we'd started dating, but she hadn't come with me before because her mother had spent the past six weeks at a cousin's condominium in Miami. So here we were, taking our first long car ride together on a sunny blue-and-yellow morning with a little bit of a breeze, and I felt like a million dollars. Sophia did too; I could tell. She said, "I should *always* go by car! You get to see so much more countryside than you do when you take the train."

I hadn't told Sophia about watching her on the train that day. I guess I thought it would make me look sort of, I don't know, sly, the way I'd engineered our meeting afterward. And besides, I was curious to see if she would bring it up on her own. In her place, I'd have bragged about it straight off. ("Want to hear how a total stranger singled me out and approached me and entrusted me with a mission?") But she never did. Either she considered it not worth mentioning or she'd forgotten it altogether. Probably things like that happened to her all the time. She must have just taken them for granted.

A lot of our trip was spent discussing her mother, who didn't sound very likable. "Every weekend of my life," Sophia said, "she expects me to stay with her, unless of course she has plans, in which case she lets me know at the very last minute: 'Oh, by the way, don't bother coming this week,' when I've practically bought my ticket already. . . ."

She was listing her mother's physical ailments when we

entered the city limits. Don't I know that kind of old lady! I drove up Broad Street and turned onto Walnut, while Sophia cataloged aches and pains and palpitations, doctor appointments, midnight phone calls . . . She interrupted herself to point out her mother's apartment building, which had a green-striped awning. I double-parked in front of it. "Oh!" she said. "There's Mother now!"

Sure enough, a big-boned, white-haired woman in a sweater set and matching skirt stood twisting her hands together on the curb. "Come and say hello," Sophia told me.

I have never been the meet-the-parents type. I said, "Oh, I'd better not. I'm blocking traffic."

But Sophia was calling, "Yoo-hoo! Mother!" as she slid out of the passenger seat, leaving her door wide open behind her.

Mrs. Maynard turned, blank-faced. Then she said, "Sophia? What on earth! You came by auto? You're so late!"

While they were pressing their cheeks together, I made a lunge across the seat and tried to shut Sophia's door without being seen. But no: "I'd like to introduce you to someone," Sophia told her mother.

So I was forced to show myself. I left my engine running, though. I stepped out and rounded the front of the car and said, "How do you do. Sorry, but I'm double-parked; I really have to be going."

"This is Barnaby Gaitlin," Sophia told her mother. "My mother, Thelma Maynard."

"I said to myself," Mrs. Maynard told her, " 'Well, that's it. Sophia's met with some accident, *I* don't know what accident, and the police will have no idea that I'm her next of kin. I'll be sitting in my apartment Saturday, Sunday, Monday, without anyone to shop for me or fetch my prescriptions. I'll run out of food, run out of pills; just get weaker and weaker, and they'll find me who-can-say-how-long after, shriveled up like a prune and lying on my—' "

"Barnaby and I have been seeing quite a lot of each other," Sophia said.

Mrs. Maynard stopped speaking and looked over at me. She had one of those rectangular faces, pulled downward at the corners by two strong cords in her neck.

"How do you do," I said again. I would have shaken hands, except that she didn't hold hers out.

See why I hate meeting parents? I don't make a good first impression.

Mrs. Maynard turned back to Sophia and said, "You might at least have telephoned and warned me you'd be late. You know perfectly well what tension does to my blood pressure!"

We hadn't been *that* late. Maybe half an hour or so. But Sophia didn't bother arguing. She said, in this forthright manner, "Barnaby has become a very important part of my life."

I froze. So did her mother. She gave me another look. "Oh?" she said. Then she said, "Mr. . . . ?"

"Gaitlin," I said.

Someone honked in the street behind me, no doubt wanting me to move my car, but I didn't turn around.

Sophia's mother asked, "Just what is your line of business, Mr. Gaitlin?"

"I'm, ah, employed by a service organization," I told her.

It came out sounding sort of smarmy, for some reason. Sophia must have thought so too, because she raised her eyebrows at me. Then she gave a sharp hitch to the shoulder strap of her bag. She said, "He works for a place called Rent-a-Back, Mother, lifting heavy objects."

"Lifting?" Mrs. Maynard asked.

I said, "Well, there's more to it than—"

"What *kind* of heavy objects?"

"Oh . . . ," I said. "In fact! I've been helping Mrs. Glynn some. Sophia's aunt. I don't know if you and she are in touch or—"

"I met him on the train a couple of months ago," Sophia broke in. "I guess you could call it a pickup."

"Pickup?" Mrs. Maynard asked faintly, at the same time that I said, "Pickup!" I stared at Sophia.

Sophia kept her gaze fixed levelly on her mother. She said, "He sat in the seat next to me, and before I knew it I had agreed to go out with him."

"Really," Mrs. Maynard said.

I wanted to explain that it hadn't been that way at all; that things had happened a good deal more inch by inch than that. But I could see what Sophia was up to here. I recognized that triumphant tilt of her chin. And I couldn't much blame her, either. With a mother like Mrs. Maynard, I'd have done the same.

Besides, the situation did work to my advantage. Because when Sophia said goodbye to me—walking me to my side of the car, ignoring the honking traffic—she kissed me on the lips and whispered, "When I get back to Baltimore, I want to come to your place."

Then she gave me a deliberate, slow smile that turned my knees weak, and she went to rejoin her mother.

By the end of April I'd saved eight hundred and sixteen dollars. I had hoped to be farther along, but no matter how hard I tried, I couldn't seem to meet my goal of a hundred extra per week. Well, at least it was a start. I got myself a savings account and a little cardboard booklet to record all further deposits.

For most of May I had this very lucrative short-term client—a young guy who'd broken his leg in four places while mountain biking. He lived alone in a two-story house, and I had to be there first thing every morning to help him down the stairs and drive him to his law office. Then I'd pick him up at quitting time, come back again at bedtime . . . Not to mention the groceries he needed bought, the shirts he needed taken to the cleaner's, and so on. When his cast was shortened to shin length and he could get around on his own, he gave me a good-bye gift of a hundred dollars. Rent-a-Back employees are not supposed to accept tips ever, under any conditions, and I told him that, but he said I had no choice. He said, "It's take it now or have it come to you in the mail, which would cost me the price of a stamp." So I took it. I confess. It would let me hit eighty-seven hundred that much sooner.

Sophia knew I was in debt. She even knew the amount, but not the reason. (Why get into the particulars? The Chinese carving and all that.) She was very understanding about it. She never expected me to buy her presents or take her anywhere fancy. Instead she ferried her Crock-Pot meals to my place after work. (We'd given up on her place, now that we needed more privacy.) First we'd go to bed and then we'd have our supper, tangled in a welter of sheets, leaning against the propped pillows that bridged the gap between my mattress and the back of the couch. I'd be in my jeans again, but she would stay naked, like that painting I have never understood where the men are picnicking fully dressed but the woman doesn't have a stitch on. Me, I tend to feel kind of undefended without my clothes, but Sophia seemed astoundingly at ease. She'd drape a napkin across her stomach and nibble on a stewed pork chop, then wipe her fingers on the napkin and toss back the loose coils of hair streaming over one shoulder. And meanwhile, I would be asking her questions. There was so much I needed to know about her. No piece of information was too small: her favorite color, favorite crab house, favorite television show . . . I guess really I was asking, *What does it feel like, being you?*

And maybe she was asking the same. She was interested in my parents. She was curious about my brother. She wondered if he and I were anything alike. ("Not a whit," I told her.) And especially, she wanted to know about my marriage. Where had it gone wrong? Why had Natalie and I split up?

"Why'd we get together in the first place, is more to the

point," I said. "A weirder combination you can't imagine. Natalie with her good-girl forehead and me fresh out of reform school."

"Oh, now," Sophia chided me. "It wasn't a reform school." But she was wearing her thrilled look, as if she hoped to be contradicted.

"Well, it was a rich-guy variation on the theme, at least," I said. "Certainly my neighbors thought as much. They pretended not to know me that whole summer after I graduated—everyone but Natalie. Natalie's family had moved in across the street while I was gone, and one afternoon I'm mowing the lawn and Natalie comes over with a pitcher and two glasses set just so on a tray. Says, 'Could I interest you in some lemonade?' Could I interest you: such a quaint way to put it. 'Why not,' I tell her, and I swig down a glass, and that might have been the end of it, except then my mother pokes her head out the door and invites us in for iced tea. As if Natalie weren't already operating her own refreshment service in the middle of our yard! Well, poor Mom; I guess the sight of a respectable girl was a little too much excitement for her. I tell Natalie, 'Cripes, let's get out of here,' and I leave the mower where it is and we walk off, just like that. So everything that happened after was my mother's fault, you might say."

"Your mother did approve of her, then," Sophia said.

"Oh, sure. Both my parents approved. It was Natalie's who objected. They'd heard stories about me, of course. Also, I was wearing my hair about halfway down my back that summer. Natalie's father called me Jesus. 'Will you and Jesus be going to the movies tonight?' This was when they were still allowing her to see me. Later, we had to sneak. I'd hired on at Rent-a-Back by then, and she would ride along on my jobs—spend the day with me while her parents thought she was swimming at their club."

"Oh, forbidden fruit! No wonder you two were attracted," Sophia said.

I was about to go on, but then a sort of hallucination stopped me in mid-breath. I swear I saw Natalie's arm, just her arm, resting on the window ledge of my car. She was waiting in the passenger seat while I was with a client. And I was stepping out the client's front door, walking down a flagstone path, heading through brilliant sunlight toward Natalie's bare, tanned arm.

Sophia said, "What happened next?"

"Oh . . . ," I said. "We got married."

"That seems awfully sudden," Sophia said.

"Well, she was about to go off to college, see. She was leaving in September."

Sophia hesitated. Then she asked, "Did you have to?"

"Have to? Oh. Have to get married. No," I said, "we didn't have to. I'm sure all the neighbors thought we did, though. To the neighbors, I was the bad guy. Natalie was 'that lovely sweet innocent Bassett girl.' It must have disappointed the hell out of them when Opal didn't come along till fourteen months after the wedding."

Sophia said, "So why . . . ?"

"But anyway!" I said. "You can imagine her parents' reaction. Mine took it more in stride. I think they hoped marriage would settle me down some. They got together with Natalie's parents and worked out all the arrangements—agreed we'd live over the Bassetts' garage and both of us would attend Towson State, and I'd keep on at Rent-a-Back in order to look like the breadwinner. Not that I really was. Our parents bankrolled just about everything. Our two mothers got into this decorating war, and pretty soon we barely had room to slither between all the furniture. And after Opal was born! They went wild. Cradles, strollers, changing tables . . . I don't know where *I* was in this. I mean, there are huge chunks of time I honestly don't remember. All at once I was standing at our front window one day, looking down at the driveway, and Natalie was buckling the baby into the car. This was a Volvo wagon her parents had given us when Opal was born. And I watched her shut the passenger door and walk around to the driver's side, and I said to myself, 'Why, great God in heaven! I seem to have married one of those station wagon mommies!' So we got divorced."

Sophia paused in the middle of licking her fingers. "Just like that?" she asked me.

"Well, no. Not instantaneously. First there was a lot of messy stuff. I admit I wasn't a model husband. Finally she took Opal and left. Didn't even warn me. Didn't even offer me a second chance. Well, you've seen Natalie. You've seen how she kind of floats along in this sealed-off, stubborn, exasperating way. Or maybe you didn't get a close enough look at her."

"No, not that close," Sophia said. "She did seem very . . . poised."

"To put it mildly," I told her. Then I said, "But why are we wasting our time on all this? Don't we have something better to do?" And I picked up our two plates and set them on the floor, and then I lifted her napkin.

Every word I had told her was true, but there was a lot I'd left out. Why we'd gotten married, for instance. I didn't tell her that I was the one who had pressed for it—that I was dying to marry, wouldn't take no for an answer, wouldn't agree to wait. I didn't tell her that at first I felt as if I'd finally come home. Hard to believe, I know; hard for even me to believe. "Did all that really take place?" I wanted to ask somebody. "Could that really have been me? How did I appear from outside? Would you say I seemed aware of my surroundings?"

The only thing I knew was, one morning I looked out the front window and thought, *Great God in heaven!* I felt as if

I'd awakened from a long, drugged sleep, and the last thing I clearly remembered was Natalie bringing me lemonade. "Could I interest you?" she had asked. And I had taken a single sip and all at once found myself married to a station wagon mommy.

Sophia started catching a morning train back from Philly on Sundays so that we could see more of each other. (The roommate spent Sundays with her family in Carroll County, and we knew we'd have the house to ourselves.) I would meet the train and drive her to her place, and we'd fix a big lunch that was really a breakfast—bacon, eggs, waffles, the works. Then we would climb the stairs to her bed, which was not a four-poster, after all. It was a spool bed—same general idea. And there was a curlicued nightstand with a silk-shaded lamp on top, and a bureau with cut-glass knobs. The drawers were packed with neat, flat layers of clothing; tiny flowered sachets were tucked in all the corners. I know because I checked when she was in the bathroom. I smoothed everything down again just the way I'd found it, though. She didn't suspect a thing.

Later in the afternoon we might watch a videotape or take a walk, but we separated earlier than other days because she had her Sunday routines to follow—her stockings to rinse out, hair to shampoo, blouses to iron for the coming week. "Go, go," she would say, and I would go, grinning, and spend the evening picturing her in her quilted bathrobe, her shower rod strung with damp nylons. Even her most mundane rituals seemed dear to me, and touching.

She had two sets of friends who were married couples. All the others were single women, and I knew them only by hearsay—their latest diets or trips or boyfriend problems. The couples she introduced me to personally. She took me to the Schmidts' for supper, and the Partons were invited as well. They were okay. Nice enough, I guess. I borrowed a khaki sports coat from Joe Hardesty, because I couldn't wear my tweed anymore now that it was summer. We talked mostly about the Orioles. I think one of the husbands had had something to do with building the new stadium.

She asked me, what about *my* friends? Couldn't we double date with someone? Oh, women get so social, sooner or later. She asked about my brother and his wife. I said, "Lord God, Sofe, you don't want to spend a whole evening looking at baby pictures." She said she wouldn't mind a bit. Well, I did want to do things right this time. I said, "I know what! I'll talk to Len Parrish. Maybe we could go out with him and one of his girl-friends."

Because I couldn't think of anyone else—any of my coworkers, for instance. Martine and Everett seemed to have broken up, or so I gathered from the fact that Martine never had the truck nowadays. Not that either one of them would have been Sophia's type. Ray Oakley's wife didn't like me; she claimed I was a bad influence. My only hope was Len. Which goes to show how desperate I was.

And he knew it too. "Well, gee, pal," he said, "I'm not sure. I'm awfully busy." In the end, though, he agreed to meet for drinks. He named a bar I'd never heard of that he had discovered downtown.

This was on a Sunday night, the only night he had free, which meant that I was at Sophia's while she was choosing what to wear. She must have tried on half a dozen outfits. Each one, I said, "That looks fine," and she'd say, "No . . . ," and shuck it off again.

"It's only Len," I said, trying to reassure her. "I don't even like the guy! He's more my mom's *idea* of my friend."

"Then why are we bothering to do this?" she asked, in a voice with a teary edge to it.

"Beats me," I told her.

By the time we left, her bedroom floor was a solid mass of cast-off clothes. She had settled finally on brown slacks and some kind of long white blouse—not much different from any of the earlier get-ups, as far as I could tell.

We took her car because mine was in the shop again. I drove, and she watched for street numbers. The bar turned out to be very easy to spot: a sheet of glass for the front, with DOUGALL'S slashed carelessly across as if the sign painter had barely found the energy for the job. We heard the music even before we climbed out of the car. I started feeling old; I'd fallen behind on the music scene a long time back. And no doubt Sophia felt even older. She paused in the doorway, patting her hair. Then we braced ourselves and walked in.

Of course Len was late. Of course we had to sit alone for half an hour—me nursing a beer, she toying with the stem of her wineglass, the two of us shouting above the din about made-up topics. ("Isn't that an unusual picture over the bar!" "Oh! My. Yes.") Finally Len breezed in with this six-foot-tall girl so blond that I thought at first she was bald; not a sign of an eyebrow on her; all languorous slouch and pouting pale lips. They were both in black turtlenecks, although it was a warm June night. "Barn!" Len said, clapping me on the shoulder. "You two been waiting long? I looked for your car out front; figured you weren't here yet."

"We came in Sophia's car," I said. "Sophia, this is Len Parrish. Sophia Maynard. And . . ." I looked toward the blonde.

"Kirsten," Len said offhandedly. "Barnaby has this incredible car that's totally wasted on him," he told Kirsten as he pulled out a chair for her.

"Yes, you mentioned that," she said. She draped herself on

the chair and reached idly for the drinks list that stood in the middle of the table. Her nails were cut in U-shapes, dipping in the middle and sharp at the corners. They made me want to curl my own fingers into fists.

"So, you and Gaitlin been going out long?" Len asked Sophia, but meanwhile he was gesturing for a waiter. She said, "Oh, five months," and he looked at her blankly. Then he asked Kirsten, "What are you having?"

"A mineral water," she told him, although she was still studying the drinks list.

He ordered two, along with a snack called Wrappin's, which he swore we were going to love. Then he turned back to Sophia. "This guy's a nut; I hope you know that. Complete and utter nut," he said. "Did he tell you about his life of crime?"

"Oh, yes," she said, smiling.

"Barnaby here is the Paul Pry Burglar," Len told Kirsten.

Kirsten merely raised her nonexistent eyebrows and turned to the other side of the drinks list, but Sophia said, "The what?"

"That's the name the newspaper gave him," Len said. "People would come home and find their silver still in place, stereo still in place; but all their mail had been opened and their photo albums rifled."

I said, "Len, *she* doesn't want to hear this."

Sophia's lips were slightly parted.

"Guy was insane!" Len told her. "Love letters missing from closet shelves, locks jimmied on diaries—"

I wanted to strangle him. "Who are you to talk?" I asked him. "You were with me! It's just pure luck you weren't arrested too!"

"*I* always tracked down the liquor cabinet," Len told Sophia smugly.

I don't know why liquor should have sounded any more

honorable, but right away her smile returned. I said, "God-dammit, Parrish—"

"Oh, tut-tut, Barnaby; language," he said. He told Sophia, "They sent him to a special-ed school to straighten out his evil ways and teach him not to curse."

"It wasn't special ed, for God's sake!"

"No, right, I guess it wasn't," he said. "They did make you repeat tenth grade. They must have had *some* kind of standards."

Sophia looked at me. I said, "I had played hooky the entire year before that, see."

I just wanted to dispel any suspicion that I might be mentally deficient, but Sophia read more into it. She got a softness around her eyes, and she said, "Oh, Barnaby. Had something gone wrong in your home life?"

"No, no. *I* don't know why I did it," I said irritably. By now I'd developed more of an appreciation for Kirsten. She was so plainly bored with all this, letting her gaze roam over the crowd that stood at the bar. "Thanks heaps," I told Len. "I just love digging up ancient history."

Len said, "Hmm?" and leaned back so the waiter could set his drink in front of him. Next came the Wrappin's, which turned out to be a sort of roll-your-own arrangement—minia-ture flour tortillas with an assortment of different fillings. Ordinarily I'm allergic to dishes with dropped *g*'s in their names, but at least these gave us something to focus on besides my unsavory character. We all sat up straighter and reached for the baby corncobs and the salsa verde. It was kind of like the activities table in kindergarten. The women fell into a separate conversation ("How long have you known Len?" I heard Sophia ask, and Kirsten said, "Um, three days? No, four."), while Len and I experimented with various fillings. The two of us got to flipping crudités off the backs of our spoons, aiming

for the sauce cups. We developed an actual game with complicated rules. "No fair!" we were telling each other. "You hung
on to your broccoli floret way past the legal limit; I saw you!" I
enjoyed myself, in fact. You miss that kind of thing when
you're not around other guys a lot. Yes, I'd say the evening
ended better than it began.

Sophia thought so too, evidently. When we said good night
to them, out on the sidewalk, she told Kirsten, "We should do
this again." (It showed how little she knew Len Parrish. If we
did do it again, it would probably be with a different girl.) And
in the car, she asked, "Do you think Len liked me?"

"I'm sure he did," I told her.

Actually, I doubt he more than registered her presence. He
had summed her up with a look and then dismissed her. But
who cared? At that particular moment, driving up Charles with
the windows down and Sophia sitting next to me, I felt completely happy.

Toward the end of July, Opal came for a week's visit to Baltimore. It was the first time she'd been allowed to do this, and
judging by all the precautions taken, you would have thought
she was being handed over to a serial killer or something. For
starters, on the morning she was arriving I had to telephone
Natalie as soon as I got out of bed, just to let her know I was
really and truly awake. (The train was a super-early one, 7:52
a.m.) Then I had to phone again from Penn Station, not even
waiting till we reached home, to say I'd met the train okay and
Opal was safely accounted for. ("Let me speak to her," Natalie
ordered, and Opal took the receiver and said, "Yes," and, "Uh-
huh," and, "I guess so," all the time eyeing me narrowly, as if
she were reporting on my general fitness as a father.) Also, she
was required to stay at my parents' house. This was only rea-

sonable, since I'd have had to sleep on the floor if she had stayed with me; but still I put up a fuss. "What," I had said to my mother, "you all think I live in a slum, is that it?"

"Now, Barnaby. You know you're more than welcome to move back into your old room while she's here," Mom told me. But of course, the very thought gave me the willies.

Opal seemed a lot older, suddenly. Maybe it had to do with being away from her mother. She was letting her hair grow out—it nearly reached her shoulders—and she wore a straight, dark dress, not so little-girlish as her usual clothes. I said, "Hey, Ope, you're getting to be a young lady!" She grimaced, clamping her mouth in a way that turned her dimples into parentheses, and I saw for the first time how much she resembled Natalie. Funny: Natalie was a beauty, but now I realized that she must have started out with Opal's plain, smooth face—unsettling in a child but attractive in a grown woman. Well, attractive in a child too. In fact, this Opal was . . . pretty, actually. I cleared my throat and said, "So!" Then I picked up her suitcase—molded blue Samsonite, an old person's suitcase—and we headed out to the car.

First I drove her to my parents' house. Big to-do: toast and home-squeezed orange juice, new doll propped against the pillows in the guest room. (Mom was really into this grandma business.) Then I took her to my place, because she'd never seen it before. I had cleaned it up spick-and-span and borrowed a few board games from Martine's nephews—Monopoly and Life and such—and alerted both the Hardesty kids, who were hanging out on the patio in this artificial way when we arrived. Joey was lying on a chaise longue with his ankles crossed, and Joy was jumping rope. Both of them were younger than Opal—I'd say six and eight or so; two tow-headed, stick-thin kids in shorts and T-shirts—but somehow they seemed the ones in charge. Joey started shrilling questions at her ("Did you come on the train? Did you ride in the engine?"), and Joy flung aside her jump rope and executed a set of brisk, efficient cartwheels across the flagstones. Opal, meanwhile, shrank closer to my side and grew very quiet.

"I'll just take her in and show her where I live," I told the Hardestys. "Then maybe you could all have Kool-Aid here on the patio." I'd mixed up a jug already and put it in my fridge—Sophia's suggestion. Sophia had been very helpful with the preparations for this visit. The board games were her idea. She had said we needed activities, something that would let us get to know each other better. That evening she was having us to dinner, and she had canceled her weekly trip to Philly.

Every day, it seemed, I saw something new to appreciate about Sophia.

Opal didn't comment on my living quarters. I showed her all around, but she said nothing. I worried she was storing up criticisms to pass on to her mother. "I know it's not fancy," I told her, "but it's affordable. And the Hardestys are super-nice landlords."

"Where's your *bathtub*?" was all she said.

"Um, I use the shower upstairs."

"Do you have to knock on the door before you go up?"

"No," I said. I wasn't sure what she was getting at. "I just walk on in. I mean, it's only their kitchen. Then I go down the hall to the bathroom. It's no big deal."

She didn't say anything more.

I brought the Kool-Aid and three paper cups to the patio, with Opal trailing behind me, but then she said she wasn't having any. She waited till I'd filled all three cups before she told me this. I felt a little put out, but I didn't show it. I said, "Okay. What would you like instead?" She said she wasn't thirsty.

Both Hardesty kids sipped their Kool-Aid, watching Opal with round, sky-blue eyes over the rims of their cups.

After that, I took Opal to work with me. We went first to Mrs. Alford's, because today was the day her nephew was coming and I had promised to help him load his truck. He was hauling her husband's tools to his cabin in West Virginia. Mrs. Alford immediately gathered Opal under her wing. "Come see the quilt of Planet Earth that I've been working on," she said. "Come see the teeny tea set my granddaughters like to play with when they visit." Opal went willingly—too willingly, I thought—not giving me a backward glance. It seemed to me she felt more comfortable with women.

Ernie, the nephew, was a beefy, muscular guy, and we made short work of the loading. He told me most of the stuff would probably have to go elsewhere. "I live in a place the size of Aunt Jessie's kitchen," he said. "No way can I fit all this in! But she's my favorite relative. I don't want to hurt her feelings."

After Mrs. Alford's, we stopped by the Rent-a-Back office, and I introduced Opal to Mrs. Dibble and a couple of the workers who happened to be there—Ray Oakley and Celeste. Mrs. Dibble invited Opal to stay and play with the copy machine while I went on my next job, but I said, "Maybe another time"—plucking a house key from the pegboard. "We're off to visit Maud May after I pick up her mail," I said. "I figure Opal will get a kick out of her."

"Well, you come by later, then," Mrs. Dibble told Opal, and Celeste gave her a stick of sugar-free gum.

But things didn't go as well with Maud May as I had expected. First off, the nursing home had all these folks in wheelchairs lining the hall. I was used to them; I hadn't thought about how they might affect Opal. She drew so close to me that her feet stumbled into mine, and she kept one finger hooked through a belt loop on my jeans. And then Maud May was in a fractious mood. Pain, I guess. She was sitting in a chair by her bed with her shiny new walker parked alongside, and, "Who's this?" she barked when we entered the room.

"This is my daughter, Opal. Opal, this is Ms. May."

"You never told me you had a daughter."

"I told you lots of times," I said. In fact, maybe I hadn't, but I didn't want Opal to know that.

"You absolutely did not," Maud May said. "I haven't turned senile quite yet, you know. What have you brought me?"

"Mostly junk, it looks like. Bunch of catalogs and stuff. Somebody left a plant on your stoop; so I took it inside and watered it. Here's the card that came with it."

"What kind of plant?" she demanded. She accepted the card, but she didn't open it.

"Something with white flowers. I don't know. I put it in the sunporch with the others."

"Did *you* go in my house?" Maud May asked Opal.

Opal nodded, still hanging on to my belt loop.

"Did you touch anything?"

"No, she didn't touch anything. Who do you think she is?" I said. "Why would you make such an accusation?"

"Good Gawd, Barnaby, simmer down," Maud May told me. "It wasn't an accusation. I was merely inquiring."

But I was mad as hell. I tossed her mail on the nightstand and said, "So anyhow. We're leaving. What am I supposed to bring next time?"

"More cigarettes?" she asked. She was using a meeker tone of voice now. "And that plant, besides, to brighten my room?"

"Fine," I said, and I walked out, with an arm around Opal's shoulders.

In the car, I said, "Next stop is Mr. Shank. You're going to like Mr. Shank. He's lonely and he loves to see kids." My voice had a loud, fake ring to it that I couldn't seem to get rid of.

"Maybe I could just go back to Grandma's," Opal said.

"Go back *now*?"

"I could watch TV or something."

"Well," I said. "All right."

It was almost noon, anyhow. I figured we could have lunch there and she'd get her second wind.

At my parents' house, I phoned Mr. Shank to push his morning appointment up to early afternoon. Then I went out to the kitchen, where Mom and Opal were mixing tuna salad. "Barnaby Gaitlin," my mother said, "what could you have been thinking of?"

"Huh?"

"Taking a nine-year-old child to a nursing home!"

"So?" I said. "You have a problem with that?"

"She says there were people in wheelchairs everywhere she looked. *Old* people! A woman with a tube in her nose!"

"Geez, Mom," I said. "What's the big deal? We're keeping it a secret there's such a thing as old age?"

Yes, we were, evidently, because my mother threw a meaningful glance toward Opal, who kept her eyes downcast as she stirred the salad. "We'll just let Opal stay with me the rest of the day," Mom said. "I'll take her to see Gram and Pop-Pop."

"Well, I don't know what you're so het up about," I told her. But I didn't argue.

I noticed a hollow feel in my car, though, for the rest of the afternoon. It seemed that just that quickly, I'd grown accustomed to Opal's company. When I was at Mr. Shank's, I thought how she could have looked through his coin collection. And I knew she would have liked playing with Mrs. Glynn's little dog.

In the last days of my marriage, Opal was just reaching the

stage where she recognized my face. I'd approach her crib, and she'd crow, "Ah!" and start wiggling all over and holding out her arms to be picked up. Then they left me. When I walked into the apartment after that, there wasn't just an absence of sound; there seemed to be an *anti*sound—a kind of, like, hole in the air.

It had been years since I had thought about that "Ah!" of hers.

Mom was miffed when I told her we'd have dinner at a friend's house. "Friend?" she asked. "What kind of friend? Male or female? You might have told me earlier. Is this a person who knows how to cook? Who'll give her fresh vegetables, and not just a Big Mac or whatnot?"

"It's someone who'll serve all the major food groups," I assured her.

"Well, I want you to know that I'll hold you to blame if Opal gets a tummyache," Mom said.

Sooner or later, I supposed, Sophia and my parents would have to meet. But I planned to put it off as long as possible.

Opal took to Sophia right away. I knew she would. Not only had Sophia gone to some trouble over the menu (Crock-Pot Chicken Drumettes and mashed potatoes, hot fudge sundaes for dessert), but she treated Opal like company: dressed up for her, in pearls and a shiny blue dress, and offered her a special fruit drink with about a dozen maraschino cherries lined up on a swizzle stick, and asked her these courteous, hostess-type questions throughout the meal. Who had Opal's favorite teacher been, so far? What kind of movies did Opal like to watch? What kind of books did she read? Opal answered gravely, sitting very straight in her chair.

As we were leaving, I told Sophia, "Thanks," and secretly

squeezed her fingers. I could see the shadow where her breasts began, above her low, scooped neckline. "You coming by later?" I whispered, and she nodded and squeezed my fingers back.

I asked Opal in the car whether she'd had a good time. "Yes," she said. "That lady was nice."

"Sophia, her name is."

"She had a nice dress on."

"She liked you too," I said.

I wondered if Opal would report all this to Natalie. You never knew what a kid that age would consider worthwhile mentioning.

We fell into a pattern. Mornings, I drove over to my parents' house for breakfast, but I let Opal stay with Mom while I went out on my jobs. Then I'd stop by the house again and have lunch. This was the most I'd seen of my ancestral home in years. It wasn't so difficult, though. I guess having Opal there sort of watered the experience down some.

After lunch, I'd take Opal to my place. She never did warm to the Hardesty kids, but she would watch TV with me or play a board game. The one called Life was her favorite. I found I couldn't abide it myself. "There's no logic to it," I complained. "Look at this: the more kids you have, the more money you collect. It should work just the opposite! Children make you poorer, not richer."

Then I worried she would take that personally; she would guess I'd been less than ecstatic when Natalie learned she was pregnant. But all she said was, "I like the little plastic people." And she set her mouth in that obstinate way she had and leaned forward to spin the arrow.

I tried to keep my afternoon jobs to a minimum, so that I wouldn't burden Mom with too much baby-sitting. Not that she complained. In fact, she put up a fight when I took Opal away with me in the evenings. I took her to Sophia's for supper, and then the three of us went on an outing of some kind—down to the harbor, or one time to an Orioles game. Things like that.

On Tuesday, Martine invited Opal and me to a birthday supper for one of her nephews. (She didn't mention Sophia, who said that she could use a little catch-up time, anyhow.) We grilled hot dogs out in the yard; Martine rented the top floor of this rickety old house with a deep backyard. The nephews were all in jeans, but Opal, not knowing, had put on a party dress—one of her Dick and Jane things, with a long, flouncy sash that tied in a bow. That was okay, though, because Martine wore a party dress too. It made her look kind of bizarre. I had never seen her in anything but overalls, till now. This dress was pink, and too big for her or something, too wide at the shoulders and long in the hem. Her hair was pulled straight back off her fore-head by a child's blue plastic barrette in the shape of a Scottie dog, and she was wearing lipstick the same garish pink as the dress, all wrong on that ferocious little yellow face of hers. I said, "Whoa! You look great." Which was an out-and-out lie, but her appearance was so startling that I thought it would be noticed if I didn't make some comment. Martine just said, "Thanks." I guess she thought she *did* look great.

The only other grownups were her brother and his wife, who seemed at least ten months pregnant, and Mrs. Rufus, the landlady. We all sat on folding chairs, and the kids sat in the grass. Mrs. Rufus did most of the talking, telling a string of bloodcurdling tales about childbirth. If you listened to her awhile, you marveled that the human race hadn't long ago died out. "But aren't you the cool one!" she said to the sister-in-law. "You don't even look nervous!"

"Thanks," Martine piped up. Apparently she thought Mrs. Rufus was talking to her. "I *expected* to be nervous, but actually I'm having a very good time."

Huh? Everybody stared at her a moment, and then Mrs. Rufus told how her fingers had swelled up like sausages when she was eight months along with her youngest. "We had to call in a plumber," she said, "to saw my wedding ring off with a hacksaw."

The sister-in-law said, "Ho-hum," and swallowed a yawn.

The brother had brought two six-packs of beer. Although he and I were the only ones who drank any, it somehow had a sort of rowdy effect on everyone else—a phenomenon I've observed more than once. Pretty soon Martine and the kids were playing Prisoner's Base, and Statues, and Simon Says, and a bunch of other games that I'd forgotten all about. Even Opal got involved. She loved it. By the time we left, she was as rumpled and sweaty as the nephews. Which made my mother throw a fit, of course, when I delivered her to the house. "How will I ever get those grass stains out?" she wailed. She should have seen Martine, if she thought Opal was dirty.

When I reached home I phoned Sophia, and she came over. "You smell like a new-mown lawn," she told me. I had this pleasantly tired, loose-jointed feeling. I let myself imagine how it would be if I lived this way permanently—watching my kid play with other kids in the yard, lying in bed later with a warm, sweet, generous woman.

After I'd walked Sophia to her car and turned off all the lights, I caught the sky doing its color-change trick, which is possible at night but exceedingly rare. And I hadn't even been trying! Maybe that was the secret, I thought. Let things come to you when they will, of their own accord. I went back to bed and slept like a baby.

Opal was due to leave on Friday morning. Thursday evening, therefore, we planned to have a farewell dinner. First it was going to be at my parents', but then it was switched to my brother's. (Recently, Jeff had developed some kind of fixation about hosting all family parties.) This irked my mother no end, because Wicky wasn't much of a cook. She wasn't *anything* of a cook, if you ask me. It must have been her Wasp background. Food was just a biological necessity, and a boring one, at that.

And then to make things worse, Mom took it into her head that we ought to invite Sophia. She didn't actually refer to Sophia by name. She called her "that friend that you and Opal have been seeing so much of." But she gave herself away when I said it was too short notice. "It's already Wednesday," I said, and Mom said, "Oh, I very much doubt Sophia will hold that against us."

I sent Opal a glare. Tattletale. She just gazed blandly back at me. "Shall I invite her, or will you?" Mom asked. "Which?"

I considered saying, "Neither." If I knew Mom, though, she would find a way of tracking down Sophia's number; and nothing could be worse than Mom on the phone unsupervised. I said, "I will." I wouldn't, of course. I'd say Sophia had turned out to have a previous engagement.

But I'd reckoned without Opal, who popped the question over supper that night. "Grandma wants you to come to my farewell dinner," she told Sophia.

Sophia turned from the stove, a pleased look lighting her face. "Really?" she asked me.

I shrugged.

"It's going to be at my uncle's, and Gram and Pop-Pop Kazmerow are coming too," Opal said.

"Your mother issued the invitation?" Sophia asked me.

"Well, she knows it's probably too short notice," I said.

"I'd love to come!"

I sighed.

"Would you rather I didn't?"

"These family things are such a drag, is all," I told her.

"You wouldn't think so if you were an only child," she said.

I could see there was no hope she would decline the invitation.

We went in her car, because we were the ones bringing Opal. (Mom had gone early, to try and wrestle some semblance of a meal out of Wicky's kitchen. Dad was coming directly from work.) For two days now, I'd been grousing about this whole idea, but as we were driving over I suddenly got in the spirit of things. Here we were, the three of us, traveling through a warm July night, with the fireflies flickering in the woods of Roland Park and faint, old-timey jazz playing on the radio. Sophia smelled of roses. Opal swung her heels in the back seat. And we were headed toward what was almost (if you didn't look too closely) a genuine family reunion, complete with parents and grandparents, aunt and uncle, cousins. Well, only two cousins. This was kind of a *miniature* reunion. But even so. When we drew up in front of Jeff's house, we found a huge tumble of silver balloons tied to the lamppost. Wicky's doing, clearly. Wicky was not half bad, I decided all at once.

Opal wanted to untie the balloons and bring them in with her. She seemed so impressed by them, you'd think she had never seen a balloon before. So our entrance was fairly crowded. The balloons filled the whole foyer, with the humans having to fit themselves in between them, and then Dad and

Jeff arrived on our heels, and a telephone started ringing, and Pop-Pop was asking where my car was. It took several minutes before we got sorted out and seated in the living room, and by that time Sophia had somehow been introduced. *I* certainly hadn't introduced her. I was already in the doghouse for getting J.P.'s name wrong. "What's new, P.J.?" I said when he toddled over, and both Mom and Wicky said, "Who?" Like a fool, I went on with it. "P.J., old buddy! Yes, sir; it's the Peej," I babbled, till I felt the disapproval streaming toward me from across the room, and I realized I had messed up yet again.

Jeff and Wicky lived in a very nice house, old-fashioned but modernly decorated, with a long white couch that fit together in an S-curve and Japanesey low tables and such. Still, I always felt it needed something. Maybe books, or pictures. It had this sort of blank feel. I knew my mother had given them a few paintings early in their marriage, but they had never hung them, and my dad absolutely forbade her to ask what had become of them. She said, "But it's such a waste! Especially the Rankleston, with the barbed wire and the Brillo pads. I could take it back and hang it in your study, if for some reason they don't like it." Dad didn't say what he thought of that idea, but you could guess from his expression.

It helped, at least, that there were so many of us. All the women wore their party clothes—even Gram, decked out in a bag-shaped shift with a rhinestone horseshoe pinned to the front. Pop-Pop had his shirt buttoned up to the collar, which was as dressy as he got, and Dad and Jeff and J.P. were in suits, and I had on my birthday necktie. A fairly festive-looking group, I'd say. The billow of balloons bobbing above Opal's head didn't hurt any, either.

And right from the start, Sophia was a hit. *Big* hit. Of course Gram and Pop-Pop already knew her. They showed off about that a little. "How's the bank?" Gram asked. "How's your *roommate*!" and then Pop-Pop said, "Stell brought the recipe for those nachos you liked so much." This made my mother go all alert and suspicious. She started edging closer to Sophia on the couch. "Oh?" she said. "You've had Mother's nachos? You've been to their house? Barnaby took you to visit?"—firing questions one-two-three, leaving her no room for answers. Meanwhile, Jeff was offering her a choice between white wine, Scotch, and ginger ale, and J.P. was lurching against her knees and trying to reach her pearls.

Not till we were settled around the table did Sophia manage to get a word in. Then she did a wonderful job. She made a little story of our trip to Camden Yards, and everyone came out well in it. (Opal had caught on to baseball so quickly; I'd been so patient in explaining the rules.) I kept saying, "Oh, it was nothing," and, "Just a routine game, all in all"—rolling my eyes at the other men and looking sheepish. Jeff asked me how Ripken had done. Dad asked if I had noticed any slacking off in attendance after the strike. I felt like some kind of impostor.

When I was a teenager, I would be eating dinner and all at once I'd imagine grabbing hold of the soup tureen and turning it upside down over my parents' heads. Noodles would snake down Dad's temples, and carrot disks would stud Mom's French twist. The image always set me to laughing, and then I couldn't stop. I'd be laughing so hard I was choking, spewing bits of chewed food, while the two of them sat staring at me grimly.

I don't know why that memory came back to me just at that moment.

Pop-Pop told Sophia I used to go to ball games with him as a little kid. "Him and Jeff; they'd take turns," he said. "Barnaby loved that *bugle* call! Loved it. Always used to say to me, 'Pop-Pop,' he used to say, 'aren't you glad we don't have organ music, like those poor other ball teams have?'"

It seemed everybody assumed that Sophia would be riveted by the most inconsequential mention of my name. And she did look entertained. She was smiling and nodding, forgetting to eat her canned pineapple ring.

"Just how did you two meet?" Mom asked, and my grandma, showing off again, burst in with, "They met on a train."

"On a train!"

The phrase gave me a vision of Sophia riding that train: her golden bun, her feather coat, her calm, pale hands accepting the stapled packet. My personal angel at last, I had fancied, but now that seemed an outdated concept. It was like when you're introduced to someone who reminds you of, say, an old classmate, but then later, when you know him well, you forget about the classmate altogether. Sophia was just Sophia, by this time—so familiar to me, so much a part of my life, that I couldn't imagine how she appeared to the people sitting around this table.

Except it was obvious they must like her. She was telling them in some detail now about our train ride. "He spilled coffee all over me," she told them, and they laughed and tossed me appreciative glances, as if I'd done something witty. She said, "First I was annoyed, but when I saw how nice he was, and how well-mannered—"

"Barnaby, well-mannered?" my mother said.

"Oh, he apologized endlessly and helped me clean myself up. And so then we got to talking, and he told me about his work—"

A few resigned expressions here and there, but I don't think she noticed.

"—and he described his clients so considerately, you know . . . And the clincher was that in Philly, I got a glimpse of Opal."

This was exceptionally kind of her. Just by mentioning Opal's name, sending her a wink across the table, she reminded the others that tonight was really Opal's night. I watched them all remember that. Gram, who was sitting on Opal's left, patted her hand and told her, "So *you* met Sophia before any of the rest of us, you smart little old thing!"

Opal smiled down at her plate.

"And then Barnaby asked for your phone number . . . ," Wicky suggested to Sophia.

"No, no. It was all left to me. I was the one who phoned, asking for him to come work for my aunt."

They laughed again, and Pop-Pop slapped his knee.

"Well, yes," Sophia said, laughing too. "I admit it was sort of trumped up. But Aunt Grace did need assistance, and so I didn't feel guilty about it."

"Of course not!" Gram said soothingly.

"He's been an enormous help to her—put her whole house in order again. You must be very proud to have raised such a caretaking person."

"Why, thank you, Sophia," my mother told her. "That's sweet of you to say." She glanced down the table to Dad. "It's not as if he hasn't caused us some worry, in times past."

"Oh, I know all about that," Sophia said. "But look at how he turned out!"

Everybody looked. I gave them a little wave that was something like a windshield wiper stopping in mid-arc.

In those photo albums I used to rifle, people were so consistent. They tended to assume the same poses for every shot, the same expressions. You'd see a guy on page one, some young father at the beach, standing next to his wife and baby with his arms folded across his chest and his head at a slight angle; and then on the last page, twenty years later, there he still was with his arms still folded, hair a bit thinner but head still cocked, wife still on his left, although the baby had grown taller than the father and was settled into some favorite stance of his own by now. Even the beach was the same, often. I would turn page after page, ignoring my friends. ("Gaitlin! What's keeping you, man? Look what we found upstairs!") I would set my sights on, say, one little boy and follow him through infancy, kindergarten, college. I'd see him slicing his wedding cake, and darned if he wasn't still wearing the same knotted-up scowl, or shamefaced smirk, or joyful smile.

What I'd wanted to know was, couldn't people change? Did they have to settle for just being who they were forever, from cradle to grave?

Seated at that table, the night of Opal's dinner, I felt *I* had changed. I waved a hand at my family as if I'd left them far in the distance—as if I'd become a whole other person, now that I loved Sophia.

Then Sophia's aunt accused me of theft.

She said I stole the cash she had been keeping in her flour bin.

"That flour bin's famous!" I said. "Everyone and his brother knows she keeps her money there. Why is she picking on *me*?"

It was Mrs. Dibble I was talking to, because did Mrs. Glynn have the decency to accuse me to my face? Oh, no. No, she went behind my back. She telephoned the office on a Sunday night in mid-August, using the after-hours number that rang in Mrs. Dibble's home. Announced right off that I had taken her money; no ifs or ands or buts. Not a question in her mind as to whether I was the culprit.

Mrs. Dibble asked her how she could be so sure. "There could be any number of explanations," Mrs. Dibble told her— or at least she claimed she'd told her, when she reported the conversation to me. I wondered what she had really said. Maybe she'd said, "Yes, that particular worker does have a history of criminal behavior."

Well, no, I decided; probably not. (It would reflect very poorly on Rent-a-Back, for one thing.)

Funny: when Mrs. Dibble broke the news to me, I felt this sudden thud of guilt, as if I might in fact have done it. I had to tell myself, *Wait. Hold on.* Why, from the first day I was hired, I had bent over backward not to meddle in our clients' private belongings. It was almost an obsession. I would go out of my way; I would ostentatiously shut a desk drawer as I passed it, and had once, while delivering a lady's diary to her hospital room, stuffed it into a grocery bag so I wouldn't be tempted to peek.

Mrs. Dibble broke the news by phone, but that wasn't her choice. First she asked if I would come see her in person. I said, "Why? What's up?"

She said, "Oh, just this and that."

"Spill it," I said.

She sighed. She said, "Now, Barnaby, I don't want you overreacting to what I'm about to tell you," and then she said Mrs. Glynn believed I'd stolen her money.

I said, "I'll go have a talk with her this minute."

"You can't. You have to promise you won't. It would only complicate matters. I just thought I should warn you first, before the police get in touch."

"The police!"

Something like a cold liquid trickled down the back of my neck.

"Do you think they're going to arrest me?" I asked.

"No, no," Mrs. Dibble said, giving a false laugh. "Arresting a person is not as easy as that! They'll probably want to question you, though, to get your side of the story."

"I hate that woman," I said.

"Now, Barnaby."

"What have I ever done to her? Why would she just up and decide it was me?"

Then I thought I knew why. I thought of how Sophia had presented me to her mother. "I guess you could call it a pickup," she'd said, with that triumphant look on her face.

She was as proud of my sins as I was of her virtues.

Mrs. Dibble was calculating aloud how I could make up for those lost hours at Mrs. Glynn's. An hour a week at Mrs. Alphonse's, she said; an hour with a man in a wheelchair over in Govans . . . She knew how hard I'd been working to save more money, she told me. But I was only half listening. I had to get hold of Sophia.

First of all, her line was busy. I tried once, tried twice, and then slammed down the receiver. Drove to her house in record time and pounded on the front door. It was after eleven o'clock by now, on a Sunday night. Normally she'd have been in bed. But all the lights were on, even the one in her room, and the footsteps I heard approaching were hard-soled and wide awake, and when she opened the door she was wearing what she'd worn that afternoon.

"Barnaby," she said.

Not surprised in the least; so I knew it must have been her aunt she was talking to on the phone.

"I didn't take that money," I said.

She pressed her cheek against the edge of the door and studied my face. She said, "Even if you did, it wouldn't change how I feel about you."

"I didn't take it, Sophia. Do you really think I'd do such a thing?"

"Of course not," she said.

Then she stepped forward and kissed me, and turned to lead me into the living room.

But after we had settled on the couch, she said, "I know you've been under some pressure, trying to pay off your debt."

"So you figured I just waltzed into a little old lady's kitchen and helped myself to eighty-seven hundred dollars."

"Twenty-nine sixty," she said.

"Pardon?"

"Two thousand, nine hundred and sixty was what she told me she had in her flour bin."

At the rear of the house, I heard the refrigerator door latch shut with a muffled, furtive sound, and then something made of glass or china clinked but was instantly hushed. Betty, trying to be discreet. No doubt they'd been discussing me before I came. ("I said all along he seemed fishy, Sophia. Didn't I have a bad feeling, way back at the beginning?")

"Level with me," I told Sophia. "Did you ever happen to mention to your aunt that I'd been in trouble with the law?"

She flushed and said nothing. She met my eyes very steadily.

"Did you?" I asked.

She said, "I might have, at some point. Maybe I did say, I don't know, you'd had some problems in the past. But I didn't mean any harm! I just wanted to show that you were an interesting person! I also said you came from a very good background. I said it was just your age or whatever, your age and circumstances, and you'd changed your ways completely and I had total faith in you."

"Well, thanks," I said.

She studied me, maybe wondering how I meant that. In fact, I wasn't sure myself. I groaned. I tipped my head back against the sofa cushions and closed my eyes.

"Barnaby," she said. She was using a tactful, delicate tone that put me instantly on guard. I opened my eyes and rolled my head in her direction. "Is it some kind of loan shark?" she asked me.

"Huh?"

"The person you owe money to."

I laughed.

"Because I know about these things, Barnaby. I see it in my business all the time: people in such deep debt they think they can't ever get out from under. Exorbitant interest rates, fees on top of fees . . . I want to help you, Barnaby. I don't have eighty-seven hundred, but I do have, let's see . . . In my savings account—"

"It's my parents," I said.

"Your parents?"

"They're the ones I owe it to."

"Well, for heaven's sake," Sophia said. "You owe eighty-seven hundred to your *parents*? And they're making you pay it back?"

"Nothing odd about that," I pointed out. "A debt's a debt."

"Yes, but your parents are so . . . affluent!"

This made me smile. It always tickles me, how people avoid the word "rich."

"I just think that's shocking," Sophia said. She was sitting very straight on the edge of the couch, practically swaybacked. "When their own son has to work weekends, even, and live in somebody's basement! That snoopy Mimi Hardesty always peeking out the window the minute I drive up, and calling down to ask if she can run a load of laundry as soon as you and I start getting intimate!"

I smiled again, but she didn't notice.

"And your clothes are practically rags," she said, "and your car is on its last legs. . . . What can your parents be *thinking* of?"

I could have calmed her down, I guess, if I'd told her about the Chinese statue and such. That would have made my parents look more reasonable. But it would have made *me* look shoddier. And besides, I enjoyed hearing somebody rail against my parents. I have to say, I took pleasure in it.

No, I was not at my best that night. I was spiteful and contrary, mean-spirited, malicious. When Sophia went out to the kitchen to get us a glass of wine, I pocketed a little porcelain bowl in the shape of a slipper that sat on her coffee table. And I didn't even like that bowl! And certainly had no use for it.

Monday, I overslept. I was supposed to run errands for Mrs. Figg, because she couldn't show her face again in half the stores in town. But I stood her up and wouldn't answer the telephone when it rang. "Barnaby, are you there?" Mrs. Dibble asked my machine. "Mrs. Figg is fit to be tied!" I just turned over and went back to sleep.

What woke me, finally, was Mimi Hardesty calling from the top of the stairs. "Barnaby?" Her voice was oddly high and childish. "There's a gentleman here to see you."

You don't often hear the word "gentleman" in everyday conversation. Especially not Mimi Hardesty's conversation. I sat up. I said, "Who is it?"

"Um, an officer. Can he come down?"

"Why, *sure,*" I said.

Meanwhile scrambling out of bed, grabbing my jeans from the floor, and hopping into them one-legged. Heavy footsteps thudded toward me. I raked desperately at my blankets. It mattered a lot, for some reason, that I should get my bed folded back into a sofa. But I had left it opened out for so long that I'd forgotten how the thing worked, and anyway, it was too late. The cop arrived at the bottom of the stairs—an older man, gray-haired, surprisingly lean considering the weight of his tread. He already had his card out to show me. Does anyone really read those cards? Not me, I can tell you. I didn't even hear his name, although he announced it in a loud, friendly voice. I looked past him to Mimi Hardesty, who was bending forward to peer at me from several steps above him. One small hand was clapped to her mouth, and her eyes were huge and perfectly round.

"Just like to ask you a couple of questions," the cop said, pocketing his card. Without glancing in Mimi's direction, he said, "Okay, ma'am."

Mimi said, "Oh! Okay," and turned to scamper upstairs. She was wearing shorts, and although the fronts of her legs were hazed with freckles, the backs were a pure, flawless white.

You notice the most ridiculous trivia during moments of stress.

But I was saying, "Have a seat," as if I weren't concerned in the least. "I can guess what you want to ask," I said. (I figured I'd be better off bringing it up before he did.) I scooped an armload of dirty laundry from the chair. "I know that one of our clients believes I stole from her."

The cop sat down and opened a spiral notebook. "So did you?" he asked mildly.

I said, "No."

He gazed at me a moment, his expression noncommittal. I wondered if that might possibly be the end of it. "Did you?" and "No," and he'd leave. But nothing's ever that easy. He had to follow protocol: take note of my name, my age, my years of employment at Rent-a-Back. Eventually I gave up and sat down on the edge of my bed. My feet were bare, which somehow put me at a disadvantage, but I worried he might think I was going for a gun if I stood up to fetch my sneakers.

I did tell him that I'd known where Mrs. Glynn kept her money. "Everybody knew," I said.

He asked, "Did you ever *see* the money?"

"No," I said. Then I said, "Hey! Do you think she could be delusional?"

But the cop just gave me a look, at that, and closed his notebook in this weary, disgusted way that made me feel about two inches tall.

When the alarm went off at the Amberlys' place, the night I was arrested, the police sent one of their helicopters putt-putting overhead. I was a little bit high. We were all a little bit high—me and Len and the Muller boys. I told the others, "Let me deal with this," and I dialed the Northern District police on the Amberlys' bedroom phone. "I wish to register a complaint," I said. "There's an extremely noisy helicopter disturbing the peace here."

The man asked what address I was at, and then he went off for a while. When he came back, he said, "Yes, sir. The helicopter is ours; we sent it out on a call."

"Well, in that case," I told him smartly, "you should know how to call it back in."

And I hung up, all dignified and haughty. Then the four of us collapsed into giggles. Then a car pulled up out front, and a flashing light revolved across the ceiling.

It was the very last moment that the world in general thought well of me.

. . .

In midafternoon, Sophia phoned. I was back in bed but not asleep. Still, I let the machine answer for me. "Barnaby, it's me," she said. "I'll try you again later. Just wanted to say hi."

"Hi," she wanted to say. "Pulled off any more grand thefts lately?"

I got up and went to pee. Ran water over my toothbrush but replaced it in the rack without brushing, as if I were still a kid trying to hoodwink my mother.

Mrs. Dibble phoned again. "Well, I don't know what's happened to you," she started out. "You are seriously disappointing me, Barnaby. Call when you get this message. Mrs. Morey wants her grill tank filled. Martine says to remind you she'll need a ride to the Alford job. Also, Mrs. Hatter would like to arrange for regular hours with you, starting tomorrow."

I couldn't even remember what Mrs. Hatter looked like, she used our services so seldom. Maybe she'd had a stroke or something. Well, tough luck. I started kicking through the clothes on the floor, trying to find my sneakers.

While I was drinking my coffee, two more people left messages. Mrs. Figg wanted me to know that I had ruined her entire morning, and Natalie asked if I could shift next weekend's visit to Sunday. It seemed Opal had been invited to a birthday party on Saturday. "I wouldn't bring it up," she said, "except the birthday girl's from the popular crowd, and it means a lot to Opal that she was included."

Yeah, right; it meant more than a visit from her own father. *Fine*, I thought. *I just won't go at all.*

By this time I was starting to feel I had died or something, listening to so many phone calls without picking up. So I grabbed my car keys and left the apartment. Went off to Mrs. Figg's to face the music.

It was hot as blazes out. I practically needed oven mitts just to work my steering wheel. I drove badly, zipping through yellow lights and honking at any pedestrian dumb enough to assume I would give him the right-of-way.

"If I'd wanted a worker who didn't show up," Mrs. Figg said when she opened the door, "someone I needed to nag about every little task, why, I could rely on my own son, for heaven's sake." She scowled into my face, pursing her raisin mouth—not an old woman, but a dried-up, drained-out one with a grudge against the universe. She went ahead and gave me her list, though, because who else could she get to do it? Most of our employees refused to deal with her anymore.

I went to the cleaner's first and picked up her husband's shirts. Ordinarily I'd have held my breath the whole time I was inside (the cancer is just swarming at you in those places), but today I took big, deep gulps of the chemical-smelling air while I waited. I wondered what Mrs. Figg had done that made her permanently unwelcome there.

At Ed's Electronics (where she had hit a salesman with her pocketbook, I happened to know), I collected her tape recorder from Repairs. Then I went to the pharmacy and the hardware, and I was done. But when I got back to Mrs. Figg's, what did she point out? The tape recorder's earphone pads were still in need of replacement. "If I'd wanted the kind of worker who did things any which way—" she began, but I was already wheeling around and stomping off. Went to Ed's Electronics again and raised such a stink, Mrs. Figg looked like a model customer by comparison. Then I drove back to her house and all but threw the pads in her face.

At Mrs. Morey's, I headed straight for the patio and unhooked the propane tank from her grill. "Wouldn't you like to see what I just persuaded to bloom?" she asked, trailing behind me, but I said only, "Mmf," and set off for my car as if I hadn't quite heard her. Got the tank filled at the gas station, reached into my pocket for my billfold, and came up with two earphone pads in a little plastic pouch. I guess they'd been clipped to the receipt and somehow worked themselves loose. Well, too late now. I tossed them in the trash bin.

At home, I found three more messages on my machine. Sophia said, "Hello, sweetie. Call me at the office, will you?" Mrs. Dibble said, "I wish you'd get in touch. Where are you?" And then Sophia again: "Barnaby, why haven't you phoned? Do you want me to bring supper tonight? Or not. I'll wait to hear."

I made myself a peanut butter sandwich and ate it standing at the bar. Then I polished off the last of the milk, drinking straight from the jug, and threw the jug in the wastebasket, even though it was the kind you were supposed to recycle. After that, I switched on the TV and watched a talk show, the outrageous type of show where everybody tries to confess to more unpleasantness than the next person. I had to sit on the bed to watch, since my chair had turned to glue in the humidity. Even my sheets felt sticky. Overhead, the Hardesty kids were carrying on a thin, shrill squabble, and their mother must have been tuned to her soaps, because at every pause in my own program, I could hear hers murmuring away.

This was the first weekday afternoon in months that I wouldn't be going to Mrs. Glynn's. The thought gave me a sort of wincing sensation. I fell back against the pillows and covered my eyes with one forearm.

I might have slept a little. When the phone rang again, the evening news was on. "Hey. Gaitlin," my machine said. (Martine's little raspy crow voice.) "Pick up, will you?"

I rolled over and reached for the receiver. I said, "What."

"Why aren't you here? It's ten till seven! You promised you'd give me a ride!"

"I did?" I said. "Where're we going?"

"Sheesh! Mrs. Alford's. We're clearing out her kitchen for the painters."

I said, "Can't you do it alone?"

"Duh, Barnaby. I don't have any wheels, remember? What's *with* you? I hope you're not hung up on that Mrs. Glynn crap."

"Oh," I said. "You heard. Great. It must be all over town."

"She's crazy; don't you think everyone knows that? Now get yourself on down here. We're running behind."

I said, "Well, okay."

It might not be a bad idea, I decided. Sophia wasn't going to wait by her phone forever. She'd come by in person, sooner or later, and I just didn't feel like facing her right at that moment.

Martine was standing out front when I pulled up—leaning against a parked car and eating pork rinds from a cellophane packet. She had on her usual overalls and what looked to be a man's sleeveless undershirt, so worn it was translucent. "At this rate, we won't finish work till midnight," she said as she got in.

I said, "You're welcome," and she said, "Oh. Thanks."

Then she slouched down in her seat and braced her boots against the dashboard and went back to eating her pork rinds. She held the packet toward me, at one point, but I shook my head.

Clearing a kitchen for painters wasn't that big a job. I could easily have done it alone. But we were dealing, I guess, with Mrs. Alford's private little affirmative action program, because her first words when she opened her door were, "Oh, I just love to see what young women can get up to nowadays!"

This evening she wore a mint-green housedress that bore an unfortunate resemblance to a mental patient's uniform. She was having one of her good spells, though, and got both our names right. "What I'd like, Martine," she said, "is, you take the small things, the pots and pans and things, and stack them in the far corner of the dining room. Barnaby, you can take the furniture and the microwave."

But Martine had to show off and grab the microwave herself. She staggered away with it, her arms straining out of her undershirt like two brown wires. I followed, with a chair in each hand, and Mrs. Alford came last, clasping a single skillet to her bosom. "You leave this to us," I told her. Already she was sounding out of breath. She said, "Oh, well, I suppose . . ." She laid the skillet on the buffet and retreated to the living room. We could hear her footsteps padding across the carpet, and a moment later, the creak, pause, creak of her rocking chair.

Before we moved the step stool, Martine climbed onto it and took down all the curtains. It was starting to get dark out, and the naked, blue-black windowpanes made the kitchen look depressing. Shadows loomed in the corners. Bare spots showed where the clock had been, and the spice rack, and the calendar. I stole a glance through the calendar after I took it down. I saw all the medical appointments—doctor this, doctor that, mammogram, podiatrist. Anything to do with her family had an exclamation mark after it. *Grandkids coming! Ernie spending night! Edward here for Labor Day!* Then I checked the times *I* had come, but she didn't refer to me by name. *Rent-a-Back 7 p.m.*, she wrote. And no exclamation mark.

"What're you looking at?" Martine asked. She was standing so close behind me that I jumped. I laid the calendar aside without answering.

When everything had been moved, Martine ran a dust mop around the tops of the walls, while I swept the floor. I found a dime, a red button, and a furry white pill. The pill didn't look all that intriguing, so I set it in a saucer with the dime and the button. Then we went out to the living room. Mrs. Alford was sitting in her rocker, with her hands folded—not reading, not sewing or watching TV—her face exhausted and empty. But when I cleared my throat, she instantly put on this animated expression and said, "Oh! All done? My, wasn't that speedy!" And she asked if we'd like a soft drink or something, but we told her we had to be going.

In the car, Martine got started on her favorite subject: Everett. How glad she was to be shed of him; how she couldn't imagine now what she'd ever seen in him. I wanted to discuss my own troubles, but she was rattling on so, I couldn't get a word in. She said Everett had given her every Willie Nelson tape that ever existed, given them as gifts, and now was demanding them back; and it was true she no longer listened to them, but still he shouldn't expect them returned just because she had dumped him.

"Mm-hmm," I said, and drove on.

I didn't want to see Sophia tonight. I just didn't; I wasn't sure why. I thought of her wide, gentle face and her kind smile, the way her blue eyes seemed lit from within whenever she stood in sunshine, and I got this wormy, shriveled feeling. I couldn't explain it.

"Here's an example," Martine was saying. Example of what? She'd lost me. "Say he's walking down the street and a man jumps off a roof," she said. Everett, she probably meant. "Know what he would say? He'd say, 'Hey! Why is this happening to *me*? Hey, isn't it amazing that someone should jump off a roof just as I'm passing by!' That's Everett for you. He thinks the world exists purely for his benefit. If he's not there, then nothing else is, either."

"Solipsistic," I said. I remembered the word from philosophy class.

"Right," she said, digging through her packet of pork rinds.

"Green light, now: figure it out," I told the car ahead of me. "What do we do when a light turns green? Ah. Very good."

Martine crumpled her packet and stuffed it in my ashtray. "So," she said. "Did you decide yet?"

"Huh?"

"About the truck. Yes, or no?"

"What truck?" I asked.

"Everett's truck; what else. It's a pretty good piece of machinery, you have to admit."

I didn't have the remotest opinion of Everett's truck, and I couldn't imagine why she thought I would. I put our conversation on Rewind. Came up empty. "Well, um," I said. "It's always looked fine to *me*. But face it: I'm no Mr. Goodwrench."

"You don't think it's a stupid idea, though."

"What idea is that?" I asked her.

"You and me going in on it."

"Going in on it?" I asked. "You mean, as in buying it? You and me? Buying a truck?"

"Jesus! Where have you been?"

"Sorry," I said. "I must have missed something."

We were on her block now, and I had been planning just to let her out in the street. Instead I pulled into a parking space. "I've got a lot on my mind," I told her. "Maybe it's nothing to *you* that I'm a victim of rank injustice, but—"

"What was the *point*! What have I wasted my breath for?"

She could have chosen a better moment for this. On the other hand, she was just about the last friend I had left in the world, and so I turned to face her and said, "Martine, I sincerely apologize. Run it by me again."

She sighed. "See, Everett bought that truck off a lady in Howard County—" she said.

"Howard County; yes." I tried to look as knowing as possible.

"—and he was supposed to pay for it in thirty-six monthly installments. Only he kept falling behind and his mom had to do it for him. And now he wants to move to New York, he says, where a truck wouldn't be any use to him; so he says to his mom, '*You* take the truck; I can't keep up the payments.' She says, 'When did you ever, I'd like to know? And what would I do with a truck?' And that's why she phoned me and asked if I wanted to buy it."

In the dusk, Martine was all black-and-white, like a photo. Black eyes slitted with purpose, black hair sticking out at drastic angles around her high white cheekbones.

"And you're suggesting the two of us should go in on it together," I said.

"Well, for sure I can't swing it on my own. But I can manage the installments, just barely, if you'd give his mom what she's already paid: twenty-four hundred dollars."

"Twenty-four hundred!" I said. "Martine. My total assets come to exactly half of that. And I'm still in debt to my parents, don't forget."

"Oh, well," she said, "but not if you sold off your car."

"Pardon?"

"Your car's worth thirty thousand, did you know that? I looked it up in a book."

I started laughing. I said, "My car's worth *what*?"

"They've got these books that give you the price of every used car ever made. So I went to the bookstore and, like, flipped through one, and there it was: a '63 Corvette Sting Ray coupe in excellent condition is worth thirty thousand dollars."

I was stunned. But I did think to say, "We could hardly claim my car is in excellent condition."

"Okay; so knock off a few thousand. You'd still be rolling in money. Haven't you always told me your car was a collector's item?"

"Theoretically, I suppose it is," I said. "But it was pretty well worn out way back when my Pop-Pop bought it, and you may have noticed I haven't exactly cosseted the poor thing."

"Oh! You're so negative!"

She bopped me on the kneecap with one of her fists. I said, "Hey, now." I took hold of her fist and set it back in her lap. Then I laid an arm across her shoulders. "I'm not trying to be a spoilsport here—"

"Well, you *are* one," she said, but a sort of grudging amusement had crept into her voice. She snuggled in closer under my arm and said, "Just listen a minute, okay? Let me tell you how I've got it figured."

"Go ahead," I said. It wasn't as if I had any pressing engagements.

"You would sell your car and, first off, pay back your folks. Quit your nickel-and-diming and just pay them back; be done with it. Get that Chinese statue off of your conscience once and for all. Wouldn't that feel good? Then take some more of the money and go in with me on the truck. It works out just about fifty-fifty—slightly in your favor, even—between what you'd give Everett's mom and what I would pay monthly."

"But meanwhile, I'd have no car," I told her.

"You'll have the truck then, idiot!"

"*We'll* have the truck," I reminded her. "And you'll be wanting to take it one place when I want to take it another."

"Don't we just about always go out on the same jobs together? And aren't you tired to death of trying to get your work done in a little, toy, baby-sized car that doesn't even have a rear seat?"

As she spoke, she was tracing a rip that ran across the knee of my jeans. Her fingertips hit bare skin and started coaxing at it. She said, "You could keep it at your place, if you like. And besides: we've been sharing it all along, more or less, when you stop to think."

"Well, shoot, with thirty thousand dollars, maybe I should just go on and buy each one of us a truck or two apiece," I said.

I was talking down into the top of her head, into her hair. It smelled of sweat. This got me interested, for some reason. Maybe she could tell, because she turned her face up, and next thing I knew, we were kissing. She had this very thin, hard mouth. I was surprised at how stirring that was. I wrapped both arms around her (not easy with the steering wheel in front of me), and she pressed against me, and I felt the little points of her breasts poking into my chest.

Then she drew back, and so I did too. I was relieved to see we were coming to our senses. (Or at least, partly relieved.) But what she was doing was shutting off the ignition. She dropped my keys in the cup of my hand, and her little face closed in on me again.

"You want to?" she asked me.

Her eyes had a stretched look, and she wore a peaky, excited expression that made me feel sad for her. I'd never really thought of Martine as a woman. Well, she wasn't a woman; she was just this scrappy, sharp-edged little *person*. So I said, "Oh—um—"

And yet at the same time I was reaching for her once more, as if my body had decided to go ahead without me. I had her between my palms (every rib countable inside the baggy denim), but she was leaning across me to douse the headlights. Then she tore free and climbed out of the car, all in one rough motion. I got out, too, and followed her toward the house. The porch floorboards made a mournful sound under our feet. The first flight of stairs was carpeted, but the second flight was bare, and so steep that I had to tag a couple steps below her so as not to be nicked by her boot heels as we climbed.

The instant we had reached the third floor—one large attic room full of a tweedy, dusty darkness—we were hugging again and kissing and stumbling toward her bed. Her bed had a headboard like a metal gate, white or some pale color, so tall it had to sit out a ways from the slant of the ceiling. It jangled when we landed on it. Martine breathed small, hot, bacon-smelling puffs of air into my neck while I fumbled with her overall clasps. They were the kind where you slide a brass button up through a brass figure eight. I don't think I'd worked one of those since nursery school, but it all came back to me.

"Martine," I said (whispering, though no one could have heard), "I'm sorry to say I don't have, ah, anything with me," but she said, "Never mind; I do," and she rolled away from me to rummage through her overall pockets. Then she pushed something smooth and warm and warped into my palm: her billfold. That made me even sadder, somehow. But still my body went hurtling forward on its own, and it didn't give my mind a chance to say a thing.

Not till later, at least, when everything was over.

And then it said, *What was that all about?*

Which Martine was probably wondering too, because already she was twisting away from me, rustling among the sheets and then rising to cross the room. A light flickered on— just the dim fluorescent light on the back of her ancient cookstove. It showed her facing me, head tilted, clutching a bedspread around her with thin bare arms. She still had her socks on. Crumpled black ankle socks. Little white pipe-cleaner shins.

"Oh, Lord," I said.

Her head came out of its tilt, and she said, "Well. I guess you want to get going."

"Yeah, I guess," I said, and I reached for my clothes. Martine turned and went off toward what must have been the bathroom, with the bedspread making a hoarse sound as it followed her across the floor planks.

I did call out a goodbye when I left, but she didn't answer.

Back when Natalie and I were still married—at the very tail end of our marriage, when things had started falling apart—I happened to be knocked down by a car after an evening class. Ended up spending several hours in the emergency room while they checked me out, but all I had was a few scrapes and bruises.

When I finally got home, about midnight, there was Natalie in her bathrobe, walking the baby. The apartment was dark except for one shaded lamp, and Natalie reminded me of some pious old painting—her robe a long, flowing bell, her head bent low, her face in shadows. She didn't speak until I was standing squarely in front of her, and then she raised her eyes to mine and said, "It's nothing to *me* anymore if you choose to stay out carousing. But how about your daughter, wondering all this time where you are? Didn't you at least give any thought to your daughter?"

Except my daughter was sound asleep and obviously hadn't noticed my absence.

I looked into Natalie's eyes—reproachful black ovals, absorbing the glow from the lamp without sending back one gleam. I said, "No, I didn't, since you ask. I was having too good a time." Then I went off to bed. I *fell* into bed, still wearing my clothes, like someone exhausted by drink and fast women.

Every now and then, I think I might have an inkling why Ditty Nolan stopped leaving her house. It may have had something to do with those years spent tending her mother. "If you make me stay home for so long, just watch: I'll stay at home forever," she said.

"If you think I'm such a villain, just watch: I'll act worse than you ever dreamed of," I said. I said it during my teens. I said it toward the end of my marriage. And I said it that whole nasty Monday, which seemed, now that I looked back, to have lasted about a month.

Back at my place, I found two more messages from Sophia and another from Mrs. Dibble. Sophia's voice was patient, without the least hint of annoyance, which made me feel terrible. Mrs. Dibble was all business. "I want you to call, Barnaby, as soon as you get in. I don't care how late it is. Use my home number."

So I called. What the hell. If she wanted to fire me, let's get it over with.

It wasn't even ten o'clock, but she must have been in bed, because she answered so immediately, in that super-alert tone people use when they don't want to let on you've wakened them. "Yes!" she said.

"It's me," I said.

"Barnaby."

A pause, a kind of shuffling noise. She must be sitting up and rearranging her pillows. "Here are your assignments for tomorrow," she said. "Mrs. Cartwright wants you to help her buy a birthday present for her niece. Mrs. Rodney needs her mower taken in for maintenance. Miss Simmons would like a window shade hung. Mr. Shank has asked for—"

"Wait," I told her. "Is this all in one day?"

"Yes," she said, and there was something unsteady in her voice—a bubble of laughter. "Package mailed for Mr. Shank, fireplace cleaned at the Brents'—"

"Fireplace?" I said. It was August. We were going through a heat wave.

The laughter grew more noticeable. "Plants moved for Mrs. Binney from the dining room to the living room—"

Mrs. Binney raised African violets, none of them over six inches tall. There was no reason on earth she should need my help to move them.

"Mrs. Portland wants you daily all next week," Mrs. Dibble said. "She's thinking of rearranging every stick of furniture she owns. The Winstons have requested—"

"What's going on here?" I asked.

"I believe they must be trying to make a point, dear heart."

I was quiet a moment. Then I said, "How did they find out?"

"How do they find out anything? Not from me, I promise."

I didn't know what to say.

"They love you, Barnaby," Mrs. Dibble told me, and now the laughter had faded. She was using a solemn, treasuring tone that embarrassed me. "It hasn't escaped their notice how you've cared for them all these years."

"So," I said. "You're not firing me?"

"Firing you!"

"Well, I know I didn't return a few of your phone calls—"

"Barnaby. I would never fire you. Did you really think I would? You're my very best worker! I tell everybody that! 'Barnaby's going to end up *owning* this company,' I say. 'You just watch: when I'm old and decrepit, it's Barnaby who'll buy me out.'"

"Who'll what?" I said.

"Oh, well, just on the installment plan or something. If only I could afford it, I'd give it to you for free! It means a lot to me to see a good man take it over."

I swallowed.

"But why are we discussing this *now*?" Mrs. Dibble asked. "For now, we have to think how you're going to manage all these assignments."

I said, "I'll find a way, Mrs. Dibble. You just leave it to me."

After I hung up, I sat there a minute, pressing my hands very tightly between my knees.

Then I phoned Sophia. I told her I was sorry. "I should have called before," I said. "I did get your messages. I've just . . . been in this mood, you know? I didn't feel all that sociable."

She said, "I understand. I understand perfectly. You don't have to explain."

"But I owe you an apology," I said. "Really. I ask your forgiveness."

"Of course I forgive you!"

Did it count if she didn't realize what she was forgiving me *for*?

Then she wanted to know if she should come over. But I thought if she came she would realize for certain, and so I said no. I said I was tired; I said I needed a shower. She didn't push it. She just said, "All right, sweetie. You get a good night's rest," and we arranged to meet the next day. I told her I was taking her out to dinner—someplace romantic.

I'd meant it when I said I was tired, but even so, I had trouble sleeping once I went to bed. I felt filled with determination. I was just about vibrating with all my plans for tomorrow.

I had to get hold of that price book. I had to sell my car and pay off my debt to my parents. And this was in addition to all those jobs for Rent-a-Back, because I couldn't let my clients down. They trusted me.

It began to seem that I really might have moved on in life.

10

"It's 'weathered and rusted,' " Len told me.

"It's 'fully drivable,' " I told him.

"It's an 'amateur restoration,' " he told me.

We were quoting from *The Collector's Automobile Prices*—the inside cover, where they explained their grading system. We were snatching the book from each other, to read aloud the phrases that supported our positions. I maintained my car qualified as Good, but Len was holding out for Poor. Secretly, I'd have been happy to settle for Adequate—the category between the two. But first I planned to put up a fight.

"If you took this to a dealer," Len told me, "he'd laugh in your face."

"Maybe I *should* take it to a dealer," I said, pretending to think it over.

A dealer would likely find about fifty things wrong with it besides what Len had already found. I knew Len was my best shot. And my bluff must have worked, because Len jumped in fast with, "Of course, no dealer would have your interests at heart the way I do."

"Or *your* interests the way *I* do," I told him. "That's why I'm giving you first refusal. You and I go back so far."

But I might have overdone it there. Len squinted at me suspiciously.

The place where I'd finally tracked him down was the Brittany Heights housing development—a series of treeless, shrubless hills out in Baltimore County. For all the snide remarks I'd made about Len's line of work, I had never actually visited any of his projects. This one was kind of eerie. Dotted about on the rolling greens, with no visible streets or driveways leading up to them and no signs of life anywhere around them, were these brand-new pastel stucco castles. They had turrets and battlements and arched front doors. The model, which we were standing in front of, flew a triangular banner from its crenellated roof. We might have strayed into a neighborhood of miniature kingdoms, all within sound of the Beltway.

"Suppose we say this," Len suggested, slapping the book shut and handing it back. "Suppose we call it Poor, but I tack on a thousand dollars for old times' sake."

The price for a Sting Ray in poor condition was forty-five hundred dollars. I shook my head.

"Two thousand?"

"Sorry," I told him. I tossed my keys up, caught them, and turned to get into the car. "Never say I didn't give you a chance," I flung back as I slid behind the wheel.

"Wait! Barn!" He grabbed hold of my door. "Where're you going?"

"Off to see the dealer," I said.

"What's your rush? We've just barely started talking here!"

"Well, hey," I told him. "You snooze, you lose." And I reached over to pull the door shut, but he wouldn't release it.

"Okay," he said. He heaved a put-upon sigh. "Just for you, then: we'll call it Adequate."

Adequate meant ten thousand dollars. I stopped hauling on my door.

Between the day we settled the price and the day I turned the keys over, about two and a half weeks passed—long enough for the red tape to be taken care of—but already it seemed to me that the car wasn't fully mine anymore. My August trip to Philly, for instance, Sophia and I made by train, because I could picture the irony of totaling on I-95 now that I had the money within my sights. And anytime I drove around town, I was more than usually aware of the salty, sun-warmed smell of the interior and the uniquely caved-in spokes of the steering wheel. I had never been a car man, never memorized all the models the way a lot of my friends had; but now I saw that a Sting Ray did have a very distinctive character. Out on the open road, it sounded like a bumblebee. Its artificial grilles and ports and vents, hinting at some barely contained explosion of power, reminded me of a boastful little kid.

I put off telling Pop-Pop. I decided I'd tell him after the fact, so that he couldn't keep me from going through with it.

On the second Saturday in September—a mild, muggy morning, overcast, the kind of day when it's hard to work up any enthusiasm—I drove to Len's garden apartment. Martine followed behind with the truck, so that I would have a ride back. Our whole transaction took place out front at the curb— Len circling the car several times, stopping to stroke a fender in this possessive, presumptuous way that got on my nerves.

He was wearing his weekend outfit of polo shirt, khakis, and yachting shoes minus the socks. I couldn't abide how he combed his hair in an arrogant upward direction. And when he got in and started the engine, it seemed to me that he did it all wrong. That first little gnarly sound was missing; he wasn't gradual enough. I called out, "Careful, there—"

But Martine, lounging nearby with her hands jammed in her rear pockets, said, "Let it go, Barnaby," and so I did.

When we left she asked if I wanted to drive, but I lacked the heart for it. I sat slumped in the shotgun seat of the truck—*our* truck, for what that was worth, with its greasy vinyl upholstery and the graying white fur dice swinging from the mirror—and told Martine everything I disliked about Len Parrish. "It isn't that I blame him for letting me take the rap alone," I said. "He'd have done me no good coming forward; I understand that. But then to act so above it all! Tut-tutting with my mom about me; mentioning the Paul Pry business to Sophia. When he was in on it! When he was just as involved!"

"Let it go," Martine said again, switching her turn signal on.

"You saw how he acted this morning. So Mr. Cool, so . . . like, uncaring. I introduce you and he says, 'Uh-huh,' and doesn't even look at you; too busy gloating over the car. Doesn't even glance in your direction."

Sneakily, I glanced at her myself. She was sitting on the cushion she used for driving, one finger tapping the wheel as she waited for the light to change. Her profile was poked forward, beaky and persistent, intent on the signal overhead.

Martine and I had developed a new style of dealing with each other lately. We were careful not to touch, not even by accident, and we never quite let our eyes meet. Our tone of voice was casual and sporty. Like now: "So?" Martine said. "He's a jerk. Give it a rest, Gaitlin." And she slammed into gear and hooked a quick left turn in front of the oncoming traffic.

Maybe I should have said something. Brought things out in the open. But how would I put it, exactly? *Hey, okay; so we did something stupid. You're not going to let it change things, are you? Could we just hit the Erase button, here, and go back to the same as before?*

But I didn't say any of that, and she went on facing straight forward. She seemed to be driving with her nose. Both hands gripped the wheel; her house key dangled from the brown leather band that was looped around one wrist. I thought of something. I said, "The key."

"What key?"

"The key to the Corvette. I left it on the ring. I turned over my whole key ring, with that Chevy emblem my Pop-Pop gave me when he put the car in my name."

"So what? You'll be driving a Ford now. What do you want with a Chevrolet key ring?"

She was right. I couldn't argue with her logic. But that emblem had been with me a very long time. The plastic surface was so yellowed and dulled, you could barely make out the two crossed flags encased beneath it. At tense moments I would run my thumb across it, the way I used to stroke the satin binding of my crib blanket. I thought of Len doing that, and it killed me.

I must be more of a car man than I'd realized.

On Monday evening, I dropped by my parents' house, choosing an hour when I figured they would both be home. Sophia offered to come with me, but I had this picture in mind: me facing Mom and Dad in the entrance hall, slipping the money from Opal's clip and saying, "Here. I just stopped by to drop this off." And then I'd lay it on the flat of Mom's palm and leave. Sophia wasn't part of this picture; no offense to her. I needed to do it alone.

But these things never work out the way you imagine. First of all, it emerged that eighty-seven one-hundred-dollar bills made a stack too thick for a money clip. I had to ask the teller to fasten one of those paper bands around the middle. And then when I got to the house, my parents did not obligingly show up together at the door. (When did they ever, in fact?) Just my mother came, carrying a cordless phone and continuing with her conversation even as she let me in. "It's only Barnaby," she told the phone. "Wicky," she mouthed at me before she turned away. So I couldn't stay in the hall. I had to follow her into the living room, and settle on the couch, and wait for her to finish talking.

"Honestly," she told me as she punched the hang-up button. "I know I swore I would always get along with my daughters-in-law, but sometimes it's an effort." She turned toward the stairs and called, "Jeffrey?"

"What?" came back dimly, moments later.

"Your son is here."

"Which son?"

"The bad one," I called, just to save her the trouble.

Mom rolled her eyes at me and then came to sit in the chair to my left. She was wearing slacks and the man's white shirt she gardened in. (I had envisioned her more dressed up, somehow. Mom in her Guilford Matron outfit, Dad in his suit. Like a dollhouse couple, hand in hand in the doorway.) "How's Sophia?" she asked.

"She's fine."

"Why didn't you bring her with you?"

"Oh, well . . ."

"Sophia would never act the way Wicky does," she said.

"Sophia's so considerate." And then she sailed into this tale about the birthday party Wicky was planning for Dad. "I said, 'We don't want you going to any bother, Wicky,' and she said, 'It won't be the least bit of bother,' and now I know why. Because first she told me all I had to do was show up, and then she told me, well, maybe I could make my artichoke dip, and then—"

"Whose truck is that in the driveway?" my father wanted to know. He walked into the room with a magazine suspended from one hand, his index finger marking a page. He did have his suit on still, but his tie was missing and he wore his velvet mules instead of shoes. "Red pickup," he told me. "Did *you* drive that here?"

"Yes; um . . ."

"You left your lights on."

"Well, I'll be going pretty soon," I said.

"Oh, don't hurry off!" my mother cried. "Stay for dinner! We're having shrimp salad. There's lots."

"Thanks, but I already ate," I said. "I just stopped by to—"

"Already ate? Ate dinner?" she asked. She checked her watch. "It's barely seven-thirty."

"Right."

"Goodness, Barnaby. You're so uncivilized!"

I looked at her. I said, "How do you figure that?"

"*We* always eat at eight," she said.

"Dine," I told her.

"Pardon?"

"You always *dine* at eight. Isn't that what you meant to say?"

She drew up taller in her seat. She said, "I don't see—"

"Gram and Pop-Pop dine at five-thirty, however," I said, "and what's good enough for them is good enough for me."

"Of course it is!" Dad told me. He bent to set his magazine

on the coffee table, as if he'd decided the situation required his full attention. "But you could join us for cocktails," he said. "Scotch, maybe? Glass of wine?" He rubbed his hands together.

"Really I just stopped by to give you this," I said, and I picked up the denim jacket that was lying across my knees. The weather wasn't cool enough for jackets yet, but I'd needed something with roomy pockets. "Here," I said. I pulled out the brick of money and leaned forward to place it in my mother's lap.

She stared down at it. My father stopped rubbing his hands.

"I don't understand," my mother said.

"What's to understand?" I asked her.

"Well, what *is* this?" she asked.

"It's eighty-seven hundred dollars, Mom. Surely that must ring a little bell."

She glanced up at my father. He gazed off over her head, suddenly abstracted.

"But . . . is it yours?" she asked me. "Where did you get it? And in cash! Walking the streets of Baltimore with all this cash! How would you have come by such a large amount, I'd like to know?"

"No trouble at all," I told her. "Though it did make kind of a mess when the dye pack exploded."

"Seriously, Barnaby. Have you been up to something you shouldn't?"

Odd that it hadn't occurred to me she would jump to this conclusion. I made a snorting sound. I said, "Don't worry. It's legal. I sold the Corvette to Len Parrish."

"You sold the Corvette?" my father asked, suddenly coming to. "Son," he said. "Was that wise?"

I wasn't going to argue about it. I told Mom, "Feel free to

count the money yourself, if you like. Make sure I didn't short-change you."

For a moment, I thought she would do it. She picked up the bills in a gingerly way and turned them over. But then she said, "That's all right."

When they gave me the wad of cash at the bank it had seemed so bulky, but now I was struck by its slimness. For all these years, that money had loomed between us. I recalled Mom's hints and reproaches, her can't-afford-this, can't-afford-that, her self-assured air of entitlement as she inquired into my finances. I recalled my old daydream that she would cancel the debt when I married, or after my first child was born. And yet it made such an unimpressive little package! Granted, it was a lot of money—a lot for me, at least—but you'd think I could have come up with it before now.

I said, "Well, then. Are we fair and square? Everything settled?"

"I suppose," my mother said faintly.

Somehow there should have been more to this. More excitement, more relief; I don't know. I stood up. I said, "Well! Guess I'll be going."

My mother went on sitting there. It was Dad who walked me to the door.

For a month after Mrs. Glynn accused me, I had nothing to do with her. Sophia didn't, either (she was never going to speak to her again, she said), but I heard a little about her from Ray Oakley. He was the one who was going there in my place. He said she had cut her hours back to one a week, and even then he hardly saw her. "I try and steer clear of her," he told me. "I'm worried she'll say *I* stole something too."

Me, I had pretty much let her fade from my mind. Sophia

thought that was incredibly charitable of me, but it was more that I just figured things always evened out, sooner or later. Look at it this way: I might have done time in jail if I hadn't had rich parents. And even rich parents couldn't have helped if anyone had discovered I stole a Buick convertible the night of my sixteenth birthday. So when Mrs. Glynn said I did something I didn't, there was a certain justice to it.

Even losing my Corvette: a certain balance, you might say.

I was still in possession of Sophia's little porcelain slipper. I brought it back one evening and put it among some doodads on her mantel, where it didn't belong, so she would think she had simply misplaced it if she'd noticed it was missing. I didn't believe she had noticed, though. I felt artful and deft and cat-like as I set the slipper soundlessly between a brass clock and a hobnail vase. I slid my hands in my jeans pockets and walked away whistling.

It wasn't entirely undeserved, Mrs. Glynn's accusing me.

Then one Friday afternoon toward the end of September, she telephoned. "Barnaby Gaitlin?" she said—pert little old-lady voice. But I knew so many old ladies, I couldn't think who she was. I said, "Yes?" in a guarded tone. When they called me direct, it was usually with a complaint.

"This is Grace Glynn."

I got very alert.

"Sophia's aunt," she reminded me.

"Yes," I said.

"How *are* you?" she asked me.

"Fine."

"Doing well?"

I waited to see what she was after.

"I was wondering," she said, after a pause. "Would you be so kind as to come to my house this evening?"

"Your house."

"Just for a little chat," she said. "It won't take long."

I said, "I guess I'll pass on that, Mrs. Glynn. Thanks anyhow."

"Please? Pretty please?"

"Sorry," I said, and I hung up.

There were limits to how charitable I was willing to be.

When the phone rang again, a few minutes later, I let the machine answer for me. But this time it was Sophia. "Barnaby, I wanted to ask if—"

I picked up the receiver. "Hi," I said. "I'm screening my calls. You'll never guess who from."

"Aunt Grace," Sophia told me.

"Oh. You knew she was calling?"

"She called me too. I just now got off the phone with her."

"What's she trying to pull?" I asked.

"She didn't say, but I guess we'll find out tonight."

"We will?"

"I told her we'd stop by."

"*I'm* not stopping by," I said.

"Oh, Barnaby. Please?"

She had a different voice from her aunt's—steadier and much lower—but the upward note at the end was the same. "I think she wants to apologize," she said.

"She didn't tell *me* she wanted to apologize."

"Well, why else would she ask us over?"

"Maybe to have me arrested," I said.

"Don't be silly. How she put it was, she wanted to 'chat.' She said, 'I know you're very cross with me, but please, please, the two of you, come for a chat.' "

"She's got some kind of ambush planned," I said. "SWAT team lying in wait for me behind her potted palm."

Sophia laughed, but dutifully, as if her thoughts were elsewhere. "How could I turn her down?" she asked. "So I said yes."

"You can't say yes on my behalf, Sophia. You had no business doing that."

"Well, but, sweetie. She's my aunt!"

I kept quiet a moment. Not to sound paranoid, but it crossed my mind that Sophia might be in on this, whatever it was. I knew she was too honorable for that, but even so, I had a little flash of doubt. Meanwhile, some other phone line seemed to be mixing in with ours—tiny distant voices I couldn't quite decipher, a woman burbling away and another woman laughing. The two of them were so lighthearted. I felt as if we'd plugged into not just another conversation but another time, simpler and more innocent; and here I was in this muddy, confused life of mine.

I told Sophia, "All right, hon. For your sake."

She said, "Oh, thank you! Thank you, Barnaby."

"But we're only staying a minute," I said.

"Of course."

"Just long enough to be polite, so things aren't awkward with your relatives."

"I understand."

Hanging up, I felt like a phony. Face it: I couldn't care less how things stood with her relatives. Underneath, my fantasy was that Mrs. Glynn really would apologize. And while she was at it, why couldn't all the others too? The Amberlys and the Royces, and Mr. McLeod with his Chinese statue. I pictured them lining up in Mrs. Glynn's parlor to say . . . what? Not that they'd wrongly accused me; that was too much to hope for. But maybe, oh, that they'd overreacted, or failed to allow for extenuating circumstances. Or that they still liked me anyhow. I don't know.

The plan was, I would drive to Sophia's after she got off work, pick her up, and then head to Mrs. Glynn's. But Martine was late bringing the truck back; she was out somewhere on a job. I had to phone Sophia and ask her to come get me. This was fine with Sophia—no doubt she preferred her Saab to my jouncing, bone-rattling truck—but it made me mad as hell. In the two weeks since I'd let the Corvette go, I'd been marooned without a ride three times and been yelled at twice when I'd marooned Martine. Also, we were stuck in a situation where we were thrown together constantly. Mrs. Dibble had always tended to pair the two of us up, for some reason, but now it was even worse. Every job assignment had to take into account that Martine and I shared a vehicle, although we lived five miles apart and couldn't stand to face each other anymore. What had I been thinking of, agreeing to such an arrangement?

And my poor little car, my little lost car. That car was my very identity—so ramshackle and rascally. I should never have let Martine talk me into selling it.

You see what I mean about my life being muddy.

Sophia arrived in her bank clothes, but I wore jeans and a stringy black sweater. No way was I dressing up for this. I climbed into the Saab, turning down her offer to let me drive. "Just gun that motor and let's get this over with," I told her.

She said, "Now, Barnaby, promise you'll be nice to her."

"Did I say I wouldn't be nice?"

"She's just a helpless old lady. Promise you won't forget that."

But as things worked out, it seemed to be Sophia who forgot.

Oh, she was congenial enough at the start. She pressed her cheek to her aunt's cheek, and she told her how pretty she looked. Mrs. Glynn wore a baggy-chested silk dress and a strand of pearls she could have jumped rope with, looped and looped again and hanging to her knees. I'd never seen her in jewelry before. Or leather pumps, either, instead of Nikes. And Tatters was yapping frantically in the pantry. The only other time I'd known him to be shut away was when the minister came to call.

"How've you been, Aunt Grace?" Sophia was asking. "How's your bursitis?" As if they were on the best of terms. It irked me some, I can tell you. When we sat down, I chose a rocker, not my usual seat beside Sophia on the couch. I tucked my hands between my knees and watched glumly as Mrs. Glynn arranged herself in her favorite chair.

"I can see just fine," she told Sophia, "except for reading. Why do you ask?"

This caused a shattered little pause, until Sophia's forehead cleared and she said, "Your bursitis, I said; not your sight."

"My bursitis. Oh. It's just lovely," Mrs. Glynn said, peculiarly. She laced her fingers together and leaned toward me. "Barnaby," she said, "I don't believe we've conversed since I discovered I was burglarized."

"No," I said, "we haven't." I felt embarrassed; Lord knows why.

"Of course, it was a *most* distressing event. Most distressing. But you know what I say: money is only money."

I'd never heard her say any such thing, but I nodded.

"In the final analysis," she said, "the human element is what counts. Wouldn't you agree?"

"Well . . ."

"You are a person my niece regards very highly. I can appreciate that. And Ray Oakley isn't half the worker that you were. I propose we let bygones be bygones."

It was while I was computing her words that Sophia's attitude changed. "If that doesn't take the cake!" she told her aunt.

"I beg your pardon?" Mrs. Glynn said.

"Let bygones be bygones? Generous of you, I must say!"

"Excuse me, dear?"

I said, "Sophia—"

"You owe Barnaby more than that, Aunt Grace. You owe him an apology. A complete and humble apology."

"Sophia, it's okay," I said.

I had never seen her like this. I felt kind of flattered. But, "We'll just put it behind us," I said. "No big deal."

"No big deal!" Sophia cried.

"Wonderful," her aunt told me. "And may I expect you to resume your regular hours?"

"No, you may *not* expect him to resume his regular hours!" Sophia cried. "Over my dead body he'll resume his regular hours!"

I said, "Hon." I turned to Mrs. Glynn. "Unfortunately, I've . . . ah, got those hours filled now," I said. "But I'm sure Ray Oakley—"

"You found the money, didn't you," Sophia told her aunt.

"What, dear?" her aunt asked quaveringly.

"You found it where you left it, and you don't have the courage to say so."

This struck me as assuming a bit too much. More likely, Mrs. Glynn had just recalled that I wasn't the only person who knew her hiding spot. I said, "In any case—"

"You are the most dishonest of all of us," Sophia told her aunt. Two scratched-looking patches of pink had risen in her cheeks. "You found that money and you won't admit it. I bet you didn't even notify the insurance company, did you?"

"On the contrary. I notified them at once," Mrs. Glynn said. "I would never commit *fraud*, for mercy's sake." She spoke very primly and evenly, somehow not moving her lips.

I stared at her.

"So there," Sophia told me, settling back in her seat.

"I don't know how I could have been so forgetful," Mrs. Glynn said. A teaspoonful of tears, it seemed, swam above each eye pouch. "I'd been listening to everybody's warnings, you know. Everybody warning me I shouldn't inform all and sundry where I kept my cash. So I took it out of the flour bin and I moved it elsewhere. Well, I'll *tell* you where: I moved it to the pocket of my winter bathrobe. Then I just . . . I don't know; I must be getting senile. I forgot! I looked inside the flour bin and I saw there was no money and I forgot I'd moved it! I hope I don't have Alzheimer's. Do you think I might have Alzheimer's? I went along for weeks not recollecting, and then this morning when the weather turned I was getting some of my woolens out of the cedar closet and I saw my winter bathrobe and I said, 'Oh, good heavens above. That's where I moved my money to!' I've been a fool, children. I've been a forgetful old fool."

"It could happen to anyone," I told her. "Don't give it another thought."

I looked over at Sophia, waiting for her to chime in, but she had this flat look on her face. "Right, Sophia?" I asked.

"Hmm?"

"We've all done things like that, right?"

"Oh, yes . . ."

"So if you've got Alzheimer's, Mrs. Glynn, I guess all the rest of us have it too."

Mrs. Glynn tried to smile, dangerously swelling the spoonfuls of tears. I said again, "Right, Sophia?"

"Right," she said after a moment.

"Well. That settles that," I said, and I stood up. "No need to show us out," I told Mrs. Glynn.

"To shout?"

"No need to *show us out*," I said.

"Oh."

I wanted to get going before she could bring up my work hours again. (I wasn't *totally* forgiving.) But Sophia stayed on the couch, still wearing that flat expression. At the door I said, "Sophia?"

She rose, finally, and so did Mrs. Glynn. They didn't kiss goodbye. "Well, Aunt Grace," was all Sophia said, "I hope next time you won't be so quick to accuse an innocent man." And she hoisted her purse strap onto her shoulder. Mrs. Glynn stood straight as a clothespin, her hands knotted tightly together.

I would have expected Sophia to act more gracious. But I felt sort of pleased that she didn't.

In the car I said, "So! Turns out you were right about why she wanted to see us."

"Yes . . . ," Sophia said. She made no move to start the engine.

I said, "How about I buy you dinner."

"Dinner?"

"What's the problem, Sofe?" I asked. "Something on your mind?"

She looked over at me. She said, "I had no idea Aunt Grace had changed her hiding place."

"Well, she'd better change it again," I said, "because already she's told at least two people where the new place is."

"And so I put the money back in the old place," Sophia went on, as if I hadn't spoken.

"What money?" I asked.

"*My* money. Two thousand, nine hundred and sixty dollars."

For a second, I misunderstood. I said, "*You* stole that money?"

Which didn't make sense, of course, since no money had been stolen, but all Sophia said was, "Me? No." She started the engine, and we pulled away from the curb.

I said, "Begin at the beginning, Sophia."

"See, I felt so responsible," she said. We arrived at an intersection, and she braked and looked over at me. "I knew Aunt Grace held me to blame for bringing you into her life. 'Well,' I said to myself, 'all right, I'll just put my own money there to replace the money she's missing.' So I took it out of my savings. I called in sick at work on a Tuesday, Aunt Grace's podiatrist day, and I let myself in with my key and put the money in the flour bin."

"But . . . how would she explain that? First her money is missing, and then it magically isn't?" I said.

"She could explain it any way she liked," Sophia said.

"And for sure the new bills would be a different denomination from the old ones. You never saw the old ones, did you? You don't know if they were tens or fifties; you don't know if they were rubber-banded, or stuffed in an envelope, or tucked away in a wallet, do you?"

"No, and I don't care, either," Sophia said. She flung her head back so recklessly that a hairpin flew out of her bun and landed in the rear seat. "All I cared about was clearing your name."

"Some criminal *you* would make," I said.

Then I saw what was bothering me. Forget the logistics; forget the question of denominations, rubber bands . . .

I said, "You believed I did it."

"No, no," Sophia said.

A car drew up behind us and honked.

"You actually believed I stole that money."

Sophia took her foot off the brake. We crossed the intersection, but on the other side she pulled over to the curb and parked. "It's not the way it looks," she said, turning to face me. "I just couldn't stand for her to suspect you; that's all."

"Well, geez, Sophia, are you going to start stashing bills every place there's been a burglary I was in the neighborhood of? That could get expensive."

"No," Sophia said, "because I don't have any more to stash. I used my whole savings account, and next month's rent besides."

I put my head in my hands.

"But, Barnaby? It's no problem. I'll just steal it back again, the next time I'm over there."

"Sure," I said, raising my head. "Unless meanwhile she goes to bake a pie or something and finds your money before you get to it."

"She won't do that. She keeps her flour in the freezer, not the flour bin," Sophia said. "I could leave it there forever!" Then she started smiling. "You know what this reminds me of?" she said. "That O. Henry story, the Christmas one. 'Gift of the Magi.'"

"How do you figure that?" I asked her.

"I mean, here I give you this gift, and it turns out you have no need of it. Still, though, it wasn't for nothing, because it proves how much I love you."

"Well," I said.

I have to admit I was touched. No one had ever done anything like that for me before.

I said, "But that story had both people giving gifts, didn't it?"

"*You* are your gift to me, Barnaby," she told me. And when she leaned close to kiss me she smelled of flowers, and her lips felt as soft as petals.

Sometimes I thought I'd been right in the first place: Sophia was my angel.

IT WAS A TRADITION in my family—I mean, my own little failed *ex*-family, family in quotation marks—that Natalie would remind me when Opal's birthday was coming up. She would phone about a week ahead, no doubt doing her best to find a moment when I was out so that she could leave a message on my answering machine. "Barnaby," this year's message went, "Opal's birthday falls on the actual day of your visit this year; so you'll be able to bring your gift in person instead of mailing it. I just thought you'd like to know that."

I imagined her congratulating herself on her subtlety. "Don't act like the cad you are and forget your own daughter's birthday," she was saying, but it came out sounding all thoughtful and solicitous. I pictured her dimples denting inward with satisfaction as she hung up the phone.

Another tradition was, my gifts were always disasters. (A goldfish that died, a storybook that gave Opal nightmares, a

pencil case that snapped shut on her thumb and made her cry.)
So this year I asked Sophia to come shopping with me. She
picked out a stuffed hedgehog—a sort of bristle ball with a button nose—and then she wrapped it for me, better than I could
have done, for sure, with a satin bow and a silver gift card. On
the card I wrote, *Happy birthday from Barnaby and Sophia*.
Adding Sophia's name was a spur-of-the-moment decision—
I'd just wanted to thank her for helping—but she looked so
happy when she saw it that I was glad I'd thought of it.

We drove to Philadelphia in her Saab, with me at the wheel
till we reached Locust Street. There I climbed out, and she
took over. "I'll see you in three hours," she said, because she no
longer spent Saturday nights at her mother's. She'd told her
mother she had her own life, now, to get back to. Her mother
had said, "Well, fine, then. Just don't bother coming at all, if
that's how you're going to be." But Sophia came anyway, every
blessed Saturday, calmly ignoring her mother's sulks and
pointed remarks. Sophia was such a *sunny* person. She didn't
let people get to her. I admired that. I wished I could bring her
to Natalie's with me.

But as it was, I had to go it alone. Stand alone at Natalie's
door like a poor relation; wait meekly for someone to answer
my ring. It was Opal who answered, thank heaven. No sign of
Natalie, although she must have been nearby, because Opal
called, "See you, Mom!" before she let herself out.

She was wearing a rose-colored jacket, so new that I had to
pluck an inspection tag from the sleeve. Beneath it she had on a
lace-trimmed dress and white lace tights and patent-leather
shoes. I said, "Don't you look nice," and she grimaced and said,
"I had to get dressed ahead of time for my party. It's at three."

"Well, happy birthday," I said. I handed her my gift.

Then we stepped into the elevator, which was still standing
there from when I'd ridden it up. Opal lifted the gift box to her

ear and shook it, but she didn't open it. Used to be, she would rip right into it. Maybe she'd lost hope by now.

"Mom and Dad's present was a canopy bed," she said as we descended.

I hadn't known she called him "Dad." It gave me kind of a jolt.

"The canopy is white eyelet, and there's a ruffled spread to match."

I said, "Isn't that—" and then stopped myself from repeating the word "nice." Instead I said, "Watch your step," because we had reached the lobby.

It wasn't till we were outdoors, heading toward Rittenhouse Square, that I realized we were missing the dog. "Where's George Farnsworth?" I asked her.

"He had to go to the kennel till we're finished with the party. If there's too many kids around, he gets all excited and wees on the rug."

"How many kids will there be?" I asked.

"Twenty," she said.

"Twenty!"

"A professional magician's coming, and after that we're having a cake with a whole ballet scene on top in spun sugar."

"Well, isn't that—"

I paused at the corner of Locust and Seventeenth. I looked down at Opal and said, "Where're we going, anyhow?"

She shrugged. The weather was cold enough so I could see the puffs of her breath.

"We don't have a dog to walk," I said, "and it's too early for lunch."

"We could sit in the park," she suggested.

This seemed kind of lame, but I said, "Fine with me," and we started walking again. Opal carried her gift in both hands, like something precious. I began to feel less confident about it.

Probably a stuffed animal was too childish. (My mother had suggested an opal on a chain—October's birthstone. Martine had suggested a video game, but I thought Natalie might disapprove.)

In the park, we met up with the usual crowd—unshaven men slumped on benches, rich old ladies tripping along with tiny, fussy dogs better dressed than I was. We found an empty bench, and I brushed the dead leaves off so we could sit. Opal placed her gift very precisely on her knees and started untying the bow. It was one of those rosette-shaped bows—I'd been impressed no end that Sophia knew how to make it—and Opal would have done better just slipping the whole thing off the box, but no, she had to untie it. I realized she must be just as worried as I was about how to fill the time. After she got the ribbon off, she wound it around her hand and tucked it in her pocket, and then she unstuck the card (first rolling the strip of Scotch tape into a cylinder and pocketing that too). "*Happy birthday from Barnaby and Sophia,*" she read aloud. She looked over at me. "Who's Sophia?"

"Sophia! You remember Sophia. Who cooked all those suppers when you were in Baltimore. And went with us to the Orioles game."

She studied the card a moment longer. Then she set it on the bench between us and painstakingly undid the wrapping, not once tearing it. Out came the box. She took the lid off. I realized I was holding my breath. She folded back the tissue and lifted out the hedgehog. Pathetic little critter, no bigger than my fist. "Thank you," she said, eyeing the button nose.

"Well. I didn't know what kind of thing you liked these days."

"This is fine," she told me.

"I could take it back and exchange it, if you'd rather."

"No, this is great. Really."

"Well. Okay," I said.

Opal put the hedgehog back in the box and replaced the lid. Then she picked up the gift card and looked at it again. Even turned it over to look at the other side, which was blank.

"So," she said. "Did you and Sophia, like, go halfsies on the money for this?"

"No, it was more that she helped me pick it out."

"Oh."

"You do remember her," I said.

"Sure," she said. Then she said, "I guess."

"You guess? You saw her every day of your visit, almost!"

"But I thought she was just a lady," she said.

"Just a . . . ?"

"I mean, is she, like, your *girlfriend* or something?"

"Well, yes, she is," I said. "I thought you knew that. We've been seeing each other for eight or nine months now."

"Seeing as in dating?" Opal asked.

"Didn't you realize?"

She shook her head. She wore this stony, set expression that made me uneasy.

"Ope?" I said. "Does that bother you?"

She just went on shaking her head.

"Did you not *like* Sophia, Ope?"

She said, "I liked her okay." Then she clamped her mouth tight shut again.

"So what's the problem?"

"Nothing's the problem!" she told me. She stood up, hugging the box to her chest. The wrapping paper wafted to the ground, but she seemed not to notice. "Could we go eat now?" she asked.

"Eat? Well, all right," I said.

Although it was nowhere near lunchtime yet.

I bent to retrieve the paper and tossed it into a trash bin, and then we walked out of the Square and headed toward a diner I knew of, a couple of blocks away. I figured we could order some sort of semi-lunch, semi-breakfast dish—French toast or something. I wondered what time it was. I kept trying to get a glimpse of people's watches, but everybody wore long sleeves and I didn't have any luck.

Then just as we started to cross the street, I caught sight of Natalie. She was standing on the opposite corner in her red coat and a long black scarf, and she must not have noticed that the light had changed to WALK, because she was gazing off to her left. I don't know why I felt so startled. This was her neighborhood, after all. She was probably running a few last-minute errands before the birthday party. But I thought to myself, *What* is *this? She pops up everywhere*—as if she'd materialized not just once or twice but anytime I turned around, flashing in and out of view like a glimmer in a pond. I stopped short and said, "Oh! There's—!" and Opal followed my eyes and said, "Mom."

We crossed to where she stood. When she saw us, she didn't seem surprised. Natalie never seemed surprised. She surveyed me imperturbably, holding her head very level on account of the scarf, which gave her a sort of madonna-like aspect. I said, "Hi there, Nat."

"Hi," she said. Her gaze dropped to Opal. "Are you having a good time?" she asked.

"I'm cold," Opal told her.

"Cold?"

This was the first I'd heard of it, and I was about to say so if Natalie accused me of negligence. All she said, though, was, "What's in the box?"

"Barnaby gave me a hedgehog."

"Stuffed," I explained, as if I needed to. "A stuffed *toy*, I mean; not taxidermy, ha ha . . ."

"Shall I carry it home, Opal, so you won't have to lug it around?"

But Opal clutched the box tighter and said, "Maybe I could come with you."

Natalie's eyes returned to me.

I told Opal, "I thought we were having lunch at the diner."

"Yes, but I'm so cold," she said. "And besides, I've got my party dress on. I don't want to spill food on my party dress. We could maybe go next time, instead. Another time we could go! I promise!"

Natalie and I studied each other a minute longer.

"Another time. Sure," I said finally.

Then I gave Opal a little, like, cuff to the shoulder to show there were no hard feelings. But even so, when I turned to leave, she called after me, "Barnaby? You're not mad at me, are you?"

I lifted an arm as I walked and then let it flop, not looking around.

Back in the Square, I sat on a bench and stretched my legs out in front of me. It *was* cold. A woman in a plaid hat and cape was feeding the squirrels. A teenage boy loped past, and I said, "Hey, guy? You got the time?" Too late, I saw he was wearing a headset and couldn't hear me. I felt kind of foolish, with my question left hanging in the air like that.

Probably I had two hours to kill. Or two and a half, even, before I could head back to Locust, where Sophia was picking me up. I ought to go to the diner after all. Order something time-consuming. But instead I kept on sitting there, expressionless as the men on the benches all around me.

This wasn't just about Opal.

I have to say, it was Natalie who weighed more heavily on my mind.

"Could I interest you in some lemonade?" she had asked on that first afternoon, and her face had been so peaceful. Her back had been so straight; her gaze so steady. But after we'd been married awhile, she turned irritable and brisk. Any little thing I did wrong, flounce-flounce around the apartment. And I did tend to do things wrong. This weird kind of sibling rivalry set in; I can't explain it. I just had to defeat her, had to prove my own brash, irresponsible, rough-and-tumble way of life was better. And yet I'd married her because *her* way was better. Just as some people marry for money, I had married for goodness. Ironic, if you stopped to consider.

When she left me, I thought, *Well, finally!* I stopped attending classes, and I did some serious drinking, and I slept till noon or two p.m., and nobody was around to nag or look disapproving.

Now I see that I went a little crazy, even. Like, the kitchen sink in our apartment had this spray-hose attachment. If you pressed the button while the faucet was running, the faucet cut off and the hose cut on; and I remember standing there on many an occasion, pressing the button and releasing it, alternating between faucet and hose, marveling at how polite they were. The faucet stopped to let the hose talk; the hose stopped to let the faucet talk. So mannerly, so genteel. I thought, *All these years, I've underestimated the qualities of inanimate objects.*

Or the view outside my bedroom window: a big, tall spruce tree leaning over the alley. Every morning, waking up, I noticed once again that it leaned at the exact same angle as the pine tree in the highway signs—those signs showing a tree and a table to indicate a picnic ground. And every morning, I went on to wonder why the tree in those signs was tilted. Was there some special significance? Was it meant to imply protection, shelter? I mean, I thought this *every single damn everlasting morning*. You try doing that sometime. It seemed my mind got into a rut, and it wore the rut deeper and deeper, and I couldn't yank it free again.

And some nights I brought a girl home and we'd be going through the preliminaries, carrying on some artificial oh-isn't-that-interesting conversation on the couch, and she would give me this sudden puzzled look, and I'd lift a hand to my face and find my cheeks were wet. Water just pouring out of my eyes. I won't say tears, because I swear I wasn't crying. But my eyes were up to *something* or other.

So many things, it seemed, my body went ahead and did without me.

Well, that stage passed, by and by. I moved out of the apartment, developed a new routine, forgot about Natalie altogether. I'd see her when I collected Opal and when I brought Opal back, but she was never really present in my mind. Not that I was aware of, at least. Not consciously.

Here I had been thinking that the train trip where I'd first glimpsed Sophia had changed my whole existence; and in fact it had, but it was Natalie who had set that in motion. I saw that now. It was Natalie in her kitchen, her face as sealed and peaceful as the day she had offered me lemonade. *Could I interest you?* It was the cookie jar on her windowsill—that humble, chipped birdcage jar we used to be so proud of when we were kids together. Oh, once upon a time I'd had all I could ask for: a home, a loving wife, a little family of my own. A *place* in the world. How could I have thrown that away?

At Rent-a-Back, I knew couples who'd been married almost forever—forty, fifty, sixty years. Seventy-two, in one case. They'd be tending each other's illnesses, filling in each other's faulty memories, dealing with the money troubles or the daughter's suicide or the grandson's drug addiction. And I was beginning to suspect that it made no difference whether they'd married the right person. Finally, you're just with who you're with. You've signed on with her, put in half a century with her, grown to know her as well as you know yourself or even better, and she's *become* the right person. Or the only person, might be more to the point. I wish someone had told me that earlier. I'd have hung on then; I swear I would. I never would have driven Natalie to leave me.

Sophia looked so light-colored, when she arrived to pick me up. I felt a little shocked, as if I had forgotten which woman I was linked with nowadays. But also I was relieved. "Sophia!" I said. "Sweetheart!" And when she stepped out to let me slide into the driver's seat, I hugged her so hard that she laughed at me.

I told her Opal had liked the hedgehog. I didn't go into the rest of it. I certainly didn't admit that I had spent the last couple of hours sitting alone on a bench. Sophia said, "Oh, good," and pursued it no further. One of the qualities I loved in her was her willingness to accept the surface version of things. I reached over to squeeze her knee—a bounteous, soft handful encased in slippery nylon.

Then, after we reached the highway, she sailed into this saga about shopping with her mother. "She told me she needed new bras," she said. "The only thing she won't buy through the mail. So we got into my car—never mind that she lives in the middle of downtown; she has to drive out to the suburbs—and right away it was, 'Oh, don't take this road; take that road,' and, 'Don't turn here; keep straight.' 'Mother,' I said, 'I promise I will get you there. Show some faith,' I said, but would she listen? 'That road is under repair now,' she said. 'Take the road I tell you.' I said, 'I'm sure they'll give us a detour route,' but she said, 'I don't want a detour route!' Then, when I turned anyhow, she fell into a pout. She sat there moving her lips for the rest of the ride—which was easy, incidentally. Nothing but a few traffic cones. But coming back, what did she do? Started the whole business over again. 'Don't take this road! Take that road!' "

It seemed to have escaped Sophia's notice that she could simply have followed her mother's instructions. What difference would it have made? But I didn't point that out. In this new, contented frame of mind, I just smiled to myself.

"Mother inquired after you, by the way," Sophia said.

"Hmm?"

"She said, 'How is that young man you've been seeing?' Then later she asked if I would be up for Thanksgiving, and when I said I didn't know yet, she said, 'You're welcome to bring your friend.' "

"Oh," I said. "Well. I guess I could come, if you want me to."

"I told her no," Sophia said.

This was fine with me. I said, "Whatever you decide."

"She'd be needling us every minute. Believe me."

"It sounds like our mothers have a lot in common," I said.

Which I used as yet another excuse to squeeze that handful of knee. I was thinking I'd like to get her into bed once we reached Baltimore, but Saturday afternoons could pose a problem. At my place, the Hardestys would be everywhere—kids squabbling on the patio right outside my door, Joe hammering away at some little task from his Job Jar. And Sophia's roommate had an annoying habit of cleaning house on Saturdays.

"She'd be sure to make all these not-so-subtle references to my weight," Sophia said, evidently still talking about her mother. " 'More turkey, Barnaby? I won't offer *you* any, Sophia. I know you wouldn't want the extra calories.' "

"Don't you dare lose an ounce," I told her.

There was a luscious little pouch of flesh on her inner thigh just above where her knee bent. It sprang back beneath my fingers like a ripe plum.

"With you, it would be your career," she said. "Mother's asked me three times now whether you've ever thought of other employment."

"She really *does* have a lot in common with Mom," I said.

"I tell her, 'Mother, drop it. Barnaby's very happy doing what he's doing,' I say, and she always says, 'Yes, but would his salary feed a family?' "

"It could," I said.

"It could?"

"It could if it weren't a very *hungry* family."

Sophia made a face at me.

I knew what we were creeping up on here—what we were skating around the border of. We had never, in so many words, discussed getting married; but I think lately it had been on both our minds. I said, "The way I see it, everyone has a choice: living rich and working hard to pay for it, or living a plain, uncomplicated life and taking it easy."

"Well, *you* work hard, Barnaby. You're practically a slave! Wakened up anytime Mr. Shank gets lonely, setting your alarm for crack of dawn on garbage days . . ."

"Yes, but it's the kind of work I enjoy," I said. "And at least it's not nine to five."

"Six to midnight is more like it!"

"Hey," I said, and I eased my foot on the accelerator. "Do *you* think I ought to change jobs?"

"No, no," she said.

"It sure sounds as if you do."

"I just hate to see you work such long hours," she said, "and not get better paid for it."

"I'm paid enough to live on," I said. Then I got bolder. "Maybe enough for a wife besides, if the wife was frugal."

The word "wife" hung in the air between us. It didn't really sound all that bad, after my meditations in the park.

"And face it," I said, hurrying on. (At heart, I was a coward.) "What other work could I do? I don't have any useful skills. My education's been a farce. All I've learned is trivia."

"Oh, that's ridiculous," Sophia said. "Of course you have useful skills! There's no such thing as trivia."

"There isn't?"

I had never heard that before. It struck me as so erroneous that I couldn't decide where to start attacking it. In the end, I said, "Well, here: During the Second World War, when butter was scarce in Germany, the Germans started eating their toast with the buttered side down. That way, they could use less butter and still taste it."

"Pardon?"

"But what's surprising is, when the war was over, they went back to buttered side up. You'd think they would have formed a new habit; but no, they reverted to buttered side up the very first chance they got. That's the kind of trivia I mean."

Sophia was silent. A truckful of chickens passed us—stacks and stacks of crates, strewing feathers.

"Well, anyhow," she said, finally. "One option I might suggest is, finish up your degree and then apply at my bank."

"Your bank!"

"They offer an excellent training program, with full fringe benefits while you're learning."

"I'd rather die than work in a bank," I said.

I felt Sophia's face whip toward me. I glanced over and saw how pink her cheeks were. "Well. Sorry," I said, "but—"

"It's all right for *me* to work in a bank, but you're above such things. Is that what you're saying?"

"Now, hold on, Sofe—"

"*I* can work nine to five, and scrimp and save up my earnings, which, by the way, I have lost every bit of, my entire savings account wiped out, and thirty dollars in my checking account to last till the end of the month; *I* can pay for the—"

"Wait," I said. "Surely you're not holding me to blame for that fool stunt you did with your money."

"Fool stunt? I did it to save you! I thought I was protecting you! I thought you would be grateful!"

"Why should I be grateful? I never robbed your aunt. And I certainly never asked you to cover for me."

"No," she said. And more quietly, she said, "No, you didn't. I realize that. It was my mistake. You had nothing to do with it. But I just feel, I don't know, frustrated when you talk about your plain, uncomplicated life and simple tastes, and I meanwhile am wishing for . . . oh, nothing fancy! Just to eat out a little more often, go to a play or a concert every now and then. Take a couple of trips together. But we can't! You don't make enough money, and mine is at the bottom of Aunt Grace's flour bin!"

This last sentence ended in kind of a wail. I put my arm around her, although I had to keep an eye on the road. "Hon," I said. "Look. First of all, I don't understand why that money is still at your aunt's."

"Well, I told you I haven't been back there. I'm very cross with Aunt Grace, and she knows it. I think she wasn't nearly as apologetic as she ought to have been."

"So? You have a key to her house. Slip in sometime when

she's out. Slip in on her podiatrist day, or her beauty parlor day. Steal your money back again."

"Oh, I couldn't do that," Sophia said.

"Why not?"

"I'm worried she might catch me."

"You didn't let that stop you when you put it there in the first place."

"But it's different, getting caught *taking* money," she told me.

"Lord God, Sophia! Not if the money's your own!"

"There's no need to shout at me," she said gently.

Then she drew away, sliding out from under my arm.

I didn't talk anymore after that, and I barely grunted when she made some comment on the scenery. "Isn't that tree a pretty shade of yellow!" Grunt. It seemed I was my difficult, unappreciative self again. For all the good it did, I might as well not have bothered with my epiphany in the park.

These little glints of wisdom never last as long as you would expect.

12

MAUD MAY had been in the nursing home for over seven months now. First it was one thing and then another. I'd begun to think she was one of those clients who go in and never come out again. Her house had taken on the faded, seedy look of a place that's been abandoned, and it gave a start and shrank back on itself whenever I walked in. The spider plant I'd been watering all this time had grown so many baby plants that some of them trailed to the floor.

But then at the end of October—Halloween, in fact—they said she was well enough to leave. I remember it was Halloween because she asked me to pick up some trick-or-treat candy before I came to collect her. "I don't want any neighbor brats soaping my windows in spite," she told me. Though how she expected to answer the door when they rang, I couldn't say. She was still exceedingly lame.

So I dropped Martine at Mrs. Cartwright's, where the two

of us were scheduled to clear out the guest room, and then I went to the supermarket. Halloween this year wasn't likely to amount to much. A thunderstorm had been threatening since early morning. But I bought three sacks of fun-size Almond Joys, along with the other items on Maud May's shopping list—the prunes and the all-bran cereal, a single grapefruit, a skinny one-quart carton of skim milk. Anyone could have told at a glance that these were an old person's groceries.

When I let myself into her house, I tried to view it through her eyes. Should that spider plant be so brownish at the tips? And how about the drawers in the sideboard: did they look *snooped into*, somehow? I hadn't snooped; I swear I hadn't; but you never know what people will imagine.

At the Silver Threads Nursing Home, Maud May was ready and waiting. She sat beside the reception desk in the wheelchair they always force departing patients to ride in. A jumble of belongings crowded the floor all around her. "At last!" she snapped when she saw me. "Bentham, we can go now."

Bentham was the orderly who was joking with the switch-board girl—a young black guy about seven feet tall, with a wedge-shaped hairdo. He threw one last remark over his shoulder and came to help me carry the luggage out. Suitcases, hatboxes, potted plants, a folded aluminum walker . . . We loaded them all in the back of the truck. A misty rain had started falling, and Bentham said, "Ms. May not going to be too happy about this"—meaning the fact of the open truck bed. "You want I should hunt up a tarp?" he asked.

But I said, "Never mind," because I figured things would get all the wetter while we waited. Besides, Maud May wasn't the fussy type.

She'd changed, though. I should have known. I'd certainly seen enough signs of it, over the months I'd been visiting. First off, as Bentham was wheeling her through the door, she barely acknowledged the staff's goodbyes. "You're leaving us?" they asked her. "Well, you take care, now, hear?" Granted, they were most of them using a honeyed, high, thin, baby-talk voice that probably drove her nuts, but still, she could have said, "Thanks." She didn't. She gave an indifferent wave, not troubling to look back.

Then, outside, she cried, "What!" so sharply that Bentham stopped pushing her. "I'm going home in a truck?" she asked me.

"It's just a short ride, Ms. May," I said.

"What happened to your darlin' little sports car?"

"Well, I sold it."

"Good Gawd, Barnaby, you're an idiot," she said.

But already beads of rain were shining on the top of her head, and she didn't protest when Bentham started wheeling her again.

Helping her into the truck's cab caused another hitch. "Damn thing is too far off the ground," she told me. And, "Jesus! My luggage is sopping!" as she happened to glance toward the rear. Bentham *tsk*ed and hoisted her up by one elbow. I said, "At least your plants'll be watered, Ms. May." She didn't smile. After I shut her in, she sat staring straight ahead, dead-faced, and she failed to lean over and unlock the driver's-side door when I came around. I had to use my key. You see a lot of that with invalids. They start out vowing they won't depend, but then they seem to get *into* it. They turn all passive. Still, I hadn't expected it of Maud May.

"You be good, Ms. May!" Bentham called as we rolled off.

Ms. May just said, "What choice do I have?"

We didn't need our wipers at first, with the rain so light and fine, but gradually the windshield grew harder to see through. I was kind of waiting for Ms. May to mention it. I thought she would order me around in that tough-talking way she used to have. But she kept quiet, staring straight in front of her. Finally I flicked on my wipers unbidden. I said, "So! How does it feel, getting sprung?"

"Oh . . . ," she said. And then nothing more.

We reached her house, and I parked at the curb. Maud May didn't even glance toward her front door. Luckily, the rain had stopped by then. I say "Luckily" because once I'd helped her down from the truck, it took her forever to inch up the walk in her walker. Step, rest, step, rest, she went, and several times she pointedly lifted one hand or the other and wiped it on the front of her coat, although I had dried the walker off after I unloaded it. Halfway along, a neighbor came out—a pudgy-faced woman with gray hair—and she took charge of Ms. May while I brought in the luggage. "Why, Maud, you're doing wonderfully. Just wonderfully," she said, but all Ms. May would answer back was, "Huh." I kept passing them, traveling between the truck and the house, and every time, Ms. May had her head down, her eyes on her feet as they shuffled behind her walker. "Sturds," she said at one point, and the neighbor said, "What's that, dear?"

"Sturds: those klutzy, thick brown oxfords they used to make us wear at Roland Park Country Day School."

Actually, her shoes were black, not brown, but I caught her drift. Till now, she'd always worn vampish heels with sling backs and open toes. Also, she used to claim she would never be seen publicly in pants, but this morning she had on not just pants but sweatpants, elastic-waisted, cuffed bunchily at the ankles.

They'd delivered a hospital bed the day before, and it was set up in the sunporch so she wouldn't have to climb stairs. I arranged her belongings nearby where she could reach them. Then I steered her up the front steps, while the neighbor followed, hands cupped to catch her if she stumbled. "Smells musty," Ms. May said as she entered.

"We'll air it out," the neighbor assured her. "Throw open all the windows and just chase those cobwebs right out of here!"

"Well, Elaine," Ms. May said abruptly, "perhaps we'll meet again sometime. Goodbye, now."

The neighbor took on a stunned look, but she was still smiling steadily, her face very bright and determined, when she turned to leave. I told her, "Thanks a lot!" to make up for Ms. May's bad manners. "She was only trying to help," I said, once the door was shut.

"Get me onto that couch," Maud May told me, "and then go."

"Yes, *ma'am*," I said.

"This is the first time in seven months that some jackass fellow human won't be sharing my breathing space."

"Hey. I can dig it," I said. I felt a tad bit better, because she was starting to sound like herself.

Even so, that experience put a damper on my day. I'm telling you: don't ever get old! Before I started at Rent-a-Back, I thought a guy could just make up his mind to have a decent old age. Now I know that there's no such thing—or if once in a blue moon there is, it's a matter of pure blind luck. I must have seen a hundred of those sunporch sickrooms, stuffed wall-to-wall with hospital beds and IV poles and potty chairs. I've seen those sad, quiet widow women trudging off alone to their deaths, no one to ease them through the way they'd eased their husbands through years and years before. And if by chance the husband's the one who's survived, it's even worse, because men are not as good at managing on their own, I've come to think. They get clingy, like Mr. Shank. They tend to lack that inner gauge that tells them when they're talking too much; they're always trying to buttonhole the nearest passerby. Ask them the most offhand question; they lean back expansively and begin, "Well, now, there's a funny little story about that that I think may interest you." And, "To make a long story short," they'll say, when already they've gone on longer than God himself would have patience for. They pull this trick where they change the subject without a pause for breath—come to the end of one subject and you're thinking at last you can leave, but then they start in on the next subject; not so much as a nanosecond where you can say, "Guess I'll be going."

And those retirement watches old people consult a hundred times a day, counting off minute by minute! Those kitchen windowsills lined with medicine bottles! Those miniature servings of food, a third of a banana rewrapped in a speckly black peel and sitting in the fridge! Their aging pets: the half-bald cat, the arthritic dog creeping down the sidewalk next to his creeping owner. The reminder notes Scotch-taped all over the house: *Lawn-mowing boy is named RICHARD. Take afternoon pill with FULL GLASS OF WATER.* The sudden downward plunges they make: snappy speech one day and faltering for words not two weeks later; handsome, dignified faces all at once in particles, uneven, collapsing, dissolving.

The jar lids they can't unscrew, the needles they can't thread, the large print that's not quite large enough, even with a magnifying glass. The specter of the nursing home lurking constantly in the background, so it's, "Please don't tell my children I asked for help with this, will you?" and, "When the social worker comes, make like you're my son, so she won't think I live alone." The peculiar misunderstandings, part deafness and part out-of-syncness—insisting that someone named "Sheetrock Mom" bombed the World Trade Center, declining a visit to a tapas bar in the belief that it's a topless bar, calling free-range poultry "born-again chicken," and asking if the postpartum is blooming when what they mean is impatiens. "Don't you look youthful!" a physical therapist said once to Mrs. Alford, and she said, "Me? Useful?" and the thing that killed me was not her mishearing but the pleasure and astonishment that came over her face.

They walk down the street, and everyone looks away from them. People hate to see what the human body comes to—the sags and droops, splotches, humps, bulging stomachs, knobby fingers, thinning hair, freckled scalps. You're supposed to say old age is beautiful; that's one of those lines intended to shame whoever disagrees. But every one of my clients disagrees, I'm sure of it. You catch them sometimes watching children, maybe studying a toddler's face or his little hands, and you know they're marveling: so flawless! poreless! skin like satin! I doubt they want to be young again ("Youth is too *fraught*," was how Maud May always put it), but I'm positive not a one would turn down the chance to be, say, middle-aged.

"Fifty was nice," Mr. Shank told me once. "Fifty was great! Sixty was too. And sixty-five; I was doing good at sixty-five. But then somewhere along there . . . I don't know . . . I said to my wife, Junie—this was when Junie was still living—'Junie,' I said, 'you know? Some days I'm afraid I might commit suicide.' And Junie, she just looked at me—she was one of those *zestful* people; energetic, zestful people—and she said, 'Well, Fred, I'll tell you. Sometimes I'm afraid I might commit suicide myself.' She didn't, of course. She passed away in her sleep, God rest her. One morning I woke up and I knew without even looking; it felt like our bedroom was quieter than it ever was before. But, now, what was I saying? What point was I trying to make? Oh. If *Junie* could feel that way, such a zestful person as Junie, then I don't see as there's any hope whatsoever for the rest of us."

He said it so matter-of-factly, like someone delivering a

weather report. And then turned in his chair and looked out the window, absently smoothing his kneecaps with both hands, the way he always did when he sat idle.

And Mrs. Cartwright: now, this was just the kind of thing I was referring to. The reason she wanted her guest room cleared out was, she had arranged for a live-in companion. Some woman from a classified ad. Companions generally mean a lot fewer hours for Rent-a-Back, but that's not what bothers me. It's that once they've moved in, they tend to take over. They leave their magazines lying around, and switch channels on the TV without asking, and throw out perfectly edible food, and smell up the air with strong perfume. I've heard it all! Still, it's not our place to argue. Mrs. Cartwright said she had to face the fact that she hadn't had a good night's rest since her husband died. Every little creak sounded like a footstep, she said. So we'd been called in to clear thirty years of clutter from the guest room, and the following week a total stranger was coming to keep her company.

By the time I got there, Martine had emptied the bureau and started on the closet—knitting supplies and sewing remnants and half-finished squares of needlepoint. "How was Maud May?" she asked, and I said, "Old," which made her pull her head out of the closet and give me a look. But instead of speaking, she tossed a ball of yarn at me. I dodged, and it landed squarely in the garbage can she'd set in the center of the room. "Ta-dah!" she said.

"Sure, at *that* distance," I told her. I moved the garbage can farther away and reached past her for another ball of yarn. It always soothes my mind if I can get some kind of rumpus going. And Martine was good at that; she was kind of rowdy herself. We started slam-dunking every dispensable item we came across, and maybe a few that weren't. A jar of buttons, for instance, which burst when it landed with a gratifying, hail-stone sound that made me feel a whole lot better.

But then Mrs. Cartwright called out, "Children? What *was* that? Is everything all right?"

We grew very still. "Yes, ma'am," I called. "Just neatening up."

After that, I sank into a mood again.

We were dragging an unbelievably heavy footlocker out to the hall when I asked Martine, "Have you ever thought of changing jobs?"

"Why? Am I doing something wrong?"

"I mean, doesn't this job get you down? Don't you think it's kind of a *sad* job?"

She straightened up from the footlocker to consider. "Well," she said, "I know once when I was taking Mrs. Gordoni to visit her father . . . Did you ever meet her father? He'd been in some kind of accident years before and ended up with this peculiar condition where he didn't have any short-term memory. Not a bit. He forgot everything that happened from one minute to the next."

I said, "Oh, Lord."

"So he was living in this special-care facility, and I had to drive Mrs. Gordoni there once when her car broke down. And her father gave her a big hello, but then when Mrs. Gordoni stepped out to speak to the nurse, he asked me, 'Do you happen to be acquainted with my daughter? She never visits! I can't think what's become of her!' "

"See what I mean?" I said.

"*That* kind of got me down."

"Right."

"But then you have to look on the other side of it," Martine said.

"What other side, for God's sake?"

"Well, it's kind of encouraging that Mrs. Gordoni still came, don't you think? She certainly didn't get *credit* for coming, beyond the very moment she was standing in her father's view. Just for that moment, her father was happy. Not one instant longer. But Mrs. Gordoni went even so, every day of the week."

"Well," I said. Then I said, "Yeah, okay."

Martine wiped her face on the shoulder of her shirt. Her sleeves were rolled to her elbows, and her house key swung from the wide leather band that circled her wrist. It wasn't *designed* to circle her wrist. It should have been hooked to a belt loop, but since she didn't have a belt loop, she wore it like an oversized bracelet instead; and all at once I was fascinated by how she'd come up with this arrangement. The workings of her mind suddenly seemed so intricate—the wheels and gears spinning inside her compact little head.

But when she said, "What," I said, "*What* what," and bent to lift the lid of the footlocker.

Just as I had suspected, I found stacks of moldering books cramming every inch. Nothing's heavier than books. These had bleached-looking covers in shades of pink and turquoise that don't even seem to exist anymore. *Let's Bake! Fun with String. Witty Sayings of Our Presidents. The Confident Public Speaker.*

"Mrs. Cartwright?" I called. "Are you around?"

Of course she was around. She was wringing her hands at the bottom of the stairs, probably longing to come supervise if only her heart had allowed. "Yes?" she said, craning up at me.

"How about those old books in the footlocker? Shall we toss them?"

"Oh, no. My son might want them. Just put them in the basement."

Yes, and that's another thing: the possessions choking the basements and clogging the attics, lovingly squirreled away for grown children. The children say, "We don't have room. We'll never have room!" But the parents refuse to believe that the trappings of a lifetime could have so little value.

We put the footlocker on a scatter rug and slid it—a trick I'd learned my first day of employment. Martine backed down the stairs ahead of me. Mrs. Cartwright stayed planted in the foyer, tugging fretfully at her fingers as if she were pulling off gloves.

When we got back to the guest room, Martine grabbed a broom while I consulted Mrs. Cartwright's list. " 'Move nightstand in from room across hall,' " I read aloud.

"I already did that."

I stepped aside to let Martine sweep where I'd been standing. She was raising a little dust cloud—too enthusiastic with her broom. Wiry tendons flickered beneath the skin of her forearms. Really her skin was more olive-colored than yellow; or maybe that was a trick of the light. I glanced back down at Mrs. Cartwright's list. "Did you turn the mattress too?" I asked.

"Not yet," she said, "because I wasn't sure what that meant. Turn it? Turn it how?"

"Flip it to its other side," I told her. "Haven't you ever done that? It's usually part of spring cleaning."

"It isn't part of *my* spring cleaning. I've never turned a mattress in my life. Do you turn yours?"

"No, but I've done it lots of times for clients," I said.

Then—I don't know why—I started feeling embarrassed. It was something about the word "mattress." I almost wondered, for a second, if that was one of those words you shouldn't say in mixed company. (These notions hit me every so often.) I hurried on. I said, "Especially back when Mrs. Beeton was alive.

About once a month, I swear, her kids would be phoning up:
'Help! Get on over to Mama's! Mama's talking again about
turning her . . .' "

Maybe I should call it a pallet. Was that too much of a
euphemism? Fortunately, Martine didn't seem to be listening.
She had propped her broom in a corner, and she was moving
toward the other side of the bed. "In fact," I told her, "that
happens to be how Rent-a-Back began. I bet you didn't know
that. Mrs. Dibble's mother was turning hers one day, and it got
away from her. When Mrs. Dibble came to check on her that
evening, she found her flat as a pancake underneath it."

Martine's eyes widened. "Dead?" she asked.

"No, no; just mad. Mrs. Dibble said, 'You should have
hired a man to do that,' and her mother said, 'I can't hire a man
just to turn one . . . mattress!' and Mrs. Dibble said, 'Well, I fail
to see why not.' And she went home and dreamed up Rent-a-
Back."

"Grab an edge, will you?" Martine asked me.

I did, finally. I heaved my side of the mattress upward and
came over to the other side to help Martine support it. We
were standing so close that I could hear the clink of one overall
clasp when she drew in her breath. I could feel that concentrated, fierce heat she always gave off; I could smell her smell
of clean sweat.

She said, "How do you get your mouth to curl up at the
corners that way?"

"Practice," I said. And then, "Whoa! Look at the time."
(Although there wasn't a clock to be seen.) "I promised to meet
Sophia for lunch," I said. "We'd better hustle."

Martine let her end of the mattress drop. For a moment I
had all the weight of it before I let mine drop too.

. . .

In the truck, she started a fight. It wasn't me who started it. She claimed that I had promised to drive her to her brother's. Her brother's wife had had a new baby. But I had promised no such thing; this was the first I'd heard of it. "How could she have a new baby?" I asked. "I seem to recollect she was pregnant just a while ago."

"She *was* pregnant just a while ago. And now she's had her baby."

"See?" I said. "This is why I should have got a car of my own. Something used, I could have bought, with the rest of my Sting Ray money. Instead I'm having to split this dratted truck."

"My heart bleeds for you," Martine said.

"Besides, a truck's a problem for old folks to climb into. It's not appropriate! That high-up seat, and Everett's silly fur dice—"

All at once, Martine reached over and swiped the dice off the mirror in one quick motion. Just snapped the string that held them, tossed the dice in the air, caught the two of them one-handed, and stuffed them into her jacket pocket.

"Satisfied?" she asked me.

"Well, hey," I said.

"You think it's easy for me, letting you keep the truck at your place? Begging you for a ride anytime I need to go somewhere? But *I* don't have any choice! I don't come from a fat-cat family! I can't just waltz out and buy myself a car if I decide a truck's not 'appropriate'!"

"You don't need to bite my head off," I said.

We had reached her house by now, and I pulled over to the curb. But Martine stayed where she was, poking her sharp yellow face into mine. "I don't know why I bother hanging out with you," she said. "You're sarcastic and moody and negative. You think just because you're good-looking you can take up with any woman you want. You think you're so understanding and sweet with those poor old-lady clients, but really you just . . . hit and run! You have no staying power! You couldn't stick around even if you tried!"

I was astounded. I said, "Huh?" I said, "Where did all *this* come from?" And when she didn't answer, I said, "You're the one who fixed it so you'd have to rely on me for your rides."

"Now, that is just exactly what I'm talking about," she said. Making no sense whatsoever.

Then she jumped out of the truck and slammed the door hard behind her.

I took off, with a screech of my tires. I went on fuming aloud as if she were still there. "Maniac," I said. "Lunatic." I asked, "Didn't I say all along this truck scheme would be a pain?"

Anyone who heard me would have thought I was demented.

13

"WE ARE PROBABLY the only family in America eating a potluck Thanksgiving dinner," my mother said, gazing around the table.

"Oh, surely that can't be true," Gram said. "Good heavens! Many's the time, in the old days, I was asked to bring my marshmallow-yam casserole when Aunt Mary had the dinner at her house."

"That's one kind of potluck, Mother. The organized kind, where the hostess assigns a dish to each guest. But I'm talking about the other kind: catch as catch can. Pot *luck*, with the emphasis on 'luck.' Who else would be doing this?"

Mom's own dish was a redundancy; that's why she was annoyed. She had made one of her famous pumpkin chiffon pies, which turned out to be what Wicky had made too. (Using Mom's recipe. I could see how that might have been a faux pas.) Also, there was no turkey. At Jeff's insistence, he and

Wicky were hosting the dinner this year, and so everybody assumed that they would supply the turkey. But they hadn't. Wicky said her oven was too small for a turkey that would feed ten people. It seemed all her efforts had gone instead into the decorations: twists of crepe paper in harvest gold and orange festooning the dining room, and an entire family of Pilgrims marching the length of the table, with lighted candlewicks sticking up out of their heads. Plus, at the start of the meal she had made us all join hands and sing "Come Ye Thankful People, Come." Except that she and Sophia were the only ones who knew the words beyond the very first line.

Our menu was: two pumpkin chiffon pies, Gram's marshmallow-yam casserole, Sophia's Crock-Pot Applesauce Cake, and a salad that Opal had tossed with a vinaigrette dressing. This was nice for Opal, because we were all so glad to see something nonsweet that her contribution was the hit of the day.

Me, I'd chosen the easy way out and brought four bottles of wine. I guess I could have complained myself, since I had specifically purchased a wine designed to complement turkey. But hey. This way, I figured, I would probably get to carry a couple of bottles home with me.

"I did inquire," my mother was saying. "I asked Wicky at least two weeks ago: 'Wicky, what *category* of food should I bring?' But, 'Oh, whatever you want,' she said. 'I'm sure it will all work out.' " Mom trilled her fingers in a breezy manner, apparently mimicking Wicky. " 'We'll each of us just *do our own thing*,' was what she told me. 'That will be much more fun, don't you feel?' "

I'd have taken umbrage, if I were Wicky, but Wicky smiled obliviously and handed J.P. a carrot disk from the salad.

"Oh, well," my grandpa said. "The important thing is,

we're together. That's what Thanksgiving is all about! Everyone gathered together. Wouldn't you agree, Jeffrey?"

My father said, "Eh? Ah. Yes, indeed," and poured himself more wine. He tended to remove himself when Pop-Pop started one of his homilies.

"And we've all got our health, knock on wood. Mother's blood pressure's under control; my eyesight's no worse for the moment. Opal is with us this year, and she's turned into a young lady! J.P.'s been upped to a booster seat. . . ."

Evidently Pop-Pop was proceeding in order around the table. Some Thanksgivings he went by age, but today he began with Gram, at his left (wearing her sequined turkey T-shirt), and then himself, and then Opal and J.P. on his right—J.P. in a miniature business suit, already smeared with pumpkin.

Next came my brother, at the head of the table. "Jeff is on the road to being a stock-market millionaire," Pop-Pop said, and Jeff leaned back with a genial laugh and laced his hands across the front of his suit. The successful patriarch; that must be the image he was aiming for. I don't know why I hadn't understood that till now. The only patriarch in Jeff's acquaintance had been our Grandfather Gaitlin, a big-bellied man who'd loved a good cigar, which would explain why Jeff was nursing an imaginary paunch and letting his laugh trail off in an emphysemic wheeze. "Well, not exactly a *millionaire*," he was saying through a smoker's cough. No wonder he was so keen on hosting all family gatherings!

Pop-Pop moved on to Mom. "Margot here's the new chairwoman of the Harbor Arts Club," he said, while Mom gave a Queen Elizabeth smile, first to her left and then to her right. "And Jeffrey, of course, continues to set an example for all of us with his philanthropic activities. . . ." My father winced, bowed, and took another sip of wine.

I never could tell who, exactly, Pop-Pop was conveying his information *to*. We ourselves already knew it. God, maybe? I glanced up at the ceiling.

"Sophia, Miss Sophia, is sharing our Thanksgiving for the very first time," Pop-Pop said, "but we're hoping it won't be the last, by a long shot." Sophia flushed and directed a smile toward her bosom. She was wearing her hair drawn up high on her head today, which made her look formal and elegant.

"We credit Sophia with helping a certain young man begin to settle down," Pop-Pop said. "Speaking of who . . ." And then it was my turn.

"Didn't I always tell everyone Barnaby would be fine? He's a good, good boy," Pop-Pop said, leaning across the table to gaze earnestly into my face. "In fact, I think some might say he's found his angel. Hah? Hah?" And he sat back and looked around at the others. "Wouldn't you agree?"

But no one would take him up on that (a Kazmerow had no business tossing around the subject of the Gaitlins' angels), and so he proceeded to Wicky. "And last but not least, our charming hostess. *Nazdrowie*, Wicky!"

"To Wicky," we chimed in, raising our glasses. (All except for J.P., who was busy with a marshmallow.) Even Opal shyly held up her Pepsi can. Wicky said, "Oh, go on. I didn't do anything much!"

I saw Dad give Mom a look from under his eyebrows, warning her not to second that.

If a meal is mainly dessert, it's hard to know when it's over. Wicky got up to clear, finally, but she refused all offers of help, and so the rest of us went on sitting around the table. I saw my reserve bottles of wine rapidly disappearing. In fact, I suspected Jeff was getting tipsy. "Pass that bottle on *down*!" he said at one point, in his new, fat-man voice. "Who's hogging the bottle?" And when it turned out to be finished, he sent me for some of his own private stock from the basement. Or the "cellar," was what he called it. "Fetch me a cabernet from the cellar, will you, Barn? There's a good fellow." His accent was becoming just the teeniest bit British.

I rose obediently—I was feeling very sober and responsible, maybe on account of Pop-Pop's speech—and went through the kitchen and down the stairs to the basement. A fully stocked wooden wine rack sat next to the washing machine. I picked out the most expensive-looking cabernet I could find and climbed the stairs with it.

In the kitchen, Wicky was scraping plates. Her dress was a beige knit, cut narrow as a tube, and she was standing in a way that made her rear end look like two small, tight grapefruits nudging against the fabric. They just called out to be cupped by two hands. They *ordered* it. I got one of my irresistible urges, and I set the wine bottle on the counter and took a step closer.

My mother said, "Barnaby."

My heart stopped.

I whirled around and said, *"What?* I was just getting wine! Jeff asked me to bring up some wine."

"Yes, but I don't think we need it, do you? We've all had more than enough," Mom said.

"Oh," Wicky said, turning. "Should I be making coffee?"

"Let me do it," Mom told her. "You go out and sit awhile."

"Why, thank you. That's so nice of you!" Wicky said.

Of course, she had no idea that Mom claimed the coffee tasted more like tea when Wicky made it.

I grabbed the wine bottle and started to follow Wicky into

the dining room, but Mom laid a hand on my arm "Barnaby," she said again.

"Yes, ma'am," I said. I still wasn't sure if she'd guessed what I'd had in mind for Wicky's two grapefruits.

"I want you to take this back," Mom said, and from somewhere in her clothing she brought out a folded powder-blue check.

I said, "Huh?"

"It's your money."

"What money?"

She pressed it into my hand. I think it was because it was in the form of a check that I was so slow on the uptake. First I set the wine bottle down on the counter; then I unfolded the check and peered at it for a moment. *Pay to the order of Barnaby Gaitlin, Eight thousand seven hundred and no/100 dollars.*

"Why?" I asked her.

"I've decided not to keep it."

This didn't thrill me as much as you might expect. I went on studying the check, hoping it would tell me something further. The space after *For* had been left blank. If only she had filled it in! I raised my eyes, finally.

"Why?" I asked her again.

"Oh . . . ," she said, and she turned away and reached for the percolator. "It just seemed the right course of action," she tossed over her shoulder.

"But you've always said I should pay it back."

"Oh . . ."

"You said *that* was the right course of action."

She noisily ran water into the percolator.

"You just want me to stay fixed in my accustomed role," I said. "You would feel more comfortable if I went on being indebted."

"Don't be absurd," she told me, shutting off the water.

"Now that I've repaid you, you've got nothing to hold over me."

"That's absurd. You can never repay me."

"Pardon?"

She wouldn't answer. She made a big show of measuring out the coffee.

"I just *did* repay you," I said.

She kept her lips clamped shut.

"Eighty-seven hundred dollars," I reminded her. "Every cent. In cold cash."

She wheeled on me. She said, "Do you honestly believe *money* will make up for what I went through? Visiting all our high-class neighbors, throwing myself on their mercy, pleading with them not to press charges?"

"I never asked you to do that," I said.

" 'Well, Mrs. Gaitlin, we'll need to think this over,' " she said, putting on a pinched and simpering tone of voice. " 'We'll need to give it some thought,' they told me. That insufferable Jim McLeod: 'I doubt if you fully comprehend, Mrs. Gaitlin, what a rare and valuable object that ivory happened to be.' They loved to see me beg! Upstart Margot Gaitlin. It goes to show, they were thinking: you can take the girl out of Canton, but you can't take Canton out of the . . . 'Just look at her son, if you need proof,' they said. Oh, always you were *my* son. I suppose I felt that way myself. Jeff was more related to Dad, but you were related to me. You I had to personally apologize for. You think you can repay me for that? You can never repay me. Not with eight thousand, not with eight hundred thousand! Take your money back."

"Don't you wish," I told her, and I ripped the check in two. Then I made confetti of it, ripping it again and again and letting the little pieces flutter to the floor. My mother just stared—her mouth open, a spoonful of ground coffee suspended between us.

I had imagined that we'd been shouting, but when I stormed into the dining room I realized none of the others had heard us. They were still lounging around the table, and all Jeff said when he saw me was, "Where's the wine, bro?"

"Oops," I said, and I made a U-turn into the kitchen and retrieved the bottle. It was no affair of mine how much he drank.

The Pilgrim candles were headless now, their shoulders curly-edged bowls of wax. They looked like torture victims. Wicky rose and blew them out, saying, "Let's adjourn to the living room, shall we?" By the time Mom brought in the coffee tray, I was on the couch, playing a game of cribbage with Opal. I waved the tray off without looking up, and no one thought anything of it.

Opal had learned cribbage just the day before, her first evening at my parents', but already she was good at it. I felt kind of proud of her. "Fifteen-two, a run of three for five, and his nobs for six," she said smartly. *I* never remembered to call the jack "his nobs." I said, "Way to go, Ope," and she sat back and grinned at me. With her legs tucked under her, you could see that the knees of her black tights were about to develop holes. I found that encouraging, somehow.

I had this sudden, startling thought: Would Opal get a visit from *her* angel, somewhere on down the line?

She was a Gaitlin, after all. Strange to realize that. She did have my last name and at least a few of my genes, even if they weren't obvious.

Wicky was rocking J.P. to sleep, humming something tuneless. Jeff was poking the fire. (Another patriarchal activity, I guessed.) Sophia sat next to Gram on the love seat, and Dad occupied the one remaining chair. So when Pop-Pop returned from a trip to the john, he had to nudge me down the couch a ways. "Ah, me," he said, sinking heavily into the cushions. "How's the car, Barnaby?"

"Um . . ."

As luck would have it, my mother approached him just then with the tray. "Coffee, Daddy? It's decaf."

"Now, what the hell do I want decaf for? What's the point of coffee if it don't have any kick to it?"

"Think how much better you'll sleep, though, Daddy."

"Ha," he said, but he helped himself to a cup and stirred in several spoonsful of sugar, while she waited.

"Jeffrey?" my mother said next, heading toward Dad.

"Yes, thanks. I will have some."

She bent to rest her tray on the lamp table beside him. "Barnaby won't let me give him back his money," she told him.

"Eh?" my father said.

"His eighty-seven hundred. He won't take it."

I felt Sophia glance over at me, but the others paid no attention. "Fifteen-two, fifteen-four, and a double run for twelve," Opal announced, while Jeff set aside his poker and took another swig of wine.

"I tried to give it back to him," my mother said, "but he tore up the check."

"We'll discuss this some other time, shall we?" my father said pleasantly.

"I want to get this settled, though."

"Another time, I told you."

"What other time? We hardly ever lay eyes on him!"

"Margot," my father said. "Do you suppose we could make it through one holiday without your tiresome fishwife act?"

Wicky stopped humming. There was a pause, and then my mother lifted her tray and proceeded back to the kitchen at a dignified pace. A second later, we heard the tray slamming onto a counter. A faucet started running. Dishes started clattering. Wicky looked over at Jeff, but he minutely shook his head, and so she stayed seated.

Gram cleared her throat. "Sophia, dear!" she said. "Tell us! What does *your* family do for Thanksgiving?"

Well, at least they didn't publicly demolish each other, Sophia could have said; but she told Gram, "Oh, nothing very exciting, I'm afraid. Usually, Mother's two cousins come for dinner, along with one cousin's husband. And then this year she's invited my Aunt Grace from Baltimore too."

"She's invited your Aunt Grace?" I asked.

But I don't think Sophia heard, because Gram was saying, "Isn't that lovely! And will they be serving a turkey?"

"Oh, yes. In fact, it's kind of like you-all's arrangement—a potluck—although Mother does assign specific dishes. For instance, Aunt Grace is bringing her chestnut dressing. She fixed it ahead of time, except for the baking, and I helped her onto the train with it, but Lord knows how she'll manage at the other end of the trip."

"You helped her onto the train?" I asked.

All this was news to me, I can tell you.

Sophia sent me an absentminded smile. "The cousins are in charge of the vegetables," she said, "and Cousin Dotty's husband makes the pies. He's an excellent cook, although in all other respects he's considered something of a—"

There was a crash in the kitchen, followed by the tinkling of glass. Sophia stopped short. The rest of us exchanged glances.

Gram said, "Yes, dear? Something of a . . . ?"

"Oh! Something of a . . . ne'er-do-well, I suppose. But—"

A metal object clanged so loudly that it gave off an echo, like a gong.

"Maybe I should go out there," Wicky said.

"Stay where you are, why don't you," my father told her blandly.

She sat back, drawing J.P.'s deadweight body closer against her.

Sophia looked from one of us to the other.

"Ne'er-do-well!" I said.

Sophia said, "What?"

"I haven't heard that term in ages!"

"You haven't heard . . . 'ne'er-do-well'?"

"It's almost Old English, don't you think?" I asked the room at large. I had to raise my voice to be heard above the racket from the kitchen. "It's almost something Robin Hood might have said! In fact, a lot of those bad-guy words are like that: so quaint and antiquey. 'Ruffian.' 'Knave.' 'Wastrel.' 'Scoundrel.' Ever noticed?"

No one had, apparently.

" 'Layabout.' 'Rapscallion,' " I said. " 'Scofflaw.' 'Scum of the earth.' "

" 'Beast of burden,' " Opal offered unexpectedly.

"Well, that's a *little* off the subject . . . or maybe not, come to think of it. And 'ill-gotten gains.' 'Misspent youth.' Or, let's see . . ."

" 'Besetting sins,' " my father said from his armchair.

"Right! Besetting sins. But it's not the same for good-guy words, at least not as far as I've—"

The telephone rang. We were all so relieved that every last one of us stirred as if to go answer it, but Mom picked it up in the kitchen. We could hear her intonation, if not her exact words. "Mm? Mm? Hmm-hmm-hmm."

Then she appeared in the doorway. "Barnaby," she said—

her voice noncommittal, her face composed, not a hair out of place—"that was that Martine person, and she says to tell you she has the truck but she'll bring it by in the morning."

"Thanks," I said.

Pop-Pop asked, "What truck is that?"

I said, "Oh, just the, you know, work truck."

"Fool kid sold off the Sting Ray," my father told my grandpa.

"He did what?"

"Sold off the Corvette Sting Ray and bought a used Ford pickup."

Pop-Pop leaned forward on the couch to peer at me. I could feel his stare, even though I had my back to him. I turned and told him, "I was planning to mention that."

"You sold the Sting Ray?"

He was so amazed, the whites of his eyes showed all around the irises.

"Well, yes, I did," I said.

"*Why?*"

I said, "I needed the money."

"The money, son: you could have borrowed money from me! I'd have been glad to lend you money!"

"Well, see . . . the whole point was, not to be in debt anymore. Not to owe anybody."

Pop-Pop's jaw went slack.

"But, Barnaby," he said finally. "That was the only year the Corvette had a split rear window."

"Oh, *damn* that split rear window!" I said. Then I said, "Sorry." I looked around at the others. They all wore the same accusing expression—even Opal. (Or maybe I was imagining things.) "I mean," I said, "I do know what a big deal it was, Pop-Pop—

"Shoot," Jeff said suddenly. "It broke my heart when Pop-Pop gave the Corvette to you."

"It did?" I asked.

"I would have killed for that car!"

"You would?"

I sat there a minute absorbing this, chewing the inside of my cheek. Dad, meanwhile, took over the conversation. "Of course, when I was Barnaby's age," he said, "I went out and *worked* if I needed money, but nowadays, it seems—"

"With all due respect, Dad," I told him, "you were never my age."

"Excuse me?"

"Times are different, Dad, okay? What I've experienced, you haven't. And vice versa, no doubt. So you can't compare us, is what I'm saying." I turned back to my grandpa. "I'm sorry, Pop-Pop," I told him. "Giving me that car was the best thing anyone's ever done for me, and don't think I don't know that. But I'm trying really hard to grow up now, don't you see? And I had to sell the car to get there. I hope you understand."

I could hear the rustle of Mom's apron as she wrapped her hands in it. Then Pop-Pop said, "Why, sure, son. It was yours to do what you liked with."

After that we had a fairly normal evening, but that was just because all of us were exhausted.

Sophia and I had driven over in the Saab, and we'd both assumed that I would go back to her house for the night, since the roommate was out of town. But on Jeff's front walk I said, "Why don't *you* drive, and that way you can drop me off at my place." Then I felt the need to invent too many excuses. "I have to get to work so early tomorrow, and Martine won't know where to pick me up, and besides, Opal mentioned something about breakfast. . . ."

Sophia just said, "All right," and we set off toward her car. I got the impression she was glad, even. Probably she could use a night alone herself.

Earlier it had been raining, and now the air had a damp, chilly feel. The car windows misted over before we'd gone a block. I grew extremely conscious of how closed in we were. Our breaths were too loud, and the tinny sound of Sophia's cake platter, sliding across the back seat at each turn, made our silence more noticeable.

Finally she said, "You didn't tell me your mother offered to give you back that money."

"How could I? It just now happened," I said.

"I don't see why you refused it."

I stared at her. I said, "What: you too?"

"It's eighty-seven hundred dollars, after all. Think what we could do with that."

"Well, lots. Obviously. But that's beside the point. I didn't want to worry about that money anymore."

"So you'd rather *I* worry about money."

"You? How do you figure that?"

"Well, I'm the one who couldn't buy a new outfit for Thanksgiving because my money's in the flour bin."

"So? Get it *out* of the flour bin. You said yourself you've been in touch with your aunt again."

"Oh, I knew you'd hold that against me!" she cried, swinging the car onto Northern Parkway.

I said, "Huh? Hold what against you?"

"She's my aunt, Barnaby. I don't have so many relatives that I can afford to discard a perfectly good aunt."

"Well, sure. I realize that," I told her.

"And it made me feel just awful, being on the outs with her.

So I called her on the phone one day last week. I meant to tell you about it; honestly I did, but somehow it slipped my mind. I asked her how she was, and she said she had a cold. Well, what could I do? Hang up on a sick old woman? I went by to see her at lunch hour. I brought her some soup and some nose drops. I couldn't just let her fend for herself!"

"Of course you couldn't," I said.

Did she think I didn't know how these family messes operated? The most unforgivable things got . . . oh, not forgiven. Never forgiven. But swept beneath the rug, at least; brushed temporarily to one side; buried in a shallow grave. I knew all about it.

I rolled down my window a quarter of an inch, thinking it might help defog the windshield. I said, "But you still haven't gotten your money out of the flour bin."

"No."

The whistling sound from my window helped to fill the silence.

"Why not?" I asked her finally.

"Hmm?" she said. She leaned forward to swab the windshield with her palm—a mistake, but I didn't point that out.

"Why *haven't* you gotten your money?"

"Oh, it's . . . never been the right time," she said.

"Now would be a good time," I told her. "While your aunt's in Philadelphia."

"Barnaby! I can't just sneak in like a thief!"

She kept her eyes on the road while she said that. It made her indignation sound fake. All at once I found her irritating beyond endurance. I noticed how the streetlights lit the fuzz along her jawline—fur, it almost was—and how large and square and bossy her hands looked on the steering wheel. Managerial: that was the word. Wasn't that why her other romances had ended, if you read between the lines? "I'm probably too . . . definite," I seemed to remember her saying. "Too definite for men to feel comfortable with." Darn right she was too definite!

And then that lingering, doting voice she used when she spoke of herself as a child—"When I was a little girl . . ."—as if she had been more special than other little girls. And her eternal Crock-Pot dinners; oh, Lord. If I had to eat one more stewy-tasting, mixed-and-mingled, gray-colored one-dish meal, I'd croak!

And her predictability: her Sunday-night shampoos and panty-hose washing, her total lack of adventurousness. (Wasn't it a flaw, rather than a virtue, that she'd been so incurious when the passport man gave her that envelope?) Her even temper, her boring steadfastness, her self-congratulatory loyalty when she assumed I had stolen from her aunt. Here I'd been hoping she would bring me up to her level, infuse me with her goodness! Instead she had fallen all over herself rushing to protect my badness.

I said, "Sophia. Let's go get that money."

"Absolutely not," she said, and she was so prompt about it, she practically overlapped my words.

"*Why* not? If it belongs to you, why can't you?"

She said, "Don't badger me, please. It's really none of your concern what I do with my own private funds."

"In fact, it is, though," I said. "In fact, every time I turn around, you're telling me how hard your life is now that you've lost your money. You're going on and on about all the things you can't afford because your money's in the flour bin, and you know what I think, Sophia? I think you *like* to have it in the flour bin. I think you feel that as long as it's in the flour bin, I owe you something. I'm starting to suspect you have no intention of getting it back. You prefer it that I'm beholden to you for your sacrifice."

"Well, that's just simply not true," Sophia told me.

You would think she'd have raised her voice, at least, but she didn't. Her tone was low and reasonable, and she went on staring straight ahead, and she remembered to signal before she pulled into my driveway. Even that I found irritating. She was just as angry as I was; I knew it for a fact, but she'd already lost two boyfriends, and she'd promised herself she would hang on to this one no matter what a . . . ne'er-do-well he might turn out to be. Oh, I could read her like a book!

I remembered what I'd told Mrs. Alford when I was describing Great-Grandpa's visit from his angel. Angels leave a better impression, I'd said, if they don't hang around too long. Or something to that effect. If they don't hang around making chitchat and letting you get to know them.

Here is how my Pop-Pop happened to give me the Sting Ray:

I was just about to graduate from the Renascence School, and I'd been accepted at Towson State, and Dad had promised to find a summer job for me. So far he hadn't succeeded, but that's a whole other story. The point is, I was doing okay for once. My life was looking up. There was a lot of talk about clean slates and new beginnings, et cetera, et cetera.

Then, at Easter, I came home for the long weekend and got into a little trouble. Well, I'll just go ahead and say it: I locked my parents out of the house and set fire to the dining room.

I can't explain exactly how it started. How do these things *ever* start? It was your average Saturday-night supper; nothing special. My brother had brought a girlfriend. He was living on his own by then, in an apartment down on Chase Street, and he wanted us to meet this Joanna, or Joanne, or whatever her name was. But that was not the problem. The girl was innocuous enough. And my parents were putting on their happy-

couple act, telling how they themselves had met and so on—
my father describing Mom as lively and vivacious and
"spunky" (his favorite word for her); my mother turning her
eyes up to him in this adoring, First Lady manner. No problem
there, either. I'd seen them do that plenty of times. Oh, I've
never claimed my parents were to blame for my mistakes. My
mother might lay it on a little thick—working so hard at her
Guilford Matron act, wearing her carefully casual outfits and
frantically dragging the furniture around before all major parties—but I realize there are far worse crimes. So, I don't know.
I was just in a mood, I guess. All through supper I kept fighting
off my old fear that I might burst out with some scandalous
remark. It was more pronounced than usual, even. (Do you
think I might have Tourette's syndrome—a mild, borderline
version? I've often wondered.) But I made it through the
evening. Bade Jeff and What's-her-name a civil goodbye in the
front hall, watched Mom and Dad walk them to the street.

Then I locked every single door behind them and stood
inside with my arms folded, listening to my parents knock and
ring and shout. ("Barnaby? Barn? You've had your little joke
now. Let us in now, please.") I didn't say a word. When my
father stepped off the front stoop, finally, and picked his way
through the azaleas to peer in the dining-room window, I
snatched up the silver box of matches my mother lit her candles with and I struck a match without a thought and set fire to
the curtains. They were some kind of gauzy material, and they
burned lickety-split. My father said, "Call the fire department!" (He was speaking to me, I had to surmise, since who
else was near a phone?) But my mother said, "No! Think of the
neighbors!" and that's when I picked up a dining-room chair
and sent it through the window. It felt spectacular. I can still
remember the satisfaction. It made such a clean, explosive

crash. Although it also provided Dad with an entryway into the house.

I didn't try to stop him. I just sort of wandered off to my room, noticing the whole while that I seemed to be behaving like a crazy man. I climbed the stairs with my hands hanging loose at my sides and my expression spacey and vacant, and I watched myself doing it or even overdoing it, the same way years ago I'd overdone my limp when I sprained my ankle once, putting everything I had into the role of a cripple.

Well, you can imagine the brouhaha. Long-distance calls to Renascence, reaming them out for sending home a dangerous individual. Telephone consultations with the headmaster and my adviser. But not my psychologist, oddly enough. I did have one, of a fair-to-middling sort; but the focus here seemed to be my criminal intent rather than my mental state. There was talk, even, of bringing in the police, although that was probably just for effect. My father went so far as to mention jail. "I saved you from jail once before, but I'm not doing it again," he said. I just kept my same vacant expression. I felt mildly interested, as if it didn't involve me. I remember reflecting on the bizarreness of jail as a punishment—like sending someone to his room, really. Just put him away! What a concept. But did it ever occur to people that getting put away could come as a relief, on occasion?

Anyhow: the next day was Easter. So we all assembled for Easter dinner—me and my folks; Jeff minus the girlfriend (I believe she'd been hastily disinvited, due to recent developments); my Grandmother Gaitlin, who was still alive at the time; and Gram and Pop-Pop Kazmerow. Of course The Event had been thoroughly discussed behind my back, and I could tell it was the only thing on anyone's mind. Much shaking of heads, much whispering in the front hall. Sidelong glances at the cardboard-covered window and the charred and blistered frame. Surreptitious sniffs of the tarry-smelling air.

Except for Pop-Pop.

He just walked straight up to me. I was standing alone in front of the unlit fireplace in the living room, feeling like a Martian, and Pop-Pop walked straight up and said, "Happy Easter, Barnaby."

"Well. Same," I said.

"It's wonderful to see you."

"It's good to see you too, Pop-Pop."

Then he reached out and put something in my hand. The Chevrolet key ring.

I said, "What's this for?"

He said, "You know about my eyesight. I shouldn't have kept on driving even as long as I have."

"But what's—?"

"I want you to have my car," he said. "She's still got a lot of miles left in her! And she's quite a machine, Barnaby. Only Corvette ever made with a split rear window."

"You're giving me the Corvette?" I asked him.

He nodded.

"You're giving it, as in *giving* it?"

"I can't think of anyone better, son," he said.

I have no idea what Jeff's face looked like at that moment. Did he, in fact, envy me? I never even glanced at him. I was staring down at the checkered flags and blinking back the tears.

14

THIS YEAR, Mrs. Alford was planning ahead for Christmas, she told us; not waiting till the last minute to get that tree of hers trimmed. So Martine dropped me off one morning in mid-December—a cold day, but sunny enough to start melting the film of snow that had fallen overnight. I climbed the front steps and pressed the buzzer before I wiped my feet, since Mrs. Alford always took some time answering. But it was her brother who opened the door. I recognized the two clouds of white hair puffing above his ears. Had I ever known his name? I'd only met him the once.

He knew mine, though. "Why," he said. "It's Barnaby. Oh, Barnaby. How very, very kind of you to call." And he held out his hand.

I hadn't been prepared to shake hands, but I did, and then I scraped my feet on the mat a few more times to show that I was ready to head on in and get to work. But it seemed he wanted the two of us to stand talking a while longer. "I can't tell you how much this means," he said. "My sister would have been extremely touched that you stopped by."

Would have been?

Oh-oh.

"But come in! Come in! What am I thinking? Please," he said. "May I take your jacket?"

"Well . . . ah, no, thanks. I'll keep it," I said.

But I did come in. I couldn't see any way out of it, really.

"Valerie will want to meet you," the brother said, leading me through the foyer. I guessed Valerie was Mrs. Alford's daughter. We passed the dining room, where a bearded man in a bathrobe sat reading a newspaper. Next to him, a baby was pounding her high-chair tray, but the bearded man paid no attention, and when he caught sight of me he just nodded and turned a page. "Richard," the brother told me. "Valerie's husband. They left the older kids at home for now; it was such short notice. And school is still in session, of course."

"Oh, yes," I said. We were climbing the stairs to the second floor. I hoped Valerie wasn't in *her* bathrobe. I said, "It's kind of early yet. Maybe I should—"

"Nonsense. We've been up for hours," the brother said. "None of us slept very well, as you might imagine." We reached the upstairs hall, and he called, "Valerie? Val! Look who's here."

In Mrs. Alford's bedroom, a woman in baggy slacks was kneeling beside a cedar chest. She didn't resemble Mrs. Alford. She was big-boned and gawky, with tortoiseshell glasses and lank brown hair, and you could see she had been crying. She stared at me blankly, which was understandable since we had never met.

"It's Barnaby," the brother told her.

"Barnaby!" she said, and she got to her feet and came over

to hug me. She smelled of cedar. "Oh, Barnaby," she said, "what'll we do without her?" When she drew away, she swiped at her nose with the back of her hand. She seemed more like an overgrown girl than a wife and mother.

"I'm sorry about your loss," I said. "Mrs. Alford was a super-nice lady."

"She thought the world of you, Barnaby. Nearly every time I phoned her, she would mention something you'd done for her or some conversation you'd had."

"I didn't even know she was sick," I said.

"Well, she wasn't, so far as anyone could tell. It was a heart attack. But I think she had some inkling, maybe. I worried all this fall, because why else did she suddenly send me those things from the attic? And her quilt: just look. She seems to have finished her quilt in a rush, after months and months of claiming she would *never* get it finished."

The quilt was draped over the edge of the chest. Valerie bent to pick it up and unfold it—a dark-blue cotton rectangle with a gaudy, multicolored circle appliquéd to the center. "Planet Earth," she said, and the brother made a clucking sound.

I'd heard about that planet quilt often, but I'd never seen it. What I had pictured was a kind of fabric map—a plaid Canada, a gingham U.S. Instead the circle was made up of mismatched squares of cloth no bigger than postage stamps, joined by the uneven black stitches of a woman whose eyesight was failing. Planet Earth, in Mrs. Alford's version, was makeshift and haphazard, clumsily cobbled together, overlapping and crowded and likely to fall into pieces at any moment.

"Pretty," I said. Because it *was* sort of pretty, in an offbeat, unexpected way.

Valerie folded it up again and smoothed it gently before she laid it in the chest.

"We're having a very small service," she said. "I'm not sure exactly when. Then afterwards, I suppose we'll need your help getting the house in shape to sell it."

"I'll be glad to help," I told her. "Just call Rent-a-Back anytime you're ready for me."

When I left, Valerie hugged me again, and the brother shook hands again at the door. "Thank you for coming," he said.

I said, "Well, I'll miss her."

It was nothing but the truth.

Of course, I had no way to get home, since Martine had driven off to mail Ditty Nolan's Christmas parcels. So I sat on the curb out front and waited for her, hugging my knees and digging my chin into my folded arms. The curb was still damp from the melted snow, and I could feel a thin line of cold seeping through the seat of my jeans.

"Oh, my! All done?" Mrs. Alford used to say when I'd finished with a job. "Doesn't that look lovely!" Her chirpy, cheery, determined voice. "Weren't you quick about it!"

And then other clients' voices—some cheery and some not, some sad, some downright cranky.

"Pasta? What's this *pasta* business? In my day we called it spaghetti."

"You'll find out soon enough, young man, it is not especially unselfish to wish on your birthday candles that your children will be happy."

"Back in Baltimore's golden age, when the streetcars were still running and downtown was still the place to go and we had four top-notch department stores all on the same one block: Hutzler's, Hochschild's, Stewart's, and Hecht's . . ."

". . . and at noon or so the phone rings, and my niece says,

'I'm waiting for Dad but he hasn't come and he said he'd be here at ten.' I say, 'Oh, now, you know how he is.' About one o'clock, she calls again; two, she calls again. 'Where can he be?' she asks me. I say, 'He'll show up; don't you worry.' Though I'm fairly worried myself, to tell the truth. Along about three-thirty, I think, *Oh!* I think, *Oh, my stars above!* Because all at once it comes to me—I can't say what brought it to mind—it comes to me that her dad had phoned me at eight o'clock that morning. 'Sis,' he'd said, 'I've been trying to reach Sue but her line is busy and I want to hit the road so you call her later on, will you, please? And tell her I've decided not to stop at her place,' he said."

Martine tapped the truck horn. I almost jumped out of my skin.

"Don't *do* that, okay?" I said, as I opened the passenger door. "A simple 'Hey, you' will suffice."

"What's up?" she asked me. She had already cut the engine. "I thought we were trimming a tree."

"Mrs. Alford died," I said.

"No!"

I hadn't meant to be so blunt about it. I settled in my seat and shut my door. "She had a heart attack," I said.

"Well, damn," Martine said. Then she started the engine again. But she drove very slowly, as if in respect. "She was one of my favorite clients," she said when we reached Falls Road.

Mine too, I realized. I wouldn't have felt that way once upon a time. It used to be that Maud May was my favorite. Maud May was so let-it-all-hang-out. But I don't know; you start to appreciate the other type of person, by and by—those ultracivilized types who keep their good humor and gracious manners even though their joints are aching nonstop and they can't climb out of their baths without help and they're not always sure what day it is. I'd be terrible at that myself.

. . .

"What are you giving Sophia for Christmas?" my mother asked on the phone.

"Oh . . . ," I said, hedging.

"Because I don't want to interfere, but if you'd ever care for a piece of your grandmother Gaitlin's jewelry—such as, say, for example, maybe perhaps a ring, perhaps, or something of that sort—you have only to ask."

"Thanks," I said, "but we've agreed not to bother with presents this year."

"Why, for goodness' sake?"

Why was a question of money, but I didn't want to say so for fear Mom would segue into the eighty-seven hundred. Instead I told her, "Just lacking in Christmas spirit, I guess."

Mom sighed. "But you do plan to bring her to dinner," she said.

"She's going up to Philly that weekend."

"To Philly? Does that mean you're going too?"

"No, I thought I'd stick around and pester you and Dad," I said.

"Oh."

"I can see you're overjoyed at the prospect."

"Well, naturally we're delighted to have you! But I was thinking her people might like to get to know you a little better."

"Evidently not," I told her.

Sophia had, in fact, invited me, but I had made up this story about how I didn't want to disappoint my parents. "For someone so down on his family," she'd said, "you certainly seem to see an awful lot of them." I told her I felt obligated, because Jeff and Wicky would be visiting Wicky's folks for Christmas and Mom was all upset about it.

Which she was, no lie, but my presence at dinner was hardly going to change that. "Christmas will be so pathetic this year!" she was saying now. "Just you and Gram and Pop-Pop. I wonder if I should invite Dad's cousin Bertha."

"You detest Cousin Bertha," I reminded her.

She said, "It's such a pity Opal's not coming."

"We'll have our turn next Christmas."

"The two of you have been getting along so well together. . . . She should start spending her summers here, don't you think? Or winters, even. We could enroll her in one of the private schools. Then for college, of course, she would go to Goucher. She could room with us, if she likes, although I suppose she'd prefer the dormitory. But dorms are so noisy! Studying in a dorm is such a struggle!"

"Mom. She's barely ten years old," I said.

She sighed again. Then she asked, "Should I invite Len Parrish?"

"I wouldn't bother."

"I could tell him to park the Corvette around the corner, where your Pop-Pop won't have to look at it."

"It's not the Corvette," I said.

"What, then?"

Someday I should get credit for all the things I *don't* say. Like, "Your hero is a sleazeball, Mom." What I told her was, "He's got other plans, I'm sure. He's a very popular guy."

"Well," she said. "All right."

This was so untypical of her—I mean, the resigned and listless tone she used—that I caught myself feeling sorry for her. I remembered what she had said at Thanksgiving: how I was more her son than Dad's, more related to her. It seemed that now I was taking that in for the very first time. Poor Mom! It hadn't been much fun loving someone as thorny as me, I bet.

So when she told me she'd better hang up because she had a hair appointment, I said, "Mom. You know what I think? I really think your hair would look great if you stopped dyeing it."

It was meant to be a kindness, but it backfired. "*You* may not like it, but all my friends say it looks lovely!" she snapped. And then she told me goodbye and slammed the receiver down.

Well, no surprise there. Just because we were related didn't mean we were any good at understanding each other.

"In the afterlife," Maud May told me, "God's got a lot of explaining to do."

"What about?" I asked. I was unpacking groceries, and she was smoking a cigarette at her kitchen table.

"Oh," she said, "children suffering, cancer, tidal waves, tornadoes . . ."

"You think those need explaining? Tornadoes just happen, man. You think God sits around aiming tornadoes at people on purpose?"

". . . old ladies breaking their hips and becoming a burden . . ."

"The most He might explain is how to *deal* with a tornado," I said. "How to accept it or endure it or whatever; how to do things right. That's what I'm going to ask about when I get to heaven myself: how to do things right."

Then I said, "Anyhow. You're not an old lady."

"Good Gawd, Barnaby, you've gone and bought those goddamned generic tea bags again!"

I looked at the box I was holding. I said, "Rats. I thought they were Twinings."

"Interesting that you imagine you'll get *into* heaven," Maud May said wryly. She blew a cloud of smoke in my direction.

"And also, you're not a burden," I added.

She inspected the end of her cigarette and then turned to stub it out. "Though who knows?" she asked the ashtray. "Nowadays, they're probably letting all kinds of people in."

Christmas fell on a Monday this year; so Friday the twenty-second was full of those last-minute chores our clients wanted seen to when guests were about to descend. Folding cots brought down from attics, wreaths hung from high-up places, major supplies of liquor hauled in. Most of this I had to handle alone, because Martine was helping out at her brother's. The new baby was in the hospital with pneumonia. I hadn't even realized new babies could *get* pneumonia. So Martine spent the first part of Friday baby-sitting her nephews, and then at three I stopped by her brother's house to collect her for a job at Mr. Shank's. Mr. Shank had taken it into his head he needed his entire guest-room furnishings exchanged with the furnishings in the master bedroom, and he needed it now, and next week or next month wouldn't do.

Only, things at Martine's brother's house were never simple. First the sister-in-law was late getting back from the hospital, and then when she did get back she was weepy and distraught, and Martine didn't want to leave her that way. So I sat in the kitchen, which was a mess, racing wind-up cars with the nephews, while Martine gave her sister-in-law rapid little pats on the back and told her everything would be fine. No mother in the world, she said, would have guessed that a tiny sniffle could go to a baby's lungs that way. And of *course* he and Jeannette would still bond; wasn't she with him in the hospital most of every day and half the night? So Jeannette brightened up and insisted on serving us fruitcake before she would let us leave. I'm a sucker for fruitcake. I like the little green things, the citrons. Why don't we ever see citrons in the produce section? What *are* citrons, anyhow? I had two slices and had just cut myself a third, when Jeannette said, "Oh, great. Hand me the breast pump, will you, Barn? I'm leaking all over the last clean blouse I own." Which reminded me in a hurry that we really ought to be going.

Martine drove, so that I could finish my fruitcake. She was still at her brother's house, mentally. She nearly ran a stop sign telling me how Jeannette was going to land in the hospital herself if she wasn't careful. "That fruitcake's the only thing I've seen her eat in the last three days," she said, "and fruitcake's not exactly what you'd call the staff of life. I tried to get her to have some breakfast this morning before she left, but she said she couldn't. I told my brother, at least she ought to be drinking fluids. You need your fluids for the breast milk."

"Must you?" I asked her. "I'm trying to eat, here."

"What'd I say? Breast milk? Big deal."

"That whole business puts me off," I told her. "I don't see how women stand it. Leaky breasts, labor pains . . ."

"Well, aren't you sensitive," Martine said. She was drifting behind a slow-moving cement truck. In her place, I would have switched lanes. "Hey," she said. "I'll let you in on a secret. There's no such thing as labor pains."

"Say what?"

"It's all a bunch of propaganda that's been spread around by women. In fact, they don't feel so much as a twinge."

"They don't?" I asked.

"They have this hormone that's an anesthetic, see, that the body releases during labor. Kind of like natural Novocain."

I laughed. For a moment, she'd had me believing her.

She glanced over at me with a glint in her eye, but her face stayed all straight lines. "Don't tell anyone else," she said.

"Women have been keeping it from men for millions of years. They like for men to feel guilty."

"Ain't *that* the truth," I said. Maybe too emphatically, because she sent me another, keener glance.

We were traveling up North Charles Street now, past huge houses where electric candles lit the windows even in the day-time—pale, weak white prickles of light that struck me as depressing. I wrapped the rest of my fruitcake in my napkin. I said, "Like Sophia, for instance."

"Oh, well," Martine said. "Sophia."

She hadn't said a word against Sophia since she first found out we were dating, but I could guess what she thought of her. Or I imagined I could guess. What *did* she think of her? I studied Martine's profile. On her head was a boy's leather cap with big fleece earflaps that reminded me of mutton-chop whiskers. I said, "Like Sophia's flour-bin money, for instance."

"Flour bin?"

"The money she put in Mrs. Glynn's flour bin when I was accused of stealing."

Martine slowed for a traffic light. She said, "Sophia put money in Mrs. Glynn's flour bin."

"Right."

"Before she learned Mrs. Glynn had changed her hiding place."

"Right."

Martine was silent.

"Two thousand, nine hundred and sixty dollars," I said, as if prompting her.

Martine said, "What: is she out of her mind?"

I had this sudden feeling of relief. I almost said, "Ah," although I didn't.

"She thought you really did steal it!" she said. "She actually thought you stole it!"

"Looks that way," I agreed.

"And so then she goes and . . . Is she out of her *mind*?"

"And the thing of it is, it's still there," I said.

"What's still where?"

"The money is still in the flour bin."

"So?"

"It's, like, hanging over my head," I said. "She keeps reminding me of it. Every time she wants to buy something, it's, oh, no, she can't, because she gave up all her savings for my sake; everything she owns is sitting in the flour bin."

"Well, that's *her* problem," Martine said.

But I rode on over her words. It was all pouring out of me now. "Talk about guilt!" I said. "That money is just . . . weighing on me! But I know she could get it back if she really wanted. Anytime she visits her aunt, she has the run of the house after all. Or if she worries she'll get caught, she could go on Tuesday, her aunt's podiatrist day. Take her own key and go Tuesday, or some Friday afternoon when her aunt is having her hair done."

"What time does she have her hair done?"

"I don't know; maybe four or so, because she always used to be home again before I got there."

The light changed to green, and Martine took a violent left turn. I had to grab my door handle. I said, "Mr. Shank's house, Martine. Straight ahead."

"We're not going to Mr. Shank's," Martine told me.

"Where are we going?"

But I knew the answer to that, even before she took a right, and another left, and came to a jerky stop in front of the Rent-a-Back office.

"Back in a jiff," she said.

I sat quiet while she was gone. I looked out my side window, watched two squirrels chase each other across the remnants of snow, listened to the ticking of the engine as it cooled. Then Martine was hopping into the truck again. "Ready?" she asked, and she gave me a foxy, sharp-toothed grin and held up her left hand. Nestled in her palm was a house key, attached to one of Rent-a-Back's oval tags. #191, the tag read. I didn't have to be told that #191 was Grace Glynn.

When we pressed the doorbell, checking to make sure she wasn't home, I had this flash of déjà vu. In the old days, I used to check by phone. I'd phone my prospective victims and listen through a dozen rings or more. (Answering machines were not so common back then.) The feeling now was the same—that strung-up feeling where you're braced for them to be there, and then the surge of energy and purpose when you find out they're away. We lounged nonchalantly on Mrs. Glynn's front porch, in case anybody was watching, but the only sound was the dog barking. So finally Martine stepped forward and fitted the key in the lock.

It was clear from Tatters's frantic little frenzy that you could just ignore him, which we did. We walked straight through to the rear of the house while he scuttled around our ankles, making busybody sounds with his toenails.

The house had a bitter smell, as if Mrs. Glynn had recently burned some toast. On the drainboard next to the sink, a clean china cup and saucer sat upside down on a dish towel. Everything else was tidied away. I opened a cabinet: glassware. I closed it and opened another. Four white canisters in graduated sizes read TEA, COFFEE, SUGAR, FLOUR. I reached for the flour canister, and it rattled. Inside I found a pale-green mug and the handle that had broken off from it; nothing more. Martine let out a small breath next to my shoulder. Tatters sniffed my sneakers.

What if Sophia had made this whole thing up? What if she had merely *claimed* she'd stowed her money here, in order to seem noble? The thought made me instantly angry. Then I reminded myself that Sophia was not the type to lie. Even so, the anger hung on a moment, like the white spot that stays in your vision after you have looked at a too bright light.

"That's not a bin," Martine said. "It's a canister."

I said, "Okay, where's the bin, then?"

She opened a lower cabinet. Saucepans. The one next to it held cookie sheets, muffin tins, and pie plates. Not a bin in sight. I felt personally thwarted, as if Mrs. Glynn were taunting me. "I could kill that woman," I told Martine.

"Forget about it," Martine said, closing the second door. "She didn't mean any harm."

"No harm! I practically lost my job!"

"Oh, you did not," Martine said. She was checking the shelf under the sink, but that held only a trash bucket. She said, "You honestly believe Mrs. Dibble would fire you? She'd have to shut down the company. You saw how all our clients backed you up."

"Well," I said. "Yes."

I walked into the pantry. There was a bin at the head of the basement stairs—a tall metal cylinder—but that contained dry dog food. I said, "I wonder how they heard."

"Heard what?"

"That I *needed* backing up."

"Oh," Martine said. "I told them."

"You did?"

I turned to look at her. She was standing in the doorway between the pantry and the kitchen, her plaid woolen jacket buttoned wrong and the earflaps sticking up from her cap at two different angles.

I said, "Well. I guess I ought to thank you."

"What for?" she asked. "Jeepers! They're the ones you should thank. Getting on the phone like they did and volleying around."

Rallying around was what she meant, but I didn't correct her. I had this vision of a crowd of old folks on a volleyball court, keeping me up, up, up and not letting me fall, stepping forward one after the other to boost me over the net. When one of them had to leave, another would take that one's place. Even if the faces changed, the sea of upraised hands stayed constant.

So, no, I didn't correct her.

Then Martine came over to the white wooden cabinet behind me. She opened the upper door, exposing what looked to be a huge tin funnel with a crank handle. She reached into the funnel and brought out a plastic sandwich bag full of money.

I said, "Whoa!"

She handed the bag to me. It had a dusty feel from the traces of old flour clinging to it.

"How did you *do* that?" I asked her.

"This tin thing is a sifter," she explained.

"A what?"

She turned the crank, demonstrating. "You store your flour inside it," she said, "and when you go to bake something, you crank the sifter and the flour falls into this box-looking place underneath. My grandmother has almost the same kind of cabinet."

I peered into the plastic bag. I saw hundreds and a few twenties, fanning out slightly because no band or clip held them together.

Sometimes when you've been looking for an object and you find it, there's a fraction of a second where you feel a kind of . . . letdown, although that's too strong a word for it. It's like you miss the suspense of the hunt. Or something of the sort.

Then I heard the front door open.

Tatters went skittering out of the kitchen, yap-yap-yapping, and Mrs. Glynn said, "Sweetums! Did you miss me?"

Martine and I stared at each other.

"Was he a lonely boy. Was he a lonesome boy," Mrs. Glynn crooned, proceeding steadily closer. "Oh, oh, oh. I wonder what I—"

A purse or shopping bag was set down on a hard surface, but she continued moving toward us. "Maybe a cup of tea," she said. "Or hot water with some lemon; that might be more . . . My, those cabdrivers talk and talk, don't they? How he did go on! I've never understood what makes cabdrivers so . . . ."

She entered the kitchen. I seemed to have run out of oxygen.

Martine said, in a normal tone, "Do you think she left a list in the parlor?"

My jaw dropped.

"Because no way would she go off and not tell us what she wanted done," Martine said, and she took a step toward the kitchen, still talking. "I bet she left a list someplace and we just have to find it, or else we could call the office and see if—"

Her voice was louder now—loud enough even for someone hard of hearing, although it had started out soft. She was letting our presence dawn on Mrs. Glynn by degrees. "Maybe Ray Oakley would know. Do you think?" she asked.

I said, "Well . . . ," and followed after her. I had no choice. I stuffed the plastic bag in my jacket pocket as we emerged from the pantry.

Mrs. Glynn was standing beside the stove, wearing this kind of flown-open expression. Both hands were pressed to her chest. She said, "Oh!" And then, "How . . .?"

"Look! There she is!" Martine told me. "Mrs. Glynn! Great to see you!"

"Why, it's . . . Barnaby," Mrs. Glynn said. "Barnaby and young . . ."

"We're just covering for Ray Oakley," Martine said. "I hope we didn't give you a scare. Ray couldn't make it today, and so he sent us instead, and when nobody answered the door—"

"But . . . today? Was he coming today?" Mrs. Glynn asked.

She had a long, drapey coat on, and her hair was screwed into those bottle-cap curls that old-lady beauty shops favor. It made her face look naked and uncertain. She said, "I don't think he was due to come *today*. Was he?"

"Well, maybe he wasn't," I said. I turned to Martine. "Do you think we made a mistake?"

"We must have," she said promptly. "Okay! Better be running along!"

"Wrong?" Mrs. Glynn asked. She stared from one of us to the other.

"Sorry about the mix-up," I said as we sidled past her. "See you, Mrs. Glynn! Bye-bye!"

And we escaped.

Before we went on to Mr. Shank's, I had Martine drive past my apartment so I could stash Sophia's money. No sense tempting fate. I ran in, leaving Martine in the truck, and hid the plastic bag behind the bar.

What had Sophia been thinking of, choosing a plastic bag? Had she wanted her aunt to know for sure that this money was a substitution?

It would serve her right if I kept it, I thought. Kept it and bought a car with it—say a used VW. One of those cute little Beetles.

No, don't worry. I wouldn't do that.

I smoothed a jumble of T-shirts over the money, and I left.

Mr. Shank, then Mrs. Portland, then Mrs. Figg. Wouldn't you know Mrs. Figg was the toughest. She wanted eight strands of Christmas lights woven around the two boxwoods beside her front door—a job that just about froze our fingers off—and then when we got done she said it looked artificial. "Artificial!" I said. "Of course it looks artificial. These are red and green and blue lightbulbs; what occurrence in nature are they supposed to imitate?"

"I mean, they're *spaced* artificially. I wanted them more random."

So Martine and I did them over. When we'd finished, Mrs. Figg said that she had no intention of paying for the extra time it took. She said anybody with half a brain would have done it right the first time. I said, "Have it your way, Mrs. Figg. Merry Christmas."

It was worth it just to see the look on her face. She hated it when someone deprived her of a good argument.

That was our last job of the day, luckily. (By now it was completely dark.) I dropped Martine at her brother's, and just as she was hopping out, I said, "Thanks for the help with, you know. The money."

"No problem," she told me, and then she slammed the

door, because her sister-in-law was on the front porch, itching to get to the hospital.

This was Sophia's last night home before she left for the long Christmas weekend, and we had talked about having dinner at some not too expensive restaurant whenever I got off work. I figured that was my chance to return her money. It did occur to me, *Oh, Lord, I hope now she won't go out and buy me a Christmas present.* But I didn't want to wait till Christmas was over, because I worried about keeping that much cash around.

She was leaving a message on my machine when I walked into the apartment. ". . . and I would just like to know . . . ," she was saying.

I picked up the receiver. "Hello?"

"Barnaby," she said. "Would you please tell me what is going on?"

"Huh?"

"What were you doing at Aunt Grace's house? Why did you and that Martine person go there when you surely must have known she would be out? I couldn't believe my ears. I said to Aunt Grace, 'Who?' I said, '*Who* did you say was there?' "

I put the receiver back down.

Then I thought, *Oops.*

It was my body proceeding without me again. I didn't hang up on purpose. I almost seemed to forget that I had to keep the receiver off the hook to continue talking.

But instead of phoning her back, I grabbed the money from behind the bar and I left the house.

The night was clear enough so the stars were out—what few of them could be seen within the city limits—but as soon as

I crossed the patio, the automatic lights lit up and doused them. On a hunch, I stopped walking and held still a moment. The lights clicked off, and then, sure enough, the sky did its color-change trick. *Loom!* it went, and that transparent midnight blue swung into focus. Of course, it lasted no longer than a second. After that, the blue started seeming ordinary again, and I continued on toward the truck.

I drove to Sophia's, parked in front of her house, and looked around for suspicious strangers before I got out. (The money made an obvious bulge in the right-hand side of my jacket.) Then I climbed her front steps and rang her doorbell.

An immediate, perfect silence fell. You know how sometimes your ear does something funny and there's an instant when the sound goes off? That's the kind of silence. Noises I hadn't even been aware of—mechanical hums and creaks, a murmur behind the curtains—suddenly stopped. And nobody came to the door.

I rang again. Cars hissed down the street behind me, and a faraway train whistle blew, but the house went on giving off its numb, dead silence.

If there had been a mail slot, I'd have slipped the money through it. What she had, though, was one of those black metal postboxes, the kind that doesn't lock, and I wasn't such a fool as to entrust her money to that. So I stood there awhile longer, and then I turned and left.

Probably she was watching me as I walked back to the street. She was peering out from behind her curtains to make sure I left. I felt self-conscious and stiff. I made a point of adding a carefree bounce to my step. Even after I reached the truck—after I was home again, parking in the Hardestys' driveway—I had a spied-upon feeling. When the automatic lights came on, I ducked my head. I scurried across the patio with my shoulders hunched, like a suspect on the evening news.

Okay, so she was mad at me. She was planning to make this difficult. But the nice thing about fussy people is, they have their little routines. You always know where you can find them, and when, if you want to track them down.

15

At 9:58 the next morning, she was sitting on a bench at the far end of Penn Station, gazing straight ahead. I know she saw me coming. But I couldn't read her expression until I got closer. (I was traveling through squares of sunlight; she was hardly more than a silhouette.) I arrived in front of her and stood there. She raised her chin. Her eyes were swimming in tears.

She said, "You hung up on me, Barnaby."

"I apologize for that," I told her.

A woman sharing the bench glanced over at us curiously. I sat down between her and Sophia, blocking the woman's view. "I don't know what got into me," I said.

"Nobody's ever hung up on me. Ever!"

I reached into my jacket and drew out the money, which I'd transferred to a plain white envelope for privacy's sake. (I'd thought of every possible scenario—even put a note inside, in case she refused to speak to me.) "Sophia," I said, and I cleared my throat, preparing to make my announcement.

But Sophia went right on. "I simply wasn't raised that way," she told me. "I'm sorry, but that's how I am. I was raised to be respected and treated with consideration. I was taught that I was a special, valuable person; not the kind that someone could hang up on."

I said, "See, it was only that I felt . . . interrogated, you know? On account of the tone of voice you used."

"Why wouldn't I interrogate you? You walked into my aunt's private home without her permission! Naturally I would wonder what you were doing there."

"Well, I should think it was obvious what I was doing there. I wanted to get your money back."

"Did I ask you to get my money back? Did I request your assistance? I tell you this much, Barnaby: I'd have thrown that money in your face if you brought it back!"

Then she glanced at my envelope. She said, "Is that what *this* is?" in a piercing, carrying tone that made me slide my eyes toward the other passengers. "Is that what you came to try and give me?"

I said, "Sofe—"

"Because I'm not accepting it, Barnaby. You'd have to ram it down my throat before I'd accept it."

This was a temptation, but I decided on a different tactic. I said, "*No*, no, no. Good grief, no! It's . . . something for Opal."

"Opal?"

"Her, um, Christmas present. I need for you to take it to her."

"Opal's Christmas present is in this envelope?"

"Take it, will you? Take it," I said, and I held it out to her. Right then it mattered more than anything that I get rid of it; I didn't care how. When she unclasped her hands, finally, and allowed me to lay the envelope on her palm, I felt a kind of lightness expanding inside my chest. I imagined I had been freed of an actual weight.

"You're asking me to carry this to Opal's apartment?" Sophia said, and she raised her eyes to look into mine.

"Well," I said, "or else . . . no." (I could see how that might get complicated.) "No, I want you to give it to Natalie at the train station."

"Natalie?"

"She knows you're coming. She'll meet you there."

Sophia blinked.

"She'll be . . . yes! At the Information island," I said. And then something about how this situation rhymed, so to speak, made me laugh. I said, "I can assure you it's not contraband."

A confused, slightly startled expression crossed her face, as if some string had been tugged in her memory, but she went on looking into my eyes.

"Goodbye," I said, rising.

"Wait! Barnaby? You're leaving?"

"Yes, I promised I'd help pack up Mrs. Alford's house today. Oh. Incidentally," I said. (My mind was racing now.) "If you and Natalie happen to miss connections, I did put her telephone number in the envelope. Just get it out and call her. But you shouldn't have any trouble."

She nodded, with her lips slightly parted. I turned and walked away.

Spink and Kunkle, Plumbing Specialists, the man's card read. "*Our Name Says It All.*"

"Your name says it all?" I asked.

"Sure does," he said. A freckled man with reddish, fizzing hair.

" 'Spink and Kunkle' says it all?"

" 'Plumbing Specialists' says it all," he told me irritably.

"Oh."

"I'm supposed to fix a leak in the master bath."

"Right." I handed back his card, and then I turned from the door and called, "Hello?" (I had no idea how to address Mrs. Alford's daughter, never having heard her last name.) "Plumber's here!" I called.

"Oh, good." She came galumphing down the stairs. Dressed for manual labor, Valerie was gawkier than ever. She wore huge white canvas gloves that made her look like Minnie Mouse. "Thanks for stopping by on such short notice," she told the man. "We're trying to get the house ready to sell, and you know how a minor thing like a drip will scare some people away."

"Ma'am," the man said heavily, "no drip on God's green earth is minor. Believe me." He was following her up the stairs, carrying what seemed to be a doctor's bag. "If you was to put a measuring cup under that drip," he said, "you would be scandalized. Scandalized! To see how much water you're wasting."

"Well, this house belonged to my mother, you see, and somehow she never . . ."

I went back to the kitchen, where I was packing the pots and pans. Martine was doing utensils. Supposedly, we'd be finished by the end of the day, but that was just not going to happen. Valerie had already asked if we could return tomorrow. I said, "Tomorrow? Tomorrow's Sunday."

"Yes, but the next day's Christmas," she said.

So I said, "Oh, I guess I could."

I felt obliged to, really, because she had told me earlier that her mother had willed me the Twinform. "That mannequin thing in the attic," she'd explained. "I can't imagine why she thought . . . But if you don't want it, just say so. Please."

"I want it! I want it," I said.

After that, how could I refuse to come Sunday? Martine said she would come too, but only for the morning. Her brother's new baby had finally been sprung from the hospital, she said. This meant that her family would be throwing their annual carol sing, after all, and she had to help them get ready. Then she told me I was invited. "You should dress up some," she told me, "now that you have a Twinform to try out your fashion statements on."

"Right," I said. "I can't wait to see her in a coat and tie."

Underneath, though, I took my Twinform very seriously. I kept going into the foyer to check on her; I'd moved her down from the attic as soon as I learned she was mine. I pretended I was just figuring out the logistics. "If we could borrow a blanket or something," I told Martine, "and wrap her up so she doesn't rattle around the truck bed . . ."

" 'Her'?" Martine teased me. " 'She'?"

"Oh, come on, Pasko: you have to admit that face has a lot of character."

She snorted, and we went back to our packing.

Place mats, tablecloths, napkins, doilies. Tupperware and empty mayonnaise jars and plastic juice containers. Waxed paper, aluminum foil, Saran wrap, freezer wrap. A lifetime supply of white candles. *More* than a lifetime supply, if you want to be literal about it.

Every now and then, in this job, I suddenly understood that you really, truly can't take it with you. I don't think I ordinarily grasped the full implications of that. Just look at all the possessions a dead person leaves behind: every last one, even the most treasured. No luggage is permitted, no carry-on items, not a purse, not a pair of glasses. You spend seven or eight decades acquiring your objects, arranging them, dusting them, insuring them; then you walk out with nothing at all, as bare as the day you arrived.

I told Martine, "I should find some other line of work."

"Not *that* again," she said, and she folded down the flaps on a box of cookbooks.

"It isn't natural for someone my age to go to more funerals than dinner parties."

Martine just smiled to herself.

Mrs. Alford's brother came in with an empty coffee mug. He rinsed it at the sink and placed it in the dishwasher. (Old folks almost always prerinse.) Then he left, slogging off with his head down, not appearing to notice us.

Overhead, the plumber was clanking pipes, and it occurred to me that the name really did say it all. *Spink!* the pipes went. *Kunkle!* In the living room, a boom box was playing alternative rock—probably the first time these walls had ever heard such a sound. "Listen to this one," a kid was saying—talking to his mother, I think. She had started packing the books. "This song comes from before their lead singer went crazy. Okay? Now, this next one . . . wait a sec. This next one is *after* he went crazy. Hear that? Can you tell the difference? Well, then, let me play it again. See, this is *before* he went crazy. This next . . ."

The bearded husband wandered into the kitchen, opened the fridge, and gazed into it. Then he closed it and wandered off. I still hadn't heard him speak. Upstairs, the baby was crying, and somebody told her, "Aw, now. Aw, now." (It sounded to me like the plumber.) I found a length of white flannel in a drawer—the kind you'd spread beneath a tablecloth for protection—and took it out to the foyer and draped it over the Twinform's shoulders. She gaped at me round-eyed, as if I'd been presumptuous.

Suppose my great-grandfather was walking down the street

one day and who did he see but his angel, the woman with the golden braid. "Miss!" he'd cry. "Miss! Wait up! I never thanked you."

She would turn and say, "Me?" She'd be this average, commonplace woman, maybe even homely, maybe chapped-lipped or shiny-nosed, depending on the season. "What for?" she would ask, and he would see then that he had been mistaken—that there were no angels, after all. Or that his angels were lots of people he had never suspected.

Where, exactly, would I get hold of a gray cloth ledger with maroon leather corners?

Martine passed through the foyer, lugging a carton. "We're running out of space," she told me. "I'm going to start stacking things here." Then she said, "Yikes." She'd just about bumped into the alternative-rock kid. He veered around her, cradling his boom box in both arms. I guess his mother had finally had enough of it.

Another boy sat at the dining-room table—so far I'd counted four boys and two girls—reading a comic book. He didn't look up until I said, "Uh . . . ," because right on the carpet in front of my feet I saw a disgusting brown mess. "Is this dog do?" I asked the kid. "Or what? Is there a dog in the house? There's dog do on the rug."

"It's fate," he told me coolly.

I said, "Oh." Then I said, "Okay." I waited a moment, and finally I decided to head on into the kitchen. It wasn't till I'd cleared another shelf that I figured out he'd said, "It's fake." I grinned.

By now Sophia would be arriving in Philadelphia. She'd be clicking across the station toward the Information island, carrying the envelope and looking around for Natalie. Of course, she'd seen Natalie once before, but that was only briefly and some time ago. She would be wondering whether they'd recognize each other. Maybe she would notice a woman in a red coat, and she would think, *Her?* and then realize the woman was too plump, or too fair. (And just then the real Natalie walked across my mind—her straight, slim figure and tranquil face, her grave, brown, considering eyes.)

I fished a screwdriver out of my pocket and removed a rusted can opener from the wall above the stove. I put it in the box we had set beside the back door for trash. Mrs. Alford's brother said, "Oh! What's this?" I hadn't even heard him arrive. He bent over the box to study the can opener. "All I have at home is that hand-grip kind; nothing that hangs on a wall," he told me.

"Then why don't you take this one?" I asked. "It's only going out to the garbage."

"Yes, perhaps . . . It's a pity to throw it away, don't you think?"

"Absolutely," I told him.

He clutched the can opener to his chest and padded off. In the dining room I heard him say, "There's dog do on the rug, Johnny," but I didn't catch Johnny's answer.

Sophia would have stood waiting for several minutes now. She'd be looking to her left and her right, biting her lower lip, her eyebrows quirked in annoyance. (I pictured her in the feather coat, although more often lately she wore something beige and belted that she'd bought on sale last spring.) Maybe she would ask the Information clerk, "Has anybody been here that you've noticed—a woman who seemed to be meeting someone?"

She'd be glancing down at the envelope more and more frequently, wondering if it was time yet to get Natalie's phone number out.

The last thing left on the wall was one of those rechargeable mixers. I unhooked it and placed it in the carton of utensils. Then I unscrewed the mounting plate, and just as I was lifting it from the wall I felt the most amazing rush of happiness wash over me. I didn't know at first where it came from. I was looking at the mounting plate, is all, not thinking of anything special. I was staring at those figure-eight-shaped holes you slide over the screws. They reminded me of something. They brought to mind the brass clasps on Martine's overalls.

Martine walked back into the kitchen, dusting off her hands, and she picked up another carton. I said, "Martine?" and she said, "What," and I said, "Haply I think on thee."

"Huh?" she said.

But I could tell she knew what I meant.

Out in the dining room, Mrs. Alford's brother was demonstrating his new can opener. "Barnaby was planning to put this in the trash," he said. "Can you imagine? Why, there's years and years of use left in it!" Upstairs, the boom box was playing something noisy and disorganized. And in Philadelphia, Sophia was opening the envelope. She was staring down at the money inside and drawing a quick breath inward. She glanced around the train station. Then she unfolded my note. *Sophia,* she read, *you never did realize. I am a man you can trust.*